Praise for Karis Walsh

Sit. Stay. Love.

"A cute and fun romance set in a small town. Great main characters that are easily relatable."—*Kat Adams, Bookseller (QBD Books, Australia)*

"This is a sweet romance about two lovely people growing together and falling in love as they help the people and animals around them."—*Rainbow Reflections*

"This is an easy romance to read. It's not overly fraught with angst, but there are some light drama to keep the plot moving forward. The obligatory separation of the leads near the end of the book didn't feel eye roll worthy, because, though dramatic, it was set up almost from the beginning of the book. I loved the characters, pacing and plot of this book. Very recommended."—*Colleen Corgel, Librarian, Queens Public Library*

Love on Lavender Lane

"Gentle romance, excellent chemistry and low angst…The two MCs are well defined and well written. Their interactions and dialogue are great fun. The whole atmosphere of the lavender farm is excellently evoked."—*reviewer@large*

"[*Love on Lavender Lane*] was very nearly my perfect romance novel. Lovely human beings for main characters who had fantastic chemistry, great humor that kept me smiling—and even laughing—throughout, and just enough angst to make my feel it in the heart. And a cute doggie, too!"—*C-Spot Reviews*

Seascape

"When I think of Karis Walsh novels, the two aspects that distinguish them from those of many authors are the interactions of the characters with their environment, both the scenery and the plants and animals that live in it. This book has all of that in abundance…"—*The Good, the Bad and the Unread*

Set the Stage

"I really adored this book. From the characters to the setting and the slow burn romance, I was in it for the long haul with this one. Karis Walsh to me is an expert in creating interesting characters that often have to face some type of adversity. While this book was no different, it felt like the author changed up her game a bit. There's something new, something fresh about this book from Walsh."—*Romantic Reader Blog*

"Both leads were well developed and you could see them grow as characters throughout the novel. They also had great chemistry. This slow burn romance made a great summer read."—*Melina Bickard, Librarian, Waterloo Library (UK)*

Tales From the Sea Glass Inn

"A wonderful romance about starting all over again in middle age. Karis Walsh creates an affirming love story in which relatable women face uncertainty and new beginnings, with all of their promise and shortcomings, and come out whole on the other side."—*Omnivore Bibliosaur*

"*Tales from Sea Glass Inn* is a lovely collection of stories about the women who visit the Inn and the relationships that they form with each other."—*Inked Rainbow Reads*

Love on Tap

"Karis Walsh writes excellent romances. They draw you in, engage your mind and capture your heart...What really good romance writers do is make you dream of being that loved, that chosen. Love on Tap is exactly that novel – interesting characters, slightly different circumstances to anything you have read before, slightly different challenges. And although you KNOW the happy ending is coming, you still have that little bit of 'oooh—make it happen.' Loved it. Wish it was me. What more is there to say?"—*Lesbian Reading Room*

"This is the second book I have read by this author and it certainly won't be my last. Ms Walsh is one of the few authors who can write a truly great and interesting love story without the need of a secondary story line or plot."—*Inked Rainbow Reads*

You Make Me Tremble

"Another quality read from Karis Walsh. She is definitely a go-to for a heartwarming read."—*Romantic Reader Blog*

Amounting to Nothing

"As always with Karis Walsh's books the characters are well drawn and the inter-relationships well developed."—*Lesbian Reading Room*

Sweet Hearts: Romantic Novellas

"I was super excited when I saw this book was coming out, and it did not disappoint."—*Danielle Kimerer, Librarian, Reading Public Library (MA)*

"Karis Walsh sensitively portrays the frustration of learning to live with a new disability through Ainslee, and the pain of living as a survivor of suicide loss through Myra."—*Lesbian Review*

Mounting Evidence

"[A]nother awesome Karis Walsh novel, and I have eternal hope that at some point there will be another book in this series. I liked the characters, the plot, the mystery and the romance so much."—Danielle Kimerer, Librarian, Reading Public Library (MA)

Mounting Danger

"A mystery, a woman in a uniform and horses...YES!!!!...This book is brilliant in my opinion. Very well written with great flow and a fantastic plot. I enjoyed the horses in this dramatic saga. There is so much information on training and riding, and polo. Very interesting things to know."—*Prism Book Alliance*

Blindsided

"Their slow-burn romance is a nuanced exploration of trust, desire, and negotiating boundaries, without a hint of schmaltz or pity. The sex scenes are sizzling hot, but it's the slow burn that really allows Walsh to shine…the deft dialogue and well-written characters make this a winner."—*Publishers Weekly*

"This is definitely a good read, and it's a good introduction to Karis Walsh and her books. The romance is good, the sex is hot, the dogs are endearing, and you finish the book feeling good. Why wouldn't you want all that?"—*Lesbian Review*

Wingspan

"I really enjoy Karis Walsh's work. She writes wonderful novels that have interesting characters who aren't perfect, but they are likable. This book pulls you into the story right from the beginning. The setting is the beautiful Olympic Peninsula and you can't help but want to go there as you read *Wingspan*."—*Romantic Reader Blog*

The Sea Glass Inn

"Karis Walsh's third book, excellently written and paced as always, takes us on a gentle but determined journey through two women's awakening…Loved it, another great read that will stay on my re-visit shelf."—*Lesbian Reading Room*

Worth the Risk

"The setting of this novel is exquisite, based on Karis Walsh's own background in horsemanship and knowledge of showjumping. It provides a wonderful plot to the story, a great backdrop to the characters and an interesting insight for those of us who don't know that world…Another great book by Karis Walsh. Well written, well paced, amusing and warming. Definitely a hit for me."—*Lesbian Reading Room*

By the Author

Harmony

Worth the Risk

Sea Glass Inn

Improvisation

Wingspan

Blindsided

Love on Tap

Tales from Sea Glass Inn

You Make Me Tremble

Set the Stage

Seascape

Love on Lavender Lane

Sit. Stay. Love

Liberty Bay

Love and Lattes

Love Takes a Village

Mounted Police Romantic Intrigues:

Mounting Danger

Mounting Evidence

Amounting to Nothing

University Police Romantic Intrigues:

With a Minor in Murder

A Degree to Die For

Big Corpse on Campus

Visit us at www.boldstrokesbooks.com

LOVE
TAKES A VILLAGE

by
Karis Walsh

2025

LOVE TAKES A VILLAGE
© 2025 BY KARIS WALSH. ALL RIGHTS RESERVED.

ISBN 13: 978-1-63679-902-5

THIS TRADE PAPERBACK ORIGINAL IS PUBLISHED BY
BOLD STROKES BOOKS, INC.
P.O. BOX 249
VALLEY FALLS, NY 12185

FIRST EDITION: DECEMBER 2025

CREDITS
EDITOR: RUTH STERNGLANTZ
PRODUCTION DESIGN: STACIA SEAMAN
COVER DESIGN BY TAMMY SEIDICK

LOVE
TAKES A VILLAGE

Chapter One

L ena Preiss dragged one last document into the Greater Metro Medical folder before saving and closing the file. She leaned back in her chair and stared at her laptop's galaxy wallpaper, waiting for the reality of her new jobless state to sink in. A few clicks of the mouse made for an anticlimactic ending to the months she had spent consumed by her work for GMM, and she didn't even have the sense of closure that would have accompanied a sad trek to her car with a cardboard box full of her belongings. Her home office hadn't changed since she was fired—although she had significantly less to do there at the moment—but she supposed she could box up her stapler and some old file folders and carry them down to her apartment's garage and back, at least for dramatic effect.

That sounded like more of a ridiculous effort than it was worth, so instead she initiated a video call with Jacquie.

"They fired me," she moaned as soon as her friend's face appeared on her screen, with her bottle-blond hair tipped with purple and piled in a messy bun, and today's glasses accented with green and yellow checkered squares. Lena knew without seeing that Jacquie's brightness continued all the way down to her toes.

She sighed and dropped her forehead onto her desk in front of her laptop. The soothing balm of sympathy from her best friend would set her right again, giving her the strength to—

"Hmm." Jacquie's voice had enough of a skeptical tone to make Lena sit upright again. "Did they actually fire you, or did they just take the first out clause in your contract?"

"Hey, whose side are you on?"

Jacquie shrugged, giving Lena one of her playful smiles that made it very difficult to remain annoyed and not give in and smile along with her. Lena managed to resist the urge and sat back in her chair, crossing her arms over her chest in a huff.

"I'm on the side of the woman who made me write the out clause into her standard contract," Jacquie said, unmoved by Lena's display of irritation. "Would you rather I was on the side of the woman who is surprised *every time* a company takes that exit opportunity?"

"Yes," Lena said, spreading her hands wide for emphasis, "obviously."

"Oh, poor baby," Jacquie said, in a poor imitation of a truly sympathetic voice. "Did the mean company fire you without any justification? Let's sue."

"Can we?" Lena asked hopefully.

"No." Jacquie returned to her normal voice. "Same answer as the last six times this happened. Besides, you know they won't be able to implement this new EHR as easily as they think, and they'll ask you back to help."

Lena nodded. That was the pattern. She custom-created her Electronic Health Record platforms for each company she worked with, and then they had the option to retain her during the implementation phase or to manage it on their own. They always came crawling back and required her assistance as they integrated the program across their system. "That's true," Lena said, feeling a small glint of hope. She'd still need to find a new full-time project, but at least this one was still possibly going to generate some income. "This one was complex, with a variety of different types of clinics in the network. They'll need help tweaking the program to make it work well for them all."

"Yes, and then they'll hire you back at a per diem rate that will be significantly lower than if they hadn't taken the out," Jacquie said, ruthlessly squashing Lena's little bud of optimism before it had a chance to flower. "For the same work. Honey, you really need to let us change your contract before you get another job."

Lena sighed again. Jacquie was right, of course, but Lena missed the good old days when her clients and her contracts were both simpler and more localized. She had started by creating EMRs for individual clinics and medical offices. They were usually smaller companies, and they couldn't afford much, but she had been just starting out and didn't charge much, so it was win-win.

Her standard contract in those days covered the entire process, from creation to integration and training in the new system, and she had been part of it all. She had gotten to know her clients, and they had even thrown her an occasional little party when her time with them was finished, to celebrate their new system and thank her for her work.

The sense of camaraderie had ended when she advanced to creating larger EHR platforms for multiclinic nationwide health-care systems.

"I got a lot of pushback on those full-service contracts once I was working with the bigger companies. I suppose I let them bully me into the less restrictive options," Lena admitted. She was nothing but brutally honest with herself about her strengths and weaknesses. She was an excellent coder, but she hated the confrontation that was too often involved with the business side of her profession, and she freely acknowledged that she sometimes took the easy way out to keep the peace. She needed to trust Jacquie's advice in these areas.

Jacquie tapped the screen with one pointy, lacquered fingernail. "Maybe so, but you were building your business and reputation, and I don't think you made a mistake by compromising. Then. Now, you're a proven entity, and your contract needs to reflect that. You can still offer the out clause, but it should come with a penalty. Plus, it should cost more, not less, to hire you back to bail them out when they can't handle the integration on their own."

"Okay, okay," Lena said in a mockingly sullen tone. She hadn't gotten platitudes and comfort from Jacquie, but the conversation still left her feeling better than she had before she called her friend. Wisdom and truth left her feeling more in control and less wallow-y than empty sympathy would have done. "I'll have a shiny new contract, but no one to sign it."

Maybe she was still wallowing a little.

"Well, I'll get Rolf to work on your new contract, and you can go pound the virtual pavement. Something great will turn up. It always does."

"Hopefully. I haven't had potential clients lining up outside my door over the past six months, but I suppose I can—" She paused and glanced at her phone screen when it chimed. "Damn. It's my dad. I should go, but I'll—"

"No," Jacquie said quickly before Lena could end the call, "put him on speaker so I can listen in. Please, please, pl—"

"Fine," Lena interrupted, making a shushing gesture at her and answering her phone. "Hey, Dad," she said.

"Hello, Lena," he said, his voice sounding deep and echoey. She figured he was talking as he walked through the hospital corridors, probably signing forms and doing CPR on ailing patients as he went. He was the ultimate multitasker. "I heard you lost your job."

Well, that story had spread fast. Her dad was the chief administrator in one of the Pacific Northwest's largest hospitals, so he had his finger on the pulse of the medical world, but this news seemed too trivial to have reached him this quickly.

"How did you know?"

He paused for a moment, and she heard him speaking to someone else in a muffled voice about a delayed shipment of a new imaging machine before he came back on the line. "Bill from GMM is an old golfing buddy, and he told me you had finished the EHR when we were on the course last weekend. He said you did excellent work for them. Good job, Lena."

"Um…thank you?" Lena said, unable to keep the questioning tone out of her voice. Her father was an unexpected source of sympathy, but Lena would take what she could get.

"Yes, this is excellent timing."

"It's…what?" Was his hospital looking to upgrade their EHR? That would be an amazing job, if not for the fact that her perfectionist father would be looking over her shoulder and watching her every move. She'd have to tell Rolf to triple her fee.

"Your aunt needs you to help with a new venture. She asked for you specifically this time."

Oh God. Aunt Cheryl routinely bought failing companies and then needed Lena's family to step in and help her with them. The task usually fell to Lena's dad, who was unexpectedly indulgent of his younger sister, but Lena's siblings had been roped into helping before, too. She had somehow managed to always be in the middle of a project when these summonses came in, but this time…

"Dad, did you get me fired?" She had to ask. The timing was too perfect…for her father, of course. Not for her.

He made an indignant scoffing sound. "Of course I didn't."

"Hmm. Do you wish you had thought of it before now?"

"No, although it would have saved me three afternoons of golf," he said with a laugh. She wasn't amused enough by the conversation to join in. "I know your work pattern. When Cheryl wrote to me about this new…" He hesitated, probably searching for a palatable word. "This new *opportunity*, I told her you were probably about to finish this latest project, and that you'd have a couple of months free before they brought you back to clean up the mess they made with it. For less money than they were paying you before. You really should rethink your contract."

Lena heard a choked laugh coming from the region of her laptop, but she ignored Jacquie's amusement and focused on her dad. She was torn between annoyance at his meddling and the resignation of *yes, this is exactly something he would do* that came from a lifetime of being Karl Preiss's daughter.

"So I've heard," she said. "How long have you known about this, anyway?"

"About a month." She heard the shrug in his voice. "Cheryl was hoping you'd be able to start right away, but I told her she'd have to wait."

"And it didn't occur to you to tell me right away?"

"Of course not. You'd have been suspicious if I started asking about when you expected to be fired."

"Not fired. Temporarily *let go*. And I certainly wouldn't have been suspicious about my own father taking an interest in my work." It was her turn to feign indignation, but she couldn't pull it off convincingly. "Okay, maybe a little, but that's because I'm not a fool. And I'm not going. I need to find another job now, so you'll have to help her with whatever scheme she's come up with this time."

"Lena," he said sternly, "don't defy me. I raised you to be more obedient than that."

Lena gave a snort of laughter. "No, you didn't. You raised me to question authority and make my own choices."

"Well, now I'm paying the price for that progressive child-raising bullshit," he said. Lena thought she detected a hint of pride in his voice, but she knew better than to think she had won the war just yet.

He paused, then continued. "I did, however, raise you to be kind to your aunt and to take care of your family."

Shit. She had no doubt about the hint of triumph in his voice this time.

"I don't want to spend the winter cleaning alpaca poop," she said, falling back on the pathetic whine of the defeated. "Send Mom."

She added the last bit as a childish jab, since Cheryl and her "shenanigans," as Lena's mom called them, were one of the few things her parents ever argued about. Besides, as chief of surgery in the hospital's neurology department, she was admittedly less able to fly to Cheryl's rescue than Lena was.

"She sold the alpaca farm years ago," her dad said, ignoring the other part of Lena's comment. "This time it's a restaurant in...Where was it? Oh yes. Leavenworth, in Washington. Cheryl remembered that you used to help your grandmother in the kitchen, and you have her old recipe book. Plus, I mentioned all those cooking classes you've taken. Apparently, Christmas season is the big tourist event for this town, so you just need to help her for a couple of months. Get some revenue coming in, then hand the job off to someone else and come back to Portland and get back to your own work. It'll be like a vacation."

Lena highly doubted that. "You mean I'm going to be expected to cook? For the public?"

"Cook, run the restaurant, that sort of thing," he said, and she pictured him waving his hand dismissively. "It's a small place in a small town. How hard can it be?"

Lena heard actual laughter from her laptop this time and hoped her phone would filter it out as background noise. "But I don't have any experience with…" She hesitated. *With any of that*, she wanted to say, but he broke into the brief moment of silence she gave him.

"Great. That's decided, then. I'll let Cheryl know and send you the details she gave me. Mom and I will drive up there and come to the restaurant for dinner once you're settled. Talk soon. Love you."

"Love you, too," Lena said out of habit, lowering the phone and looking at Jacquie, who was still overcome with mirth.

"I adore your family," she said, wiping her eyes and scanning her screen, obviously searching the internet on a different tab. "You're the weirdest blend of control and acceptance, and criticism and support that I've ever seen."

Lena allowed Jacquie's fascination with her family, since she knew Jacquie's parents provided only the criticism and attempts to control, with none of the kinder aspects, in their relationship with her. Lena sometimes had to look hard to find them in her own interactions with her parents.

"I don't know how to cook," Lena said, interjecting her words with despair. At least cleaning alpaca poop didn't require any skills beyond holding a shovel. Or a rake? Okay, she wasn't qualified for that one, either.

"Are you kidding?" Jacquie stopped scrolling and returned to their chat screen to make eye contact with Lena. "You're a wonderful cook. Wasn't the sauerbraten you made a couple of years ago from one of your grandmother's recipes? It was possibly the best meal I've ever had."

"Thank you, but that was a meal for four friends, not a restaurant full of people. Plus, it took me six hours and every pan I owned." She shook her head, remembering the state of her kitchen when she was done. She had even thrown out a couple of the worst pans rather than attempt to scour off the burned-on bits of sauce. She had enjoyed the cooking classes she had taken at local adult centers and community colleges whenever she had a chance, but in those she had always cooked one dish at a time, with all the ingredients thoughtfully laid out before her. At that rate, it would take her a full day to get all the orders out to customers.

"You'll get faster with practice. Besides, won't you have assistant chefs and dishwashers to help?"

"I don't know," Lena said warily, unsure what all was covered under her father's *that sort of thing*. She might well be doing it all on her own. "I might be able to handle a food truck, I suppose. If we're only selling sandwiches, or something easy like that. But entire meals, with garnishes and everything? There's no way."

"I'm going back to searching for this town," Jacquie said, changing tabs again. "Isn't it close to Seattle? You love Seattle. I'm sure you can go there once in a while for a concert or nice meal out, or…Oh. Well, that's kind of far away, I suppose, and over the pass. And with unpredictable winter weather…Do you like to ski?"

"Not really," Lena said, pulling up a map herself and hunting for Leavenworth. The first one she tried didn't have enough detail to show the tiny town, so she searched another. It wasn't a long drive from Seattle, distance-wise, but it was hemmed in by the Cascades and the Wenatchee Mountains.

"At least you'll have plenty of time to get to know your aunt better," Jacquie said. "She sounds awesome. Alpacas? German restaurants? She must have some great stories."

Lena sighed. Of course Jacquie, with her diverse hobbies and unique taste, would find Cheryl's life somewhat appealing, but to Lena and the rest of her family, her aunt's eccentric choices were absolutely not aspirational. She had no idea how this highly focused, driven, and type-A family tree had spawned a twisty, aimless branch like her aunt's.

"I don't know any of her stories, except hearsay when Dad or one of the sibs comes back from helping her," she admitted. "She's always traveled a lot and has started businesses all over the country, so I rarely saw her when I was growing up. Just occasional holidays, I suppose." She paused, thinking back to those deeply buried memories of her aunt's visits. They had tended to be stressful times for her family, with her mother's barely concealed disdain and her dad's failed attempts to lecture his sister about settling down in a conventional, sensible job. They'd had paintings in their homes, but few family photos, so Lena couldn't even call to mind an accurate picture of her aunt.

"She's a really good hugger," Lena said thoughtfully. "I remember that much, at least."

Jacquie regarded her skeptically. "A good hugger compared to normal people, or compared to your family? Because I'm guessing that a chainsaw would be a good hugger compared to your family."

Lena couldn't argue with that. Her parents were definitely not the demonstrative sort. They were free enough with verbal praise—when they believed it was warranted—but there tended to be a lot of teeth grinding and grimacing if they tried to show physical affection. Lena admitted that her assessment might be slightly exaggerated, but not much. "Compared to normal people," she said.

She opened the Wikipedia page for Leavenworth and scanned it quickly. Apparently, they celebrated the holiday season from Thanksgiving through the end of February. The official line was that this gave more people a chance to come visit and see the festive lights, but Lena could easily discern the true motive behind the three-month span. This was a small town with what looked like little draw beyond this one season, and they extended it to give local businesses a chance to make as much money as possible during that period. Enough to carry them through the much lighter influx of tourists through the rest of the year.

Which meant that if Lena was truly going to help her aunt, she was signing on for an intensive few months of work in the restaurant. There wouldn't be leisurely weekends and afternoons available for skiing or heading to Seattle for some nightlife and entertainment.

Three months. That was about the usual length of her aunt's obsessions, so they'd both be ready to pack up and leave Leavenworth by the time her sentence was up. Then Lena would be free to return to her normal life, to her annual job search, with family guilt assuaged. And her aunt would be free to move on to whatever new enterprise caught her fancy. Whatever the hell it was, Lena would have done her part, and someone else in the family could step in and help her.

"Make sure you save me a reservation," Jacquie said. "I can't wait to meet this aunt of yours and experience some fine Leavenworth dining."

"You'll come? Really?" Lena asked, bypassing the obvious joke that the reservation would need to be at a different restaurant than hers if the dining was expected to be *fine*.

"Of course I'll be there. And I'll ask to compliment the chef, and when you come out of the kitchen, I'll lavish praise on you so loudly that people two doors down will come in and leave you tips."

Lena laughed, feeling marginally better. "I'm not setting my aspirations as high as receiving tips. I'll just be glad if none of the diners throw their food at me. Oh, and once Rolf is done with my new contract, let him know I'll be needing a restraining order against my family, keeping them yards away from my career."

CHAPTER TWO

Devin Meyer rolled up the sleeves of her light blue shirt before slipping an apron around her neck and tying it at her waist. When the shop was closed, she always wore one of her old white cotton half aprons she'd had since pastry school wrapped around her hips, but when customers might come in, she chose the more formal royal blue option with *Meyer's Fine Chocolates* slanted in gold embroidery across the bib.

She was just pulling out a set of candy molds when her phone buzzed on the counter beside her. She stifled her flash of annoyance because now she'd have to wash her hands again after answering—which seemed to be an entirely inappropriate response to a call from her girlfriend—and picked up the phone.

"Hey, Criss," she said, forcing a smile in the hope that it would imbue her voice with cheerfulness. She had left Seattle a week ago to spend this last holiday season helping her dad with the shop before he retired, and she was feeling the stress of the looming tourist hordes. Not to mention all the side jobs she was accepting to make the store seem more enticing and flourishing to prospective buyers. The thought of having to add the task of entertaining her high-maintenance girlfriend—and Criss applied the term to herself as if it was a badge of honor—had her ready to lock herself in the pantry and eat their entire stock of milk chocolate. Well, maybe not the new shipment from their favorite supplier in Belgium. She had plans for that and didn't want to waste it in a self-soothing spree.

"Hey, sweetie," Criss said, dragging out the syllables in a way that might have been meant to sound calming. Devin had a sudden premonition that her sanity—and their chocolate supply—might be safe. "Look, I know I was supposed to be there this weekend, and I really hate to disappoint you, but some stuff has come up at work, and, well, I just can't get away right now."

"Work is important. I understand," Devin said. And she did. Criss was an optometric assistant in an office that was open on weekdays, normal hours. She was great at her job, but she hadn't worked a minute of overtime in all the months Devin had known her, and she doubted that a sudden eyeball emergency had popped up. One that could wait for the weekend.

"And, well, you know I'd have been bored out of my mind there," Criss added, which was much more plausible to Devin than the work excuse. "I don't get how you were able to stand living there all those years growing up, but I suppose that's a sign of how different we are…"

Her voice faded to a stop.

Here it comes, Devin thought. She felt a rush of emotion in anticipation of Criss's next words. Surprise wasn't one of them. Relief was, as well as the familiar conviction that something was very wrong with her if she never felt more of a connection to the women she had dated.

"Maybe this time apart will be good for us, so we can think through our relationship. We've seemed to be growing apart…"

Devin lost track for a moment when her dad, Ron Meyer, came out of the back room with their assistant Shay on his heels and saw her on the phone. He was slightly shorter than her, with carefully trimmed salt-and-pepper hair and a near-constant smile for everyone. His blue apron was tied around a belly that provided physical testament to how passionate he was about his job and the product he made. He mouthed *Criss?* at her. When she nodded, Shay giggled and made kissing noises as they walked by.

"And I need time to work on myself for a…Oh, sweetie, are you crying?" Criss asked, apparently hearing and misinterpreting the kissing sounds. "Please don't cry."

"I'm not...well, maybe a little," Devin said. That would be the normal response, wouldn't it? Rather than this empty lack of any true emotion? She gave a tentative sniff to prove it, rather than admit that she really just wanted to end the call and get back to her work.

It took another ten minutes to reassure Criss that Devin would survive the breakup, and then she was finally off the phone. By that time, both her dad and Shay had figured out that this wasn't the time for teasing.

"So, she's not coming this weekend?" her dad asked as she put her phone on the back counter and started washing her hands again.

"No."

"Did she break up with you?" Shay asked, with all the pathos of a teenager who probably thought a breakup was the worst thing that could happen to someone.

"Yes." Devin dried her hands on a clean white towel and went back to the molds she had set aside when she got the call.

Shay and her dad exchanged glances in what they might have thought was a surreptitious manner. The shop was too tiny for that to work, though.

"Do you need to cry?" her dad asked. "Drown your sorrows in a pint of ice cream from Tucker's?"

Devin paused at that one. "I wouldn't say no to a bowl of ice cream," she said. "But mostly I just want to get back to the chocolates for this Friday's wedding."

"I'm on it," her dad said, heading for the door, looking relieved to have some way to help her through her barely felt pain. "One bowl of cherry chip coming up. Shay?"

"Ooh, a hot fudge sundae, please."

He left, not even bothering to take off his apron. Devin went into the walk-in fridge to grab a few ingredients and came out to find Shay leaning against her work counter.

"Are you sure you're okay?" she asked hesitantly, as if not wanting to intrude. It was typical in such a small town—and in an even smaller, family-run shop—that people were very careful about not pushing past boundaries. Small-town residents might have a reputation of being overly involved in everyone else's personal business, but Devin had always found it to be the opposite from what people saw on television and in books.

She smiled at Shay. "I'm sure. And thank you for asking. Criss is a wonderful person, and we had fun together, but she wasn't the great love of my life."

She had serious doubts about ever finding that kind of love, but she wasn't about to start looking right now. She needed to get the shop sold and her dad settled into retired life, make some decisions about the trajectory of her own career, and then maybe she'd make more of an effort in her relationships. Give them more of a chance. Change who she was? She wasn't quite sure what it would take to become the kind of person who found true love, but at the moment she needed to keep her focus on more important things.

"Can you teach me how to make these?" Shay asked as Devin started picking through a pile of fresh mint leaves.

"Oh, sure," Devin said, a little surprised. Her dad always hired local students to help during the holidays. Most just wanted to work the register and make some extra cash, and they had likely applied to every business in Leavenworth, not really caring which job they got. Some of them, though, were actually interested in learning more about the process involved in being a chocolatier, and she was always willing to share what she knew. Shay was peering at the ingredients with what seemed like genuine interest. Her light ginger hair was pulled back in a ponytail, and she had masses of freckles across her arms and cheekbones. Devin thought they were adorable, but she wondered how the girl felt about them since too many teenagers hated anything that made them look unique or different. Judging by the greatly increased number of teenage male customers they'd had lately, Devin was quite certain that her opinion was shared on the matter. Shay was bright and friendly with all their customers, and Devin was glad to see that she wanted to get more involved in the shop.

She slid a bunch of the leaves in front of Shay. "I'm just picking off the tiniest of leaves right now. We'll candy them and use them as a garnish. About this size, or smaller."

She held one up as a model, and they quickly sorted through

the bunches, and then she set a pan on the burner and added heavy cream. "We're going to steep the rest of the leaves and infuse the liquid with their flavor, just like you would for tea, but with cream instead of water so we can use it to make a ganache."

Her dad came back as she and Shay were mixing raspberry puree with glucose, and after taking a look at where they were in the process, he wordlessly stashed their ice cream containers in the freezer until they were at a good stopping point. He joined them at the counter and seamlessly entered the conversation about the properties of pectin and citric acid while Devin carefully poured a cascade of rich chocolate coins into the stainless steel bowl on the scale. She loved hearing her dad talk about the art of chocolate making, and he used to read books about confectionary technique to her instead of bedtime stories when she was young. Her mother used to joke that her first word wasn't *mama* or *dada*, but *cacao*...

Devin had to force herself to relax and gently fold the raspberry-mint concoction into the chocolate. This shop was full of memories of her mother and her grandparents—and the two generations before them, even though Devin hadn't known them. It wouldn't be easy for her dad to walk away from this place, but he seemed convinced it was the right thing to do. Maybe he was even relieved to have the burden of running such a high-maintenance shop lifted from him. She hoped he was. And then Devin could focus on her own career, not worrying about whether an employer would let her leave for two or three months every year to come back and help him, and not feeling guilty in those seasons when she couldn't get here.

She had struggled all her life against the expectation that she would continue to run the store, but even when she had managed to get away from Leavenworth and the family business, she had still felt driven to come back. Usually by guilt, but also force of habit. She had been making chocolates at this counter since she was old enough to stand on a stool and hold a spatula. She always said, though, that while she was very knowledgeable about chocolate, for her dad—and for her mom, when she was alive—it was truly a passion.

They took a brief break to eat their ice cream, and Devin and her dad took turns explaining terms like *couverture* and *tempering* to Shay. She seemed interested, and Devin decided to get her more involved in filling orders and making some of the simpler truffles and pralines. She usually was just relieved to have someone else watching the register and boxing up chocolates for customers so she could concentrate on making the confections, but she didn't want to ignore the girl's desire to learn. If nothing else, Shay would end the holiday season with some go-to recipes for chocolates that she could bring to parties and use to impress her friends. Devin also thought it might be an additional selling point for the shop if they had a ready-made local assistant who had some knowledge and experience.

The scented ganache was the right temperature when they had finished eating, so Devin brought the heart-shaped molds and piping bags over to their workstation. She filled the bags and handed one each to her dad and Shay.

"You'll want to go slowly with this, making sure you're filling the entire mold and not leaving air pockets," she said, demonstrating with her own mold. "Don't go all the way to the top."

"Wait, you're letting me make some? What if I mess them up?"

Devin shrugged. "You'll be fine," she assured her. "And Dad will eat the mistakes."

He patted his stomach. "Best part of the job," he said. "I was real disappointed when Devin got good enough so all her chocolates were fit to sell."

They were silent for a few moments as they concentrated on carefully filling the molds, and then her dad took over and showed Shay how to cap the truffles with a layer of chocolate that would become the base when they were unmolded. Devin used a spatula to scrape the excess chocolate off the mold, subtly marking a few of Shay's that had too thick a layer of chocolate on the bottom. Devin would show her the difference later, once they were finished. They wouldn't be good enough to serve at the wedding, but they'd still be delicious, and Shay could take them home to share with her family.

Devin set the trays aside to rest before they were unmolded and fully encased in chocolate, and then she pulled a tray of already enrobed truffles out of the freezer.

"Cool," said Shay. "It's like a cooking show, where they put something raw in the oven and pull out an already cooked one at the same time. But wouldn't it be easier just to do all the batches at once, like an assembly line?"

"Well, in some ways, yes," Devin said, prepping a spray gun with a canister of red-colored cocoa butter. "That's what we used to do when I worked at a bigger candy company. But we also had less variation in our product. We'd make a bunch of shaped candies, and then use an enrobing machine to coat them all with the same chocolate. We really don't have the space here to make hundreds of candies at a time, especially since these ones are for the wedding, and we're also making chocolates for the store at the same time."

"Plus, we're more focused on small-batch, artisan confections here, rather than mass-produced candy," her dad added, bringing the focus back to passion and off logistics. "We'll often use different techniques and different flavors for each type of chocolate. Just watch what Devin does with these ones."

Devin turned on the sprayer and gently moved it across the surfaces of the frozen treats. As soon as the cocoa butter hit the little hearts, the chocolate crystallized, and its texture transformed.

"Oh, they look like velvet," Shay said.

Devin smiled at the excitement in her voice, remembering how she had felt every time she learned some new technique or how to use a new candy-making tool from her parents. She looked at the bright red confections with pride. She had missed being so in touch with her creations when she worked for the larger company in Seattle during pastry school, often feeling like she was merely running the machines while they were the ones actually making the chocolates. Here, she was hands-on with every single truffle. By the time Friday arrived, she would have dozens of these little hearts ready to go, as well as a variety of other shapes and flavors for the fancy dessert table.

At the thought of the weekend, she realized that she hadn't spared a thought for Criss in over an hour. She opened a jar of teensy mint leaves that she had already cooked in a sugar solution and used a pair of tweezers to place one on each heart while her dad let Shay practice with the spray gun on a piece of parchment paper. She wondered what Criss would have thought of Devin's work. Would she have been impressed? Intrigued? Eager to try something Devin had created with her own hands and expertise? Or just bored and ready to go back to Seattle?

Likely the latter, she thought, setting the hearts aside to fully set and putting a pan on the little burner to start crystallizing the new leaves she and Shay had separated.

"Say, Dad," she said, looking at the texture on the hearts. "I've usually only done this for hearts and Valentine's Day candy, but wouldn't this technique make cute little Christmas stocking truffles? They'd look like those plush, old-fashioned ones."

"Oh yes. Maybe flavored with chestnut puree?" he agreed eagerly. "And some chopped dried cranberries."

"And piped white chocolate to make the little cuff on the top," Devin said, practically able to taste them already. "I'll make a batch this weekend and we can see how they sell."

CHAPTER THREE

According to her car's GPS, the trip from Portland to Leavenworth should have taken four and a half hours. Lena managed
to more than double that. She ignored the computerized voice's suggestion to follow the Columbia River Gorge and then head north
toward Yakima, preferring instead to remain along the I-5 corridor
for as long as possible, where she was rarely out of sight of some
city or town. Civilization. She even disregarded the advice to take
the Auburn exit off I-5, once she had passed Tacoma, and held out
until she reached the turnoff for 405, just south of Seattle. Of course,
that meant she had to crawl along in heavy traffic with everyone else
headed toward Bellevue, until she eventually had to admit defeat
and merge onto I-90.

Of course, she didn't bother stopping in any of these cities
along her way. She just wanted to *see* them as long as possible.
To be surrounded by shopping malls and billboards and bars, all
promising an abundance of clothes, food, and nightlife before she
was surrounded by nothing but trees and mountains. And random
ingredients that she'd be expected to spin into edible meals for
strangers. Maybe she'd find Rumpelstiltskin hiding in a nearby
cave, and he would grant her a few wishes.

Even though she was dragging out her trip, the time between
her father's summons and her departure from Portland had been
dismally brief. According to her aunt's email, forwarded to her
by her dad, they only had the few weeks before Thanksgiving to

work the kinks out of the restaurant before it would be a full house every night. Lena thought *kinks* was an overly optimistic view of the difficulties she was about to face. Gordian knots seemed more apt.

To the annoying delight of her scheming father, she and Jeanine had broken up a couple of weeks earlier, so Lena hadn't had any reason not to get to Leavenworth right away, to give her time to learn in a handful of days what professionals spent years studying in culinary school and apprenticeships. Yeah. That was going to happen.

She had briefly considered reconnecting with Jeanine just to give herself a reason to stay in Portland, but she had quickly dismissed the idea. Partly because it wasn't in her to use someone that way, and mostly because Jeanine was unlikely to care whether Lena went to Leavenworth or not. In fact, Lena wasn't sure if they had actually broken up or if they had just gotten so busy that they forgot they were dating in the first place. Between her intensive work in the final stages of the GMM project and Jeanine's never-ending responsibilities as the head of a nationwide children's charity, they had basically communicated by texts and sticky notes in the last month of their relationship. Somehow, her parents had made that kind of relationship work, but Lena so far hadn't been able to keep a romance alive when both she and her partner were consumed by work.

She felt a momentary surge of hope as she neared Snoqualmie Pass and the raindrops hitting her windshield took on more substance, containing droplets of ice and eventually turning into full-fledged snow. She could call her aunt with the disappointing news that she wasn't able to make it across the pass in this blizzard, and she would have to return to her snug little apartment in Portland. Unfortunately, the longed-for snowstorm never materialized, and all she saw as she reached the summit were clear roads with a light dusting of snow on the shoulder. With her luck, the blizzard of the century would arrive next week, stranding her in Leavenworth until spring.

She was rapidly running out of ways to prolong her trip as civilization grew sparser. She stopped in Cle Elum for gas, getting a bag of chips and a surprisingly good cup of coffee for her late lunch, when she spotted an eagle in a tree across the highway. She managed to waste an hour backtracking until she found an access road that ran along the tributary of the Yakima River, and then she coaxed her gutsy little Saab over the ruts and potholes until she was able to park directly below the majestic bird. She took a few photos and sent one to Jacquie before getting back in her car and realizing that she didn't have room to turn around. She had to go another half mile before there was room to maneuver.

All too soon, though, she was back on the highway, turning onto 97, and winding along steep roads toward her destination. She had been feeling smug about her delaying tactics, but she had really only added a few hours and a lot of miles to her trip, plus possibly some new dents to her car's undercarriage, and now she was here. Her home for the next couple of months. Less, perhaps, if her aunt tired of this venture before Christmas. Fingers crossed.

She drove down Front Street, feeling the disorienting sense of having been magically transported into the Alps. Or at least a Disney, fairy-dust-sprinkled version of the Alps. Snow-sugared foothills bristling with evergreen trees surrounded the town, looming so close that they seemed as much a part of it as the buildings themselves. She had been picturing Leavenworth as a one-pony town, with nothing to recommend it besides the brief Christmas season. Judging by the number of turnoffs for hiking trails that she had passed on her way in, and the encroaching mini-mountains that looked manageable for an intermediate hiker like herself, the area would be a joy to visit in the warmer seasons. She definitely would love to come back in the summer or fall, once her aunt had moved on to a new venture and the board of health had shut down the restaurant because of her cooking.

But those promising seasons were months away, and she was here now, with snow and cold and an overwhelming cooking schedule that wouldn't leave her much time to explore. She had to admit, though, that the winter season had a unique beauty all its own. The shops she passed were all decorated within an inch of their lives in the Bavarian style. She saw the usual mix of stores common in tourist-heavy areas, most with German names and window decorations, as well as some more place-specific offerings, like entire shops devoted to Christmas tree decorations and German kitsch and souvenirs. There were art galleries and clothing stores and restaurants crammed side by side on the short main street. She made note of a couple of bookstores and an enticing chocolate shop to visit while she was here. A good number of wine-tasting rooms and quaint pubs looked promising, as well. She wouldn't die of boredom, but the cuteness might be the end of her.

She was contemplating how she would look in a Tyrolean hat, slowly starting to reconcile herself to her exile in this quaint-on-steroids town, when she saw it. Haus Bavaria. Her restaurant.

It was just as charming as the other buildings on the street, its ornate woodwork and gabled roof not giving any indication of the potential for food poisoning lurking inside its sweet, timbered walls. The name was unimaginative, but Lena was just relieved her aunt hadn't called it Lena's Good Eats or something equally embarrassing. She tried to put the place out of her mind as she turned off Front Street and located her small hotel. She only had reservations for the first week of her stay since she had learned that most inns and other accommodations were booked out months in advance, but she hoped she'd be able to find a last-minute opening somewhere, now that she was in town.

If not, Portland was only a few hours away. She had a place to stay there, and she knew she'd make the return trip in record time.

Lena checked in and made two trips from her car to get all her belongings into the hotel room—Bavarian-themed, of course. She had haphazardly thrown some clothes and toiletries into a suitcase, and she had her laptop, but the bulk of her car's trunk was filled with books. Uncertain about the internet service she would have in the mountains, and definitely not wanting to be spotted in a Leavenworth shop buying cookbooks, she had made a trip to Powell's Books before she left Portland. She already had an e-reader filled with novels to help her pass the time in the middle of nowhere, but she wanted some physical cookbooks with photos and explicit, step-by-step instructions to help her build some sort of repertoire.

Hopefully, one of them would contain an easier version of her grandmother's sauerbraten. She had also added a few memoirs from chefs to her basket, deluding herself that some of their skills might miraculously rub off on her while she read.

And then she was done. Her clothes were in drawers, her books were carefully arranged on the tiny desk, and the extended drive to Leavenworth was over. She had nothing left but to get to the restaurant and let the fiasco begin.

The rain had lightened into a steady drizzle, and it was colder than it had been in Portland, so Lena pulled on a thick wool sweater and a fleece-lined hoodie and walked the four blocks between her hotel and the restaurant. Glass half full said her commute was a breeze. Glass mostly empty said that her usual commute was the walk from the bedroom where she slept to the one where she kept her desk. When she arrived at the Restaurant of Doom—a much more fitting name than Haus Bavaria, and much more informative for potential diners—she found a sign on the door, lettered in a delicate script font and stating that they would be open to the public for limited seating on the weekends until Thanksgiving, with their grand opening happening on the Saturday after the holiday. Then they would be open daily through February.

Lena rested her hand on her suddenly queasy stomach, reading the notice with the same sense of despair as if she was reading the details of her prison sentence. She started to calculate how many meals she would be making over that period of time but quickly put an end to that endeavor, while also trying to ignore the fact that their first night of business was only five days away. Before she could lose her nerve completely, she reached for the door handle and, finding it unlocked, walked inside.

She stood for a moment in the empty dining room, looking around and feeling her lips twitch into the first smile she could recall over the past week. If someone had asked her to describe her expectations of the interior of Haus Bavaria, she would have nailed it. The walls had a similar stucco and timber look to the exterior—in case any of the patrons forgot they were in Simulated Bavaria—and they were covered with pictures of placid, flower-bedecked

Alpine cows, Heidi look-alikes with their sheep, and snow-covered mountain peaks. Rustic wooden shelves held a large collection of highly decorated beer steins, which gave Lena her first glimmer of hope. If they served enough beer, maybe the patrons wouldn't notice her cooking.

The tiny area next to the register was crammed with more income opportunities for the restaurant. Postcards, keychains, Haus Bavaria T-shirts—even with all her stress, Lena really wanted one of those—and steins embossed with Alpine decorations and the town's name. There was even a rack of Tyrolean hats, and Lena couldn't resist choosing one of the felt-and-feathered concoctions to try on. She peered into the small mirror at the top of the rack and grinned at her reflection. Snap a pic of her next to a sheep or cow, and she'd fit right in on these walls.

"Lena. Darling. You're here."

Lena spun away from the mirror to find Aunt Cheryl walking toward her from the back of the restaurant. For the second time that day, she felt a sense of disorientation, of being thrust into some different version of her reality. She could have been watching herself emerging from the future in a time warp. She shouldn't have been surprised by the family resemblance since she clearly favored her father's side in looks more than her mother's, but she hadn't seen Cheryl since she was a child, when the similarities between the two of them were less pronounced.

Cheryl had her same light blond hair, cut in an eerily similar style to hers, so the gentle waves just reached her jawline. Cheryl's hair had more gray flecked through it, giving hers an ashier tone than Lena's, but she figured she'd catch up on those gray hairs during her time in Leavenworth. Cheryl's eyes were hers, too—or hers were Cheryl's, she supposed—wide eyes with the same greenish-hazel, gold-flecked color and frame of unexpectedly long, dark eyelashes. Lena was torn between a kind of creepy sense of observing herself and the more cheerful thought of *Damn, I've aged well!*

Cheryl caught her up in a big hug, warm and enveloping. They were practically the same height, but Lena still felt like a child in her aunt's arms. Cheryl held her for a couple of heartbeats longer than most hugs, then gave her an extra squeeze before letting go. Just like Lena remembered.

Cheryl stepped back and looked at her. "What has it been, ten, twelve years? You've grown up," she said.

"I've grown into you," Lena corrected her with a laugh. Her awkward anticipation of meeting her aunt again after so long had dissipated with the hug.

Cheryl grinned, her eyes crinkling at the corners exactly the way Lena's did. "True. There was always a resemblance when you were young, but now it's...uncanny."

"Were you going to say creepy? Because that's how I felt at first."

"Maybe I was," Cheryl admitted. "My first thought when I saw you was *Hey, give me back my face!*"

They laughed, and Lena wished she was just here for the weekend, visiting a relative she hadn't seen for a decade or more and catching up. Then going home. No cooking or months-long stay required.

"Let me give you the grand tour," Cheryl said. She waved her hand around. "Dining room, obviously. We also have a private room for larger parties that seats up to a dozen people. But I'm sure you're more anxious to see your kitchen. It's right through here."

Anxious was one word for it. Sick with dread might be a better description of her internal state. She carefully avoided picturing the dining room full of hungry guests—with another dozen off in some room in the back—and followed her aunt through the swinging door.

"Ta-da!" Cheryl said, spreading her arms wide as they entered the kitchen. Lena struggled to find something to say. It was spotlessly clean and had the required fridges, stoves, and industrial-sized dishwasher—at least Lena was familiar with the basic appliances. That was as far as her knowledge of professional kitchens extended, though.

"It's really...I mean, it's..." Lena sighed and shook her head at her aunt. "I can't do this, Aunt Cheryl. I have no idea what I'm doing here, except that you and Dad seem to think I somehow absorbed all of grandmother's talent and skills just because I watched her cook every once in a while and because I've taken a few amateur cooking classes. I'm going to fail."

Cheryl shrugged. "I'm sure you will."

Lena frowned, unsure how to handle that response. She wasn't sure what she had expected after her little speech—recriminations because her skills had been oversold, or the same dismissive platitudes she had received from her father. *Oh, I'm sure you'll be fine.* But an acknowledgment that she was going to fail? Not what she thought her aunt would say.

Cheryl smiled and patted her cheek. "I know what you do for a living, Lena dear. I'm not under the impression that you're a professional chef, or that you'll earn a Michelin star by next weekend. You're going to make mistakes, probably some really impressive ones, but you're smart, and you'll learn from them. This is a chance for us to work on a project together and get to know each other again, or, really, for the first time. Besides, if you're anything like your father, you're accustomed to being good at everything you do. It will be good for you to be a beginner at something."

Lena was not going to share this conversation with her mother. It would only corroborate all the less than complimentary things she said about Cheryl. Flaky, impulsive, impractical to the extreme. Who else would buy a restaurant and then uproot her inexperienced niece to come run it, when she could have just as easily come to Portland and asked Lena to go to dinner or for a walk in the park if she just wanted to reconnect with her? This was further proof—if any were needed—that Lena and Cheryl might look alike, but the resemblance didn't go below the surface.

"Do your customers realize they're guinea pigs in my character-building experience?" Lena asked. It was all very well for her aunt to be blasé about her probable kitchen failures, but Lena was the one everyone who ate here would blame. And pelt with food.

"Well, we're certainly not going to advertise that," Cheryl said with a laugh and a shrug. "You'll make mistakes. If they're inedible ones, we won't charge the patrons. If they're moderate ones, well, I'm sure you've had plenty of mediocre dining experiences. It's part of the gamble of eating someone else's cooking."

Lena shook her head. She was definitely considering this experience as her one and only contribution to her dad's let's-help-Cheryl project. She would give it a try until the tourists and citizens of Leavenworth banded together and drove her out of town—not that she'd put up a fight when they did.

"Okay," she said, giving in since she was already embroiled in the mess. "I'll do my best. Where do we start?"

"I've already stocked the fridges and pantry with some staples, and I found a local source for meat, but you'll want to check out our local store tomorrow for more specialized ingredients. Here's an inventory of what I bought and a credit card for you to use. You'll have the kitchen to yourself tomorrow, and the staff will be here in the evening to meet you and do a tasting of what you've prepared. I'll also need a finalized menu for the printers by tomorrow afternoon, and if you give me the receipts from your shopping trip, I'll figure out prices for the dishes. Now, what about dessert?"

"Oh yes, please," Lena said, distracted by the way her aunt had shifted from seeming flaky to professional in a single moment. She logically knew that Cheryl had a lifetime of experience running different businesses as she rambled from interest to interest, but she hadn't given a thought to the fact that she might actually know how to run a business. Clearly, even though she seemed unperturbed by the idea of Lena muddling her way through the process, she expected her to really make an effort.

Cheryl was watching her with an indulgent smile. "I wasn't asking if you wanted dessert, dear. I was asking if you know how to make them."

"Oh," Lena said. Right, she was being a professional here. "Not really. I can make decent cookies, I guess."

"Well, we'll need to bring those in for now, since we don't have anyone with pastry experience on the staff. Why don't you stop by Meyer's while you're out gathering ingredients tomorrow. They do some outside catering, I believe, and they make excellent tarts and cakes. Two or three offerings per night should be sufficient. Now, let's get you moved in."

"Moved in?" Lena repeated, the switch in her aunt's tone from businesslike to cozy catching her off guard again. "I have a hotel room."

"For the season?" Cheryl asked. Lena shook her head. "Well, there won't be anything available in town after Thanksgiving, and why pay for a room when we have an apartment above the restaurant? You'll have your own space, but it will give us a chance to get to spend time together."

"Well, okay. Thank you," Lena said, wondering when she had lost all agency in her life. "But I've already prepaid for the week at my hotel, so I'll move here once my time is up," she added, clinging to some small remnant of autonomy.

"Of course, dear," Cheryl said, handing her the credit card and giving her another squeezy hug. "I'm just so very glad you're here."

Lena smiled and nodded, thinking *I'm not* but not saying it out loud. She made it out the door and stood in the cold air for a few moments, dragging icy breaths deep into her lungs to calm herself. She tucked the lists and credit card into her back pocket and retraced her steps to her hotel, uninterested in doing more than passing through the town. She soothed herself with the thought that she could keep looking around for other rental options, just in case. Somehow, the fact that her aunt was willing to accept mistakes but was still expecting her to put serious effort into the process made it seem even more daunting. She had been ready to use the excuse that she didn't know what she was doing to get her through the holiday season, giving her the ability to shrug off her mistakes as belonging in part to others. To her dad, for forcing her here. To her aunt, for coming up with this scheme in the first place. To her cooking teachers who had praised her food because they were paid to be encouraging, leaving her with absolutely no clear indication of whether she was a success or a disaster in the kitchen. Now it was all on her.

She was halfway back to her hotel before she figured out why the passersby kept smiling at her, with their gazes flicking to the top of her head. She had apparently stolen a Tyrolean hat from her own restaurant gift shop. Oh well. She was keeping it. Her aunt could take it out of her nonexistent pay.

CHAPTER FOUR

Devin used a sharp, serrated knife to carefully slice the domed surface off a round chocolate genoise to make it perfectly flat, and then she gently cut it in half. She moved the scraps to one side and set the two thick layers next to the ones she had already finished. Although she usually did all the chocolate making on the steel and marble counters behind the display cases, so customers could watch the process, she used the small kitchen in the back for making cakes and tarts—mostly for special orders—as well as the tartlets and mousse cups they sold in the store. The space was cramped, but she had everything at hand and usually did this work when only she and her father were here, and their assistants and patrons hadn't yet arrived. She loved the coziness of the space, preferring it over the big, more industrial kitchens she had worked in during school. She was dabbing the surface of the first layer with a rich dark rum syrup when her father came into the small kitchen and pounced on the extra bits of cake. Devin smiled as he leaned against the counter and tried one of the pieces—he'd always seemed to have a built-in radar that let him know when scraps of cake or chocolate were available.

"Mmm, delicious," he said, quickly finishing off the genoise. "Is this for Maggie Duncan's birthday cake?"

"Yes," Devin said as she spread bittersweet ganache over the genoise with a spatula, making sure the chocolate covered the surface evenly. "It's kind of a chocolate overload, but you know how much she loves rich desserts."

"Bless her for that," her dad said as he went over to the counter next to the oven and returned with a large tray of meringues, setting them in Devin's reach. "It means I get to eat well today."

Devin laughed. "You eat well every day," she said. She used a paring knife to trim the edges of the chocolate hazelnut meringue until the flat disc was the size of the cake layers. She slid the discarded, crispy edges toward her dad. "I've seen you sneaking chocolates when you think nobody's looking."

He laughed as well, but Devin thought she noticed a sad note to it. "I'll miss this," he said, with a definite air of wistfulness.

Devin set the meringue on top of the ganache and then added another layer of genoise. She used her hands to align the layers neatly and picked up the rum syrup and brush. "This?" she asked.

"All of this," he said, waving his hands to encompass the small kitchen and the entire store. "The chocolate, the creativity, the customers. Working with you."

Devin sighed. Although she had spent a good portion of her life trying to get away from the family shop and the weight of expectation it laid on her, she felt pangs of nostalgia and sadness at the thought of selling the place, too. But there was relief there as well, and she was certain her dad felt the same way.

"If you always have chocolate at hand, you can make candy and experiment with new flavors, but without the stress of customers and money. Just think how easy it will be for you to make new friends, wherever you decide to live, once they find out what your hobby is." Devin repeated the steps on her cake until all the layers were complete, and then she spread the rest of the ganache on the top and sides. "And we'll be able to just spend time together without worrying about the store and getting enough product made for the day. It'll be nice. We could even go on vacation together sometime, with no responsibilities or customers dragging us down."

She scooped up a handful of chopped roasted hazelnuts and pressed them into the side of the cake, slowly spinning it until she had every inch covered. She glanced at her dad, who hadn't responded to her comments. "Dad?"

He was toying with a scrap of meringue but looked up when she spoke. "Oh yes. It will be nice. And what a relief not to have to run the shop. I'm just feeling maudlin, I suppose, but I'll get over it."

"I wish you'd change your mind and come to Seattle instead of staying on this side of the mountains. I'd be able to see you more often, even if I get a job that doesn't let me take much time off for traveling over here."

"Maybe," he said, giving her a kiss on the cheek. "Probably. Now, I'm going to go open up and let you get finished here."

Devin watched him go through the swinging door to the front of the shop, and then she moved to the other side of the island, placing a sheet of acetate next to a bowl of chocolate she had already tempered and set aside to rest. They had been having this discussion ever since they had decided together that it was time for her dad to sell the shop and retire. He loved his snowy winters and hot summers and wasn't keen on trading them for the more temperate, rainy western side of the Cascades, but most of the reason they had decided to sell was because she couldn't count on having the time or ability to get across the mountains to help him as much as he needed. She'd feel better if he was settled into a retirement community nearer to Seattle.

She put that argument aside for another time, though, and concentrated on the decorations for her cake. She needed to get this done and then get a few dozen more wedding chocolates finished, not to mention the extra salted caramel and maple pecan candies she should make for the shop. They were always the best sellers. She exhaled, feeling the tension of a long to-do list tightening her shoulders, but as soon as she began freehand piping some fir trees and a grazing deer, she felt her muscles release and her mind settle. The chocolate was the perfect consistency, and the deer's head didn't look proportionately too large—something she often struggled with. Of course, as soon as she set the piping bag down, her concerns flooded in again, but they were muted, somehow, by the little woodland scene she had created.

By the time her dad popped his head in the door and said he was going to get them coffee, asking her to listen for the bell on the door in case customers came in, she had fully assembled the cake and the decorations on top of it. A marbled white and dark chocolate mountain and base formed the backdrop for the trees and deer. She had dusted them with confectioners' sugar to give a snowy effect, and the chopped hazelnuts looked like rocks on the mountain slope.

She put the rest of her supplies away before she wiped an errant drop of ganache off the glass plate she had used as a base and slowly picked up her heavy creation, backing through the swinging door and into the main area of the shop just as the bell above the front door chimed. She swore under her breath as she startled a little, pausing to get her balance back before stepping into the showroom and letting the door swing closed behind her as she turned to greet the customer.

Devin knew everyone in town by sight and would have recognized this woman as a tourist, even without the Tyrolean hat as a clue. Instead of looking silly in it, though, she looked adorable. Her golden hair fell in a soft wave over her left cheekbone, and her eyes were a perfect blend of all the mossy greens and rich browns of a hike through a forest. There was something warm and silky about her, calling to mind Devin's favorite honey-almond nougats, dripping with milk chocolate.

"Wow," the woman said, echoing Devin's thoughts. Unfortunately, she wasn't exactly looking at Devin when she said it.

"Are you talking about me or the cake?" Devin asked wryly, easing the cake and its glass base into a cardboard box.

"What? Oh, both...I mean, you, of course...You're really... um..." She stuttered to a stop and then grinned, her eyes crinkling in the corners. The good-humored smile seemed natural on her. "You have beautiful eyes," she offered.

"Yes, and you were looking about a foot south of them when you said wow," Devin said, giving in and laughing with her. Her ego might have been more bruised if she hadn't been so proud of the cake. Besides, she had been thrown off guard by her immediate physical reaction to the woman, and she was glad to have some humor bring her back down to earth. She was here to sell chocolate, after all, not to drool over a tourist who would be gone in a day or two.

"Sorry," the woman said sheepishly. "I haven't eaten all day, and that cake looks delicious." She looked around the shop, at all the trays of multicolored and delicately shaped confections. "Everything looks amazing in here. Do you make all these candies yourself?"

"My dad and I make everything by hand," Devin said. She couldn't resist plucking one of the honey nougats out of the case. "Here, try a sample."

The woman took the treat from her, with slender fingers that trailed a ghost of warmth along Devin's palm, and popped it in her mouth. Devin smiled at her expression—she might get tired of working in the shop after so many holiday seasons, but she never got tired of seeing the looks on people's faces when they tasted a Meyer's chocolate for the first time, especially if they were accustomed to only store-bought bars wrapped in foil and paper.

She closed her eyes as she chewed. "Oh my God. I love you," she said after she swallowed. She opened her eyes again and grinned at Devin. "Okay, I was talking to the chocolate that time, too."

Beautiful and charming. Dangerous. Time to get her out of the shop. Devin wiped her hands on her apron and belatedly realized she was wearing one of her chocolate-smeared white ones instead of the official blue one. Oh well. She was behind the cases with all those distracting chocolates between them. The woman probably wouldn't even notice her enough to see what she was wearing. "What can I get for you?" she asked.

"Oh, I really didn't come in to buy anything," she said. She scanned the cases again with a sigh. "But I'll take a dozen of anything. Pick your favorites. I'm Lena, by the way. The new... well, I'm the new chef at Haus Bavaria." She fell silent, biting her lip, her smile fading away.

Devin got a box and made her selections on autopilot without really needing to think about what she was choosing. So she wasn't a tourist, and she'd be here all season? Devin was a little uneasy about that, but Lena looked even more upset about it than she was.

Lena sighed. "I'm new at this," she said, trying to smile, but it didn't have any of the naturalness as before. "We need someone to make desserts, and my aunt—she owns the restaurant—suggested I talk to you about making something for us. Or two or three somethings per night, I guess."

Devin managed to keep her groan inward and not audible, although she doubted Lena would have noticed. She seemed locked in some internal struggle about this restaurant. Almost without thinking, Devin handed her another piece of dark chocolate–covered candy.

"Kirsch and coconut," she said, giving herself time to think while Lena ate. On the one hand, even though her dad had run the shop successfully, he wasn't the best with financial decisions, and there was an equity loan on the shop. The premium quality ingredients they used were expensive, and the tourist season was short. Even though he sold chocolate year-round, they'd needed to supplement their income by taking on other jobs like making specialty chocolates for weddings or the increasing number of wine-tasting rooms in town, or taking on jobs like the one Lena was proposing. Devin was desperately trying to make the shop look as solvent and ripe with potential as she could for prospective buyers.

On the other hand, she had been accepting every offer that came along since she'd been back in town. She was already overbooked and overworked, even without factoring in the day-to-day effort of keeping their own cases full in the shop. She'd be a fool to take on another big job right now.

On the other, other hand—or foot, whatever—Lena upset her equilibrium. Devin had been internally moaning about not being able to feel an emotional, romantic connection to other women, and now here was someone who made her believe that maybe it hadn't been a character flaw after all. Maybe she just needed the right person to ignite…No, she didn't. Not right now.

"Thank you, that really helped," Lena said after she finished the chocolate. "Look, I'm not really a chef. This whole idea is just another spur-of-the-moment scheme of my aunt's, and I don't know what I'm doing. But what you've made here…well, if we could serve something like this for dessert, it might make people forget how disappointing the rest of the meal was." She gave a weak laugh, as if she was joking, but not really. "You'd really be helping me out if you say yes."

Lena looked a little forlorn as she spoke, and Devin had a feeling it wasn't a natural state for her. She closed the box of chocolates and tied a blue satin ribbon with gold edging around it. "How many seatings?" she asked, giving in to the inevitability of taking this job, even though she still hoped something in their conversation about logistics would let her turn it down.

Lena scrunched her nose and seemed to be thinking about her answer. "About forty, I think?"

"Forty seatings," Devin repeated. "A week?"

"No, a night. We're open weekends until Thanksgiving, then daily after."

"Seatings, not seats," Devin clarified.

Lena smacked her forehead with her palm. "Of course. *Seatings.* My aunt said two per night. Maybe three later in the season if I figure out what I'm doing. I misunderstood—I've never worked in a restaurant."

"But I assume you've eaten in one before," Devin said, fighting her grin.

Lena laughed, with a little less strain than before. "Yes, and I know what a seating is. I'm just not accustomed to it having anything to do with me and my cooking."

"Okay, two seatings and about forty seats. A German restaurant in the middle of town is going to be full every night during the season, so be prepared for that. Are you expecting authentic German food, or are you okay with vaguely European, general dessert sort of options?"

"Whatever you want to make," Lena said with a permissive wave of her hand. "I honestly don't think I'd know the difference, and I'm hoping to attract a clientele with undiscerning palates."

Devin laughed. "I'm sure you'll be a success with that kind of can-do attitude. I can make a couple of sample desserts and bring them by sometime for you and your aunt to try."

"That'd be great," Lena said with a bright smile, looking happier than she had since the topic of the restaurant had come up. "I'm supposed to be making dinner for the staff tonight, to get to know them and let them sample what we'll be serving. Is that too short of notice? They might be more inclined to be kind if they get dessert out of the deal."

"Oh. Yes, I can pull something together by then." She mentally ran through some options while she rang up the chocolates and swiped the credit card Lena handed her. "How many staff do you have, so I know how much to bring?"

"I have no idea," Lena said with a cheerful shrug, picking up the box and heading toward the door. "And you're welcome to stay for dinner, but you might want to eat something before you come, just in case."

She held the door open for Devin's father, who was holding two paper coffee cups in his hands, and then waved good-bye to the two of them as she left.

"My, she's pretty," he said, coming behind the counter and handing Devin her latte.

Devin didn't respond to his comment, but he had always been more perceptive than she liked, and he just chuckled at her silence.

"She's the new chef at Haus Bavaria," she said, bypassing the discussion of Lena's looks. She had already spent too much time thinking about them. "We're going to be making their desserts for the season."

"That'll be a good gig," he said, washing his hands and putting on a fresh apron. Devin took off her stained cotton one and did the same. "You've been adding so much to your plate since you got here, though. Do we have time to add a full restaurant service to all the other jobs you've taken on?"

"No," Devin said wearily, leaning her hip against the register counter and taking a sip of her latte. "But the added income will look good on paper for the sale."

She didn't have much faith in Lena's ability to run the restaurant for an entire season, mostly based on Lena's own palpable lack of faith, but that didn't matter to Devin. She only had to last a few weeks, until the sale of the store was final. Surely, Lena could manage that much?

"We'll make a few easy tarts," she said, thinking through her usual repertoire. "Simple ones that Shay can help us make. I can start a little earlier each day and get some fancier cakes made, too. We'll be fine," she assured him.

"We'll be fine," he repeated, with less conviction in his voice. She patted him on the shoulder with what she hoped was a confident smile and went into the back room to scrounge ingredients for tonight's desserts.

Chapter Five

L ena sat in the midst of chaos and opened an imported bottle of hefeweizen, then poured it into one of the fancy steins from near the register. She apparently wasn't bartender material, either, because the foam cascaded over the rim of the mug, and she had to mop it up with a towel while she surveyed the kitchen. The day had started out rough—meaning she had still been in Leavenworth when she woke up, and it hadn't been a dream after all—and it had been going steadily downhill ever since.

Except for the chocolate shop.

Lena sighed, thinking back to the one bright spot in her morning. She had to admit that she had been mesmerized by that cake at first since she hadn't eaten much since her coffee and chips in Cle Elum the evening before. She'd been feeling too nauseated and anxious to eat. But once she saw past the cake, well, *wow* definitely applied to the woman holding it, too. She was gorgeous, with eyes so deep blue they almost shaded into indigo, and straight brown hair that was as glossy as one of her chocolates. The old apron wasn't the type of clothing Lena would usually picture if she was thinking *sexy*, but it had somehow managed to emphasize her curves.

Lena was no stranger to dating successful women—in fact her usual type was the highly driven, no time for anything but work kind of person. Like her family. And like her. But this woman had been a different sort of successful, creating works of edible art. She obviously was talented and incredible at her job—which was quite a turn-on—and she had a quiet confidence in herself that had been a marked difference from Lena's current insecurities. Plus, she had been kind, feeding Lena soul-reviving chocolates and taking pity on her plea for help.

She sighed. If only she had been less preoccupied with her anxiety about tonight, she would have asked her name. Now it would be an awkward question to bring up when Ms. Chocolate arrived with her desserts. Maybe her aunt would know?

Lena decided to ask her later. Right now, she needed some moral support, so she called Jacquie.

"Hey, sweetie, how's it going?" Jacquie said when she answered, with a breezy, no-worries type of attitude that Lena longed to share.

"I lasted a day," Lena said morosely, taking a swig of the hefeweizen. It was excellent—slightly citrusy and wheat-y, with a light fizz on her tongue. The perfect accompaniment to some fine German food. Too bad she didn't have any at hand. "That's good enough, isn't it?"

"Are you quitting already? It doesn't seem like you've been there along enough to even serve a single dinner yet."

"I haven't," Lena said, looking around the once-spotless kitchen. Now it was uniformly covered in gravy. "Not to the public, at least. I'm just making sample dishes to serve to the staff, but it's not going well."

Understatement of her lifetime. She wasn't meant to be serving the food for another hour, but two of her dishes were already finished and were drying out in a warm oven—possibly a better alternative than letting them get cold on the counter, but she wasn't one hundred percent convinced of that. The roast was still cooking and likely wouldn't be cooked through for another four hours, judging by its current internal temperature. She had turned the heat up on that oven to speed up the process and might be able to salvage some of the outermost meat.

Jacquie made a tutting sound. "You're always so hard on yourself, Lena. I'm sure it'll all be better than you're expecting."

"Oh, I really doubt that," Lena said, taking another drink. "I did some reading about these staff tastings, and I need to describe the dishes to them so they'll be familiar with my menu when customers ask questions. Do you mind if I put you on video so I can show you around and practice my speech?"

"Oh yes, please," Jacquie said, with obvious excitement. "I was going to ask to see what you've made, but I thought it might seem too schadenfreude of me. See? I'm already in character."

"Go ahead and laugh at my misery," Lena said, waving weakly at Jacquie when she switched to video. "At least someone should get some joy out of this meal, since my staff and I aren't likely to."

"What's all over your face?"

Lena swiped at her cheeks with the beer-scented towel. "Does it look like gravy? It's probably gravy. I had a slight disagreement with the immersion blender."

"Ah. Did you forget about the part where it's meant to be immersed?"

Lena scowled. "It was partially immersed. You'd think that would be good enough, but apparently not."

She hoped she had managed to salvage enough to serve over the schnitzel, but she also needed it for the sauerbraten since she hadn't had time to make her grandmother's lovely wine and sour cream sauce. It was going to have to stretch, so she was planning to add more cream. Who'd complain about that?

Her aunt had volunteered to act as her sous-chef tonight, but Lena had thought she'd be better off scrambling around on her own, without anyone else watching and making her nervous. She had barely spent time with Cheryl so far, since she had been busy planning the menu, shopping for ingredients, and then trying to beat them into submission. Her aunt might have seen this restaurant as a way for them to reconnect with each other, but Lena just wanted to form a meaningful relationship with a few aspirin and another beer. She blamed her aunt and her dad for getting her in this mess, and she wasn't in the mood for turning it into a family reunion. Those were supposed to be potluck, anyway, weren't they? And not completely her responsibility.

She used a towel to pull one of the dishes out of the warming oven. "This is pork schnitzel," she told Jacquie, keeping her camera pointed toward the food and avoiding looking at her friend's expression. "I pounded it thin, breaded it, and fried it. It's served with parslied noodles and red cabbage."

She swapped the dish for the other one from the oven. "This is bratwursts and hot potato salad. This one should be okay. Who can mess up bratwursts? And here's the sauerbraten, which is still kind of raw."

"Shouldn't you be trying to sell me on these?" Jacquie asked, her voice sounding tinny since Lena was holding her phone as far in the oven as she dared.

Lena shut the oven door and faced her friend. "There's bacon in the hot potato salad. Yum yum!"

Jacquie laughed. "Oh, that's much better. Is it meant to be hot, or did you accidentally put it in the oven instead of the fridge."

Lena wanted to act insulted, but it really was a fair question, given her abilities. "It's meant to be served warm. It's probably the best part of the meal. So, tell me honestly. How bad does it look?"

She steeled herself for Jacquie's criticism since she was never less than honest, but her friend just shrugged.

"It looks like food, Lena. You could maybe tidy up the presentation a little so it doesn't look like you slopped it on the plate for your family, but I'm sure it will all be good. You just need to believe in it more than you do. If you describe it to your staff in that gloomy voice, they're going to be predisposed to think it's bad. Use some more positive words than *okay* and *still raw*, and you'll hook them. Get them excited about working with you."

"I suppose I can pretend I'm on a job interview," Lena said. "Then I'll—oh, hi."

She faltered to a stop when the woman from the chocolate shop came through the door carrying two white boxes tied with bright blue ribbons.

"Hello," Jacquie said. Lena started and realized she had swung the phone toward the door.

The woman pushed aside a few dirty pans and set her pristine boxes on the gravy-smeared counter before waving at Jacquie with a friendly smile.

"Hello," she said, then glanced at Lena.

"Oh, right. This is Jacquie. Jacquie, this is…um. Ms. Meyer?" Damn. She should have asked her aunt about this before calling Jacquie.

"Nice to meet you, Jacquie. I'm Devin. Lena hired me to make desserts for the restaurant."

"And she didn't even ask your name?"

Devin laughed. "She was too busy flirting with a chocolate cake at the time," she said, giving Lena a wink.

"That sounds like something she'd do," Jacquie said.

Lena turned the phone back to face her. "In what universe does that sound like something I'd do?"

Jacquie just laughed. "I'll let you two get back to work. Let me know how tonight goes, and do you remember what I said?"

Lena sighed. "Yes. If I sell the food with the right words, they won't notice the taste."

"Well, that motto inspires my confidence in the chef," Devin muttered dryly as she undid the ribbon on one of the boxes and lifted out a glistening tart.

"Fig and frangipane," she said when Lena had ended the call, setting it down and opening the next box. "And this one is chocolate hazelnut. Nothing fancy, but it's always a popular flavor combination."

Nothing fancy? Lena stared at the perfect fluted edges of the tart, the shiny chocolate surface that was scored to make slicing it easier, and the circle of miniature truffles—each topped with a hazelnut coated in caramel—that nestled on each neat triangle.

"Did you really make these today? After I came to your store?"

"Yes. Tarts are simple once you have the basic technique down. I'll be able to make Black Forest cakes for you, too, since those are always a hit around here, but I'll need to plan ahead for those. I didn't have time today."

"Wow," Lena said, then she caught Devin's eye and laughed. "That one was for you," she said. She leaned forward and lowered her voice. "Maybe we can just serve these tonight, and skip dinner? Or, better yet, we can run out the back door and take them back to my hotel room so we don't have to share?"

Devin gave her a playful shove in the shoulder. "I'm sure your food will be great. It actually smells pretty good back here. Can I help you get the plates ready?"

Lena was torn between wanting Devin to stay because she loved her throaty laugh and she had started to feel marginally less freaked out about tonight since she had arrived, and wanting to shove her out onto the street so she wouldn't witness what was about to happen once the food was served.

"I don't think we need to get started quite yet," she said, stalling for time.

Devin patted her on the arm. "It's time, Lena. People were starting to arrive when I came in. Your aunt asked me to bring these back and tell you to come out and introduce yourself as soon as you were ready."

As if on cue, Cheryl came through the swinging door and clapped her hands. "Less chatting, you two, and more plating. Oh, Devin, those tarts are beautiful! Almost too pretty to cut, but we have to because I can't wait to taste them." She looked around the kitchen, her smile fading slightly and then returning full force. "Let's find you some plates that don't have gravy splatters on them."

Cheryl and Devin busied themselves with dessert while Lena loaded her plates onto a serving cart. She had only managed to make a few out of the ten entrées and six side dishes she had given her aunt for the menu. She had several plates of each and would give everyone small portions after she attempted to sell them, according to Jacquie's advice. She pulled the roast out of the oven and sliced off some of the worst burned parts, stopping when she got to the undercooked center. She had enough of the in-between, relatively nicely cooked meat to spread over two plates, and she drizzled gravy over the roast, the bratwursts, and the schnitzel. She had meant to make a different sauce for each dish, but well, she had meant for everything to look and taste wonderful, too. The best laid plans, and all that.

"Let's get this done," she said grimly to Devin and her aunt, who were watching her with what she could only interpret as trepidation. "These people need to get home and update their résumés, after all."

"It's your first night, dear," Cheryl said. "You'll get better with each one."

"Yes," Devin said, obviously trying desperately not to laugh. "What she said."

Lena looked at the cart filled with lovely slices of mouth-watering tarts. "Would you mind squishing some of those so my plates don't look as bad by comparison?"

"Not a chance," Devin said, giving in to the laughter and blocking her cart from Lena's reach.

She sighed and wheeled her sacrificial offerings out to the dining room where the staff were seated around three tables pushed together. Oh great, she thought. Teenagers. The epitome of tact. They were going to roast her alive. And they'd probably do a better job than she had with the sauerbraten.

Her aunt introduced the five teens who would be the waitstaff, and then Kirby and Layla, who would be her sous-chefs. Those two at least looked like they had already graduated from high school— maybe a year ago. Lena smiled at everyone, hoping she looked confident, but her smile faded as her aunt introduced her. Cheryl would have made Jacquie proud with the way she sold Lena and her mad culinary skills, emphasizing the hours she had spent at her grandmother's side, absorbing these family recipes and her love of cooking. Lena was tempted to look over her shoulder in case there was a real chef standing behind her, one who would be able to live up to her aunt's words. One who had magically turned a few community center classes into an advanced culinary degree in a single afternoon.

And then it was her turn to describe the dishes. By this point, she was so tired from all the culinary cramming she had done the night before, and on edge after not eating much more than half a box of Devin's chocolates all day, that she was merely hoping she would be able to string some coherent sentences together, let alone market her food with any sort of enthusiasm.

"Well, um, this is the sauerbraten. My grandmother's specialty. It'll have a different kind of sauce when we serve it, and there will be more than this on the plate. The bratwursts are pan fried and served with German potato salad. And it really is supposed to be warm, not cold, so that wasn't a mistake. And this is a pork schnitzel that I coated in seasoned panko and fried so it's crispy and golden brown." Hey, she was getting the hang of it. "It's served with a mushroom gravy that…oh, damn. I forgot to put the mushrooms in it."

A couple of the teens snickered at that, and Lena heard a snort of barely contained laughter from Devin behind her. She gave the kids a lopsided grin and a small shrug.

"Thank you, Lena," Cheryl said, clapping her hands. A few of the others joined in half-heartedly. "I'm sure we're all excited to taste everything. And on an unrelated note, I'll be installing a jar in the kitchen, where we can add a dollar every time one of us swears. I imagine that Lena will be funding a lavish pizza party for all of us before the season is over."

There was more enthusiastic clapping for that comment. Pizza? Lena figured she'd put enough in the jar to buy everyone a steak dinner. She turned back to her cart and made eye contact with Devin. She was looking a little teary-eyed and had her phone held out in a way that looked suspiciously like she was taking a video of Lena. But she put it away and gave Lena a thumbs-up sign, coming over to help her dole out the food.

"I'm not sure that was exactly what your friend Jacquie had in mind, but I loved the speech. You need to give me her number so I can send the recording to her."

"You wouldn't dare," Lena said, trying to sound menacing even though she wanted to laugh, too.

"Oh, I would," Devin said with a wicked grin, walking with several plates balanced on her arms and setting them in front of the staff.

Once everyone had a plate, there was a moment of quiet while they each looked around the table, as if waiting for someone else to take a bite and not die, before they tried the food. Cheryl and Devin both dug in with enthusiasm, though, and the others followed their lead, a bit more tentatively.

"The schnitzel is very flavorful, Lena dear," Cheryl said. "And the potato salad is tasty, too."

"The bacon is a great addition," Devin agreed. She took a bite of cabbage and quickly schooled her expression back to neutral, but not before Lena caught her wince. She raised her eyebrows, and Devin smiled encouragingly at her. "It's…sweet. That helps to balance the vinegar."

"Can we try dessert now?" one of the kids asked, leaning over to stare at Devin's cart.

"Yes, let's," Cheryl said. "Devin, would you mind describing the tarts for us? And Lena, everything is delicious. Thank you for cooking for us tonight."

She led another round of applause, and everyone joined in this time. Probably because Lena was taking their partially eaten plates of dinner away.

"Would it make you feel better if I swear when I talk about the figs?" Devin whispered as she wheeled her cart closer to the table and passed Lena with her armload of dishes.

"Don't patronize me," Lena said haughtily, even though her lips quirked in a smile. "Just make sure I get double portions of everything."

She piled the plates on her cart and turned to watch Devin happily chatting to the staff about frangipane and tempering chocolate. She was embarrassed about how the evening had gone, and doubtful that she would actually improve as much as her aunt seemed to think she would, but those emotions faded when she watched Devin smile. She still wanted to put as much distance between her and Leavenworth, this restaurant, her aunt, and anything remotely Bavarian as possible, though. She wasn't interested in small towns or the beautiful chocolatiers who lived in them. When the restaurant inevitably failed, she would put all this behind her without a second glance.

CHAPTER SIX

Devin helped Lena and Cheryl stack all the dirty plates and leftover food on the carts and wheel them back into the kitchen. She really didn't need to stay and help clean up—honestly, all she had meant to do was drop off her tarts and leave before the tasting—but she had found herself lingering, talking to the kids and watching Lena navigate through what were quite clearly unfamiliar waters for her. She had told Devin that she wasn't a professional chef, but Devin had assumed that she had been exaggerating about how little she knew about running a restaurant.

No, not even close.

Lena had clearly felt awkward talking about her food and serving it, and she couldn't possibly have missed the way everyone picked at her offerings, then devoured every crumb of Devin's desserts, but she had gone through the evening with what seemed to be a genuine smile on her face. She had talked easily with her teenage waitstaff and had been enthusiastic in her praise of Devin's food, even though the tarts had managed to make the rest of the dinner seem even worse in comparison.

She seemed to have an underlying confidence and self-deprecating good humor that had let her make it through a bad night without needing to sulk or tear Devin down in an attempt to make herself feel better. And that kind of attitude was too damned sexy for Devin's comfort. So, of course, instead of leaving like a sensible person and vowing to let her dad or Shay deliver the desserts to

Haus Bavaria for the rest of the season, she was hanging out after the party with Lena and her aunt like she was one of the family.

The three of them stood just inside the kitchen door and surveyed the disaster zone. Even though Devin had stayed this long because she was having a difficult time pulling herself out of Lena's compelling orbit, she knew she couldn't just walk away now and leave the other two to deal with this gravy-bedecked room alone. Naturally, the staff wouldn't be expected to clean up after a chef's tasting, since they were considered honored guests at the event, but Cheryl had wisely kept them from even walking into the kitchen for any reason at all. If they had seen what was left in the wake of Lena's cooking, Devin would guarantee that less than half of them would show up on opening night.

Lena turned her back on the mess and faced Devin and Cheryl. "All right," she said, crossing her arms over her chest and then uncrossing them and putting her hands on her hips instead, as if unsure what to do with her limbs. "No sugarcoating. Tell me honestly how that went." She held up her hands, palms facing out, as if to hold off the criticism a moment longer. "Obviously, I know it was an awful meal. But was it awful with a scrawny little possibility that I could make it better, or awful with absolutely no chance that I can make edible meals for the public, and I should just go back to Portland right now?"

She heaved a big sigh, as if mentally preparing herself for the worst, and dropped her hands to her sides. Devin and Cheryl looked at each other, and Lena's aunt gestured for her to go first. Devin knew she wouldn't be doing Lena or the restaurant any favors by holding back her suggestions, but still, she led with the most positive comments that came to mind.

"Your flavor profiles are very good," she said, meeting Lena's gaze so she knew Devin wasn't lying. "And you've come up with some nice, basic German-style dishes that will be appealing to a lot of people, especially tourists who want a meal that complements the town itself."

"But…" Lena prompted, although Devin thought she seemed to relax a fraction at her words.

Devin shrugged. "But your timing is off. Parts of the meal were cold, parts were warm but dried out from sitting too long. That's fixable."

"Okay," Lena said with a nod. "Timing. That sounds like something I can handle. Cher...Aunt Cheryl?"

"Well, the schnitzel was tasty, but very greasy."

"Your oil probably wasn't hot enough," Devin added. "When that happens, the food cooks too slowly and absorbs too much of the grease."

Cheryl nodded in agreement. "That sounds right." She paused and looked around. "And I know you meant for more of this gravy to be on the food than splattered on the walls, but you really need to have different sauces and gravies for each dish, not just one type poured over everything."

"Oh, and the cabbage," Devin said, remembering the shock of her first bite, when copious amounts of sugar and vinegar went to war in her mouth. "I'm sure it will be delicious tomorrow, but the flavors were too strong since it didn't have time to mellow."

"I'm afraid that's my fault," Cheryl admitted. "She had less than a day's notice about the tasting."

"Anything else?" Lena asked, looking between the two of them.

"I loved the potato salad," Devin said, and Cheryl nodded in agreement. "But if you're talking to customers," she continued, "don't say things like *Really, it's supposed to be warm. That isn't a mistake.* That just makes it sound like it really was a mistake, and you forgot to put it in the fridge or something."

Cheryl laughed. "Luckily, I wrote the descriptions for the menu and didn't leave that to her."

"That was smart of you," Devin said, joining in her laughter. Cheryl seemed much more relaxed about the fiasco of a tasting than Lena was, which was surprising since it was apparently her business. Maybe she just had an abundance of faith in her niece's abilities. Devin deepened her voice, as if she was narrating an imaginary menu. "The schnitzel is coated in panko and topped with a delicious gravy, but dammit, sometimes I forget to add the mushrooms."

"The sauerbraten is usually served in a generous portion and covered in a special sauce…but not tonight," Cheryl said, matching Devin's menu-narrating voice.

Lena took a towel off the counter behind her and swatted playfully at the two of them. "All right, that's enough," she said. "But seriously, thank you for the feedback. I can work on those things, and I'll try again this weekend. But Cheryl, if it isn't any better than tonight, then I'm done, okay?"

"Okay," Cheryl repeated, her voice subdued. "I won't ask more than that."

Lena just shook her head, and Devin wondered if she thought Cheryl had already asked an excessive amount from someone who wasn't a chef—and who, even though she honestly seemed determined to improve, didn't act like someone who even *wanted* to be a chef.

"Now I need to get this kitchen clean so you two can go get some rest." She turned to survey the mess, and Devin and Cheryl exchanged another glance behind her back.

"Do you really believe I'm going to go upstairs and leave you alone with this, Lena?" Cheryl asked, and Devin heard something indefinable in her voice. Hurt? Surprise? "Devin dear, you've done more than enough to help tonight, so please don't think we expect you to stay."

Devin had just been handed the opportunity to get away from Lena and the complications she embodied, but she shrugged it off. "It's really not as bad as it looks," she said. "A few loads of dishes and a little wall scrubbing. With the three of us working, it'll be done in no time."

Lena sagged against the counter, looking relieved, as if she had truly thought they were going to walk away without helping. "Thank you, again," she said, with an audible sigh. "I'll do the walls, since they're the worst of it."

"There's a stepladder in the walk-in pantry," Cheryl said. "Let me get that for you."

"I suppose this is yet another thing I need to improve," Lena said with a forced-sounding laugh. "Managing to cook without completely destroying the kitchen each time."

Devin was surprised by her unexpected desire to reach out to Lena. To rub her shoulders, or to brush her fingers over Lena's forehead and help to ease the visible tension in her. She went over to the dishwasher and turned the machine on, hoping it would start producing enough steam to hide her suddenly warm cheeks.

"Well, yes, especially since you're having two seatings. You won't have time to do a major overhaul like this in between. But it's something every cook or baker struggles with," she added quickly, when Lena seemed to deflate at the reminder of what a dinner service would be like. "You should have seen our kitchen when I was done with the tarts."

Lena laughed again, but more real this time. "Was it spotless and shiny, and you were sitting at the counter sipping a nice cup of tea?"

"No," Devin said, with unconvincing indignation. She had learned from the start to clean as she baked, and she hadn't left a mess in the kitchen since she was ten. Of course, her parents—and now just her dad—always seemed to be magically on hand to help her with dishes and other tasks. She gave Lena a guilty grin. "I was sitting at the counter eating the leftover ganache out of the bowl."

Cheryl returned with the ladder and a bucket that she filled with soapy water at the sink, and then Lena got to work on the dried-on gravy while Devin and Cheryl started sending trays full of pans and plates through the industrial dishwasher. Cheryl changed the subject to Leavenworth, asking Devin about local attractions and activities and occasionally attempting to draw Lena into the conversation. Devin talked about summer hikes in the wine country near Peshastin while taking the opportunity to observe the dynamic between aunt and niece.

Lena was attacking the walls with focus and determination, even though she seemed interested in Devin's stories and asked questions now and then about local wildlife and geology, while Cheryl was more sporadic in her attention—not to Devin, which was unwavering and felt genuine, but to the cleaning itself. She would load half a tray of dishes, then notice a counter that needed cleaning and go start that job, and then take an armload of towels to the laundry basket. She worked hard, and if left alone would probably have gotten the kitchen just as clean as any of them, but she took a haphazard approach. She zigzagged toward their goal, while Lena worked methodically from one wall segment to the next and seemed to get annoyed every time her aunt switched tasks.

Devin couldn't help but compare the two of them with her and her dad. Where the two of them easily switched between conversation and comfortable silence while they worked together, Lena and Cheryl carried a tension between them. It was obvious in the way Cheryl's voice changed from normal when addressing Devin to a forced cheerfulness when she spoke to Lena. Lena did the same thing, but something far different from cheerfulness seeped in when she talked to her aunt. Devin thought she heard irritation, or maybe even disdain, creeping in around the edges, although Lena was unfailingly polite to Cheryl. Polite, but distant.

She wondered what a stressful season of working side by side would bring for the two of them. A new closeness that didn't seem to be present at the moment? Or a family rift that would take years to mend, if it ever did?

Still, even though their working styles were different—or maybe because they were—they had the kitchen back to what Devin presumed was its baseline appearance in less than two hours. She had borne most of the conversational burden since she wasn't emotionally invested in whatever tense dynamic was simmering between Lena and her aunt, so she had mentally walked them through most of the hikes within a few hours' drive from Leavenworth. Once she had gotten started on the topic, she found she had more to say about it than she ever would have guessed. Although she had returned to Leavenworth for nearly every holiday season since she had left home, she had rarely come back during the other three seasons. She had forgotten how much she loved being surrounded by the beauty of the mountains and lakes, and she hadn't realized how much she missed being in touch with nature in that way. She rarely saw more than cultivated parks in the city these days.

She might have felt guilty monopolizing the conversation, but both Lena and Cheryl had seemed intrigued by her stories, interjecting relevant questions now and again. Whenever Devin paused, giving one of them a chance to change the topic, they remained in a silence that was, while not necessarily hostile, also not companionable.

But eventually the final pan had been tucked into its cupboard, and the last of the leftovers were wrapped and stowed in the fridge— Devin's, at least, since Lena had dumped her own food in the compost bin. Lena stuffed a couple of large, illustrated cookbooks into a canvas satchel and slung it over her arm.

"Come on, Dev," she said, with a familiarity that just felt right to Devin, which ironically made it disconcerting. "I'll walk you home on the way back to my hotel."

"Remember that Kirby and Layla will be here tomorrow for training," Cheryl said, following them through the empty dining room and to the front door. "And thank you, Devin, for helping clean and for the lovely desserts."

Cheryl squished Devin into a really nice hug as they left, but she and Lena sort of waved good-bye at each other from just a few feet away. Devin shivered as they went outside and into a light snowfall, and she tugged her fleece-lined hood over her hair. Lena left hers down, turning her face toward the sky and letting the tiny flakes settle in her hair, where they sparkled like glitter under the old-fashioned streetlamps.

Devin licked her lips and faced forward again, watching for icy patches on the sidewalk, not wanting to trip and fall, either physically or romantically. Not only was Lena a temporary fixture in town, but she was also working through challenges in the restaurant and likely with her aunt. Definitely not relationship material, especially since Devin herself had too much going on at the moment to devote herself to romantic fancy.

"You're staying in a hotel?" she asked as they walked along the nearly empty sidewalks. In a couple of weeks, people wouldn't be able to walk side by side and carry on a conversation on Front Street, but instead they would shuffle along through the crowds in single file.

Lena sighed audibly. "Just for the week. I couldn't get a

reservation anywhere after that, plus I suppose it'll make more sense for me to be at the restaurant once we open."

"So, you and your aunt aren't close?"

Lena laughed, her breath making a cloudy puff in the cold. "That's a tactful way to put it. No, we're not." She looked over at Devin, her hazel eyes warm with concern. "I'm sorry if it seemed tense between us. The last thing I'd want to do is make you feel uncomfortable."

Devin shook her head, lost for a moment in those eyes. "I didn't. You were both friendly toward me, but just...careful, I suppose, with each other."

Lena shrugged. "We never really spent much time together. When I was growing up, Cheryl would come visit every once in a while, but she spent most of her time flitting from job to job, starting businesses and then selling them. She never seemed to be in one place for very long, and when she was, it wasn't anywhere near Portland. I really can't believe how different she is from my dad, her brother. From all of us, really. We're all driven and focused, and all of us work in the medical profession." She laughed, but with a hint of bitterness. "Except me, in a way. I'm seen by my family as sort of medical-adjacent since I design electronic records platforms for clinics and health care systems. I never could stand the sight of blood, and I'm the only one who didn't go to medical school. Anyway, I suppose that if it wasn't for Cheryl, I would have been considered the family eccentric, so I should be grateful to her for making me seem normal to them by comparison."

She gently nudged Devin with her shoulder. "You must understand the type of people we are, even though your career is so different. You're just as focused and single-minded about chocolate as they are about blood."

Devin heard the unspoken words she had lived with all her life. The expectation that she would follow in the family's footsteps and take over the shop, just one more in a long line of chocolatiers. Living her life based on the choice someone else had made generations ago.

"I work in the finance department of a telecommunications company," she said. It never sounded as intriguing as saying even the simple sentence *I make chocolates for a living.* "I only come here during the Christmas season when I can, to help my dad with the shop." She hesitated, never comfortable voicing the words even though she knew the time was right for the action behind them.

"This is my last season, too. My dad is selling the shop."

"No! Really?" Lena said, looking as forlorn as if she had just been told that Santa didn't exist. "I mean, I hope you're happy at your job, but it is a crime against humanity that you're not devoting every minute of your life to creating your chocolate masterpieces. But selling the—oh, wait. I've seen this movie. Is it an evil developer, coming to Leavenworth to build a resort where the beloved candy shop used to be? If someone is blackmailing your dad and forcing him to sell, I'll help somehow."

Devin laughed at the dramatic scene Lena was envisioning as they stopped in front of the shop. The store was closed, but still brightly lit, and the cases glimpsed through the windows were filled with decorated chocolates that glistened as if they were gemstones.

"The potential buyers are empty-nesters who want to run the store as it is. Besides, this would be the tiniest resort ever," Devin said, gesturing at the shop's miniscule footprint. "And there are strict building codes here, to keep evil developers at bay. Thank you for the offer, though. Out of curiosity, what were you planning to do to fight them?"

Lena shrugged. "I didn't have time to work out details, but it would have something to do with my food. I'd either throw it at them or make them eat it."

Devin laughed, ignoring the opening to tease Lena about her cooking. "After a couple of weeks, your cooking will be so great, it will no longer be able to be weaponized. From the way you described your family, I'll bet you see this as a challenge you need to overcome. I have a feeling you can do anything once you put your mind to it."

Lena smiled and reached out to touch Devin on the shoulder. "Thank you. You're right, too. Not that I'm superwoman and can do anything, but that once I start a project, I won't let go until I've accomplished it or knocked myself out trying. It's the competitive drive in the Preiss genes, I guess." She paused and frowned. "I think that's why I was a little angry with Cheryl tonight. I can feel myself starting to get invested in this restaurant, even though it was never my dream, and I honestly never cared if I became a great chef or not. But now that I've started, and failed, I know I'm going to do whatever it takes to succeed."

Devin wondered if it was Lena's genes, or the messages she had gotten from the rest of her family about what success really meant. "Sometimes conquering a goal isn't the important part. It's the people you meet and the things you learn along the way. I'll bet you'll be surprised by the way you feel when you start getting more comfortable in the kitchen."

"Maybe," Lena said, looking unconvinced. "But either way, I'm stuck in it now, and I really want to improve. Look, I know you've already done more to help than I should expect, and you have your own business to run, but could you possibly find the time to give me some pointers? You talked about needing to improve my timing, and I understand that it needs to be fixed, but I really don't know where to start. I'd pay you for helping, of course."

Devin glanced in the shop window, knowing exactly how much time and effort went into each of her chocolates, not to mention the extra projects she had taken on this season. She really should say no, but would it really hurt to spend a couple of hours more with Lena, just giving her some pointers on kitchen management? She enjoyed sharing the knowledge she had learned from watching her parents. And Lena...well, Devin needed her to stay in business, at least until the shop was sold. That was her main motivation, after all. Pure economics.

"I can help," she said, turning back to Lena and being rewarded with her relieved smile. "And you don't have to pay me. I'd like you to stay in business longer so I can sell you more desserts."

She said the last part in a joking way, hiding her real motive. She knew her time and expertise were valuable, but she also didn't want to lock herself into a commitment to Lena. Lena's smiles were too distracting, and her story too intriguing. Devin wanted to keep the ability to walk away if she felt herself falling too deeply under Lena's spell, and if she was being paid, she wouldn't have the same freedom. Once Leavenworth filled with tourists, time would fly by in a hectic rush, and then she and Lena would both be consumed by their own businesses. And then they would go back to their real lives. She didn't want to get so involved with her that the inevitable parting would hurt her.

"I'll come over to the restaurant tomorrow, once school is out and our assistant gets here."

Lena nodded, reaching for Devin's hand and giving it a brief squeeze. "I appreciate it," she said as she let go of her hand. "I promise to be a diligent and well-behaved student."

"I have no doubt," Devin said with a laugh. "But be sure your aunt has the swear jar in place, just in case."

Lena laughed, then walked away through the gentle snow. Devin sighed and unlocked the door to the shop, her mind switching to the tasks she still needed to complete before she went to bed. At least the work would get her mind off Lena and the curve of her lips...

Her dad came through the door that led upstairs to their living space and interrupted her thoughts.

"Have you been waiting up?" Devin asked.

He shrugged. "I wanted a chance to talk to you. How did the tasting go?"

Devin gave him a brief description of the food. "I told her I'd help her for a few days, before they open. She just needs to learn how to organize a kitchen and her time, and then I think she'll be just fine."

"You always were generous that way," he said with a fond smile. "But I worry about you. You're already working harder this season than you ever have, and now you're taking on the responsibility of helping her run a restaurant? Is it going to be too much for you?"

"Probably," she said with a light laugh, thinking of Lena and how much she was looking forward to spending more time with her. The work she was doing this year was manageable, but the complication of Lena might be a danger to her heart. Besides, Lena only respected her as the dedicated chocolatier, not as the aimless person she actually was.

Not many jobs would give her the opportunity to leave for three months each year to come make chocolate in Leavenworth, and she had occasionally needed to make the choice between quitting and not coming back here to help. Especially in the first few years after her mother had died, the option of quitting had been both the necessary and easy choice. As a result, she had a résumé that would more likely resemble Cheryl's than Lena's. Their relationship wasn't going anywhere beyond a few weeks of friendship, though, so she didn't need to worry about that.

"We need her to stay in business," she continued. "At least until the shop is sold, so we can show how profitable it can be. Besides, this is my last season to do this. I can manage the extra workload for just a couple more months."

He sighed. "You've always sacrificed a lot to help me here. It will be good when you can just live your own life and don't have to worry about me and the store."

She kissed him on the cheek, trying to keep the melancholy emotions that she felt when she talked about this being their last season hidden from him. He was likely feeling them, too, but even more strongly than she was. "I haven't minded coming home to help. You know I love this shop, and you, of course. Now, what did you want to talk to me about?"

Her dad gave her a sad smile and then reached for an apron. "I was just wondering if you wanted help getting another batch or two of those key lime truffles done tonight."

Devin breathed a sigh of relief. The truffles on their own weren't difficult to make, but they were tricky to decorate, with a delicate bright green and silver swirl that needed to be painted into the molds before they were filled. They were going to be the centerpiece of the dessert table since they were in the wedding colors, so they needed to be flawless. "Oh yes, please," she said, grabbing one of her school aprons out of a cupboard and following him into the kitchen.

CHAPTER SEVEN

Lena sat at the island in the restaurant's kitchen, tapping her foot against the metal leg and flipping through another of her cookbooks. She felt mentally worn out after the day before, with its wild swings from highs to lows. She was someone who tended to live on an even keel, with occasional spikes of annoyance when dealing with her family and mild anxiety when she was between jobs. She wasn't prepared to handle the emotional roller coaster that was Leavenworth.

Her inborn need to drive toward success and not accept failure as an option had been triggered into action last night. She really didn't care about this restaurant or whether a bunch of people she didn't know raved or complained about her food, so she should be able to throw her hands in the air and quit. Drive away without guilt or second thoughts. This definitely wasn't *her* dream, and it was only Cheryl's dream for a fleeting moment in time, so why did she care? Well, she didn't. Would that stop her from driving herself to learn more and master at least some culinary skills? Of course not.

At least yesterday's performance had left plenty of room for improvement, and the memory of it made her wince. The experience had been as humiliating as her first piano recital. She hadn't cared about the instrument or enjoyed her lessons, getting by using her naturally strong memory and ability to pick up new skills fairly quickly rather than practicing like she was supposed to. She had managed to make it through her lessons, but she hadn't accounted for the additional nervousness she would feel when she was alone onstage and expected to perform. She had memorized the notes, but when the spotlight fried all her brain cells, she didn't have the muscle memory she should have built through practice to help her through the simple piece she had to play.

Looking more closely at the memory, though, she started to understand the drive to excel that had kicked in after her failure the night before. After her recital, first her dad and then her mom had delivered lectures about what it took to succeed in life and what she needed to do to gain their approval. She'd never complained again about disliking a school subject or extracurricular activity. She simply did what she needed to do in order to win the trophy or get the grade or shine during a recital. She was an accomplished pianist now. Still hated playing, but she could entertain a crowd at a party if she needed to.

She sighed, shutting the cookbook and pushing it aside. She had come into this preprogrammed with a trigger, and she had ended up blaming her aunt when it was activated. If Devin had noticed Lena's stiffness around her aunt, surely Cheryl had felt the waves of anger as well. As different as she and Cheryl were, and as little as Lena approved of her aunt's chaotic lifestyle, Lena had no right to hold her responsible for her own overly driven nature. She'd make amends the only way she knew how. By making her aunt's restaurant a success, no matter what it took. Plus, she could be kinder to her. They didn't have to be best friends or agree on every aspect of life, but Lena couldn't use her own hang-ups as a reason to be snippy.

Lena went to the fridge and took out one of the leftover slices of Devin's fig tart. She had only managed to salvage a few pieces from the kids who had suddenly become ravenous only after dinner was over and it was time for dessert. She sat on her stool again and ate a big forkful. Devin's desserts were amazing, but it was the woman herself who had been the one bright spot in Lena's night. Lena could hear the conflicting emotions in Devin's voice when she spoke about selling their family shop, and she knew it must have been a difficult decision for her and her father to make. She was so talented at candy making, but she had moved away from it as her career. Lena maybe understood that in a small way. Even if a Christmas miracle occurred and she was voted the best chef in town, she still would be glad to burn her apron and go back to her regular job after the season was over. Just because Devin was a skilled chocolatier didn't mean she needed to devote her life to that career.

Still, Lena thought there might be more to that story than she knew, and while she was tempted to spend enough time with Devin to learn more about the layers beneath the surface, she knew she should be careful about getting too close. Aside from the fact that merely getting by in this kitchen would likely take all the time and energy she had, she had never dated someone whose talents were more in the creative realm. She usually dated successful businesswomen because she thought they would be better suited to her lifestyle and nature, but also—and she hated to admit this— because they would be more likely to get along well with her family and get their approval. If they ever had enough time in their lives to accompany Lena to family events and actually meet them. This hadn't happened yet, so it was all still theory.

Lena shook her head, polishing off the last bite of fig tart. For all Devin's complexity and depth, being with her was surprisingly easy, even though Lena hadn't known her long. She was intelligent and funny. She could imagine her seamlessly fitting in with Lena's few close friends and could even picture her winning Lena's parents over with her artisan chocolates and thoughtful, perceptive manner.

Those flights of fancy had no place in her life right now. She was doing something she didn't particularly care about, and was facing humiliation and hard work in the process of getting better at it, so it was only natural that she would be looking for some kind of distraction. She wouldn't use an attraction to Devin as a convenient way to avoid focusing on the restaurant. She got up and put her plate in one of the trays for the dishwasher. It looked tiny in the massive plastic container, but Lena needed to do some practice cooking today, so it would soon be joined by every available pan in the building. A night of making disgusting food and having to clean the mess afterward should subdue her libido and get it back under control.

Still, when the swinging door opened, her heart beat a little faster at the thought of Devin coming into the kitchen. Unfortunately—or luckily, since she had just lectured herself on controlling her impulses where Devin was concerned—it was her aunt.

"Hello, Lena," Cheryl said, sounding much more cautious than she had the night Lena had first arrived. Lena knew whose fault that was, and she made up her mind to fix it. She might be feeling laden by doom and gloom, but she didn't need to bring her bright and flighty aunt down with her. "The menus just came back from the printer, and I thought you might want to see them."

Lena took one of the laminated menus from her and looked it over. It was only a single tall page with the food listed on the front—with her aunt's admittedly superior descriptions of the items—and beer, wine, and desserts on the back. It had all the Bavarian bells and whistles around the edges, which made it kind of gaudy, but it fit with the town and the holidays, and Lena was surprised by how professional it looked. Like a real menu for a real restaurant. Which, of course, it was, but Lena had been expecting something different from her aunt. Maybe something scrawled on printer paper with a felt-tip marker? She switched her focus to the writing instead of the decorations.

"There aren't as many options as I had on my list," Lena said, counting six entrées and four sides.

"Oh…well, yes," Cheryl said, sounding uncertain about Lena's reaction. "I thought ten entrées and six sides might be overwhelming for you at first. You can always add more specials to the menu if there are other meals you want to make. I hope that was okay."

Lena looked them over again, feeling slightly better about their upcoming public opening. She even liked the idea of creating some sort of off-menu option if she found ingredients that interested her. She nodded. "This looks more manageable than what I had before, although you maybe should have whittled it down even more if you want me to…Holy shit, do you honestly expect people to pay these prices for my food?"

Cheryl laughed, looking more like herself when she did.

"These are competitive prices for the area, dear, especially during the season. You've seen the price of groceries."

"Well, yes, but I didn't think…I guess I expected us to offer to pay customers five bucks or something if they ate the food without complaining."

"You're planning to bribe your customers?" Devin asked from the kitchen doorway. She must have come in while Lena was distracted by the menu. "You'll be the most popular but least profitable restaurant in town. I'm glad you paid me in advance, Cheryl."

Lena slumped down onto her stool. "I forgot to talk to you about payment for the desserts, didn't I?"

Devin and Cheryl looked at each other and shook their heads, as if she couldn't see them. "That's my job, Lena," Cheryl said. "You're the chef, I'm management."

Luckily, her dad had been wrong about Lena running the entire restaurant on her own. She was so focused on making a few plates of schnitzel that she didn't seem aware of the business side of the restaurant. But her aunt didn't seem to mind taking charge of menus and expenses, so Lena could leave those aspects to her. Maybe she didn't need to do it all but could just focus on trying to do one part of it fairly well.

Devin set a beribboned box on the counter and picked up the menu. "It's pretty," she said, turning it over to see both sides. "And this seems like a reasonable number of dishes. You should be able to handle it with some practice."

"Unfortunately, this weekend's patrons will be part of that practice. I won't be an expert by then."

"No," Cheryl admitted. "But you'll learn what to expect with a dinner service, and you'll be even more prepared by the next weekend. Devin, Lena said you were going to help her with timing, so I can leave the two of you alone."

"No," Devin said, at the same time as Lena. They looked at each other, and Devin continued. "It might not hurt for you to hear this, as well. Then the two of you can work together to plan how to manage the menu. It can be easy to overlook some steps in a recipe during the planning stages and get behind when you're in the middle of a service, but between the two of you, you ought to catch mistakes before they happen."

"That makes sense," Lena said. "I thought you should stay because if Devin takes some fancy chocolate dessert out of that box, I'll get so obsessed that I won't hear another word she says. You can listen while I eat, and fill me in later."

Cheryl laughed and pulled two more stools over to the island, for her and Devin. She seemed happy to have been included, and Lena didn't feel guilty about the reason she had given to keep her here. What she had said was true. Equally true, though, was that she was more likely to be distracted by Devin, not the dessert she had hopefully brought with her.

Devin grinned and opened the box, taking out a tart that was covered with a rainbow of glossy berries and fruits. "I'm used to teaching our assistants about dessert making, and they're usually kids from the local high school. I discovered that if I offered them the chance to eat something after the lesson, they tended to pay more attention to me."

"I'll pay attention," Lena said. "Just don't expect me to be able to make anything like that."

"This is just for demonstration purposes," Devin said, but she correctly interpreted the crestfallen look on Lena's face. "Don't worry. You'll still get to eat it. Now, here's the recipe. Go ahead and read through it, and I'll give you some estimates on how long each step takes."

She set the paper between Lena and her aunt, and they leaned over to read it together.

"I can usually get the pastry dough together in about ten minutes, and it cooks for twenty-five," Devin said, while Lena skimmed the headings. Flaky pastry dough. Pastry cream. Apricot glaze. "The pastry cream takes about twenty, and chopping the fruit fifteen. Putting the elements together and glazing the top is another fifteen. Say I want to have this done by three o'clock in the afternoon, what time would I need to start making it?"

Math? Lena could do math. "One thirty-five," she said quickly.

"Oh, wait," Cheryl said, pointing at one of the lines. "The dough needs to chill for up to a day."

Lena reread the sentence. "Then you'd make the dough the day before and start at one forty-five."

"And when I poured hot pastry cream into a crust straight from the oven, I'd have a soggy mess," Devin said. "You're right that I need to make the dough the night before, but I have to give myself enough time to let it rest before I roll it out. Once it's in the pan and getting ready to chill overnight, I need to clean the floury mess in the kitchen, or we won't be able to get anything done the next morning. After it bakes the next day, it needs to cool completely before I can assemble the tart, and the pastry cream needs to be chilled, as well. I can make the crème pât while the dough is cooking, which will save time, and I should also be chopping the fruit and cleaning the counter and dishes then, too."

Lena read the recipe over again. "I sort of glossed over a lot of what's here," she noted, surprised by how little she had paid attention to the instructions. Making her grandmother's sauerbraten had been an all-day event, but most of the dishes she had made in her classes had been designed to fit neatly in the allotted hour or two time slot, from start to finish. "I suppose that's how one ends up with raw sauerbraten and schnitzel that's been dehydrating in the oven."

"Exactly," Devin said with a nod. "And I was just talking about a single dessert. You'll need to fit the steps for making all your dishes together like a puzzle. And you'll always want to add more time than you think you need, plus don't forget that you'll need to clean as you go as much as possible, so you're not still doing dishes and wiping the walls when the second seating begins."

Lena tried to imagine how she was going to juggle all the components of her dishes, feeling herself spiraling into a deeper anxiety. Hadn't she been thinking, mere minutes ago, that the menu looked doable? There was no way she could get one perfect plate of food onto a table, let alone eighty per night.

Cheryl got up, hurried over to one of the cupboards, and pulled out a few plates, while Devin got a knife and cut a generous slice of her tart. She put it on the plate Cheryl handed her and shoved it in front of Lena.

"Eat," she ordered. Lena took a bite, and the buttery crust crumbled in her mouth, combining with the silky pastry cream and the tangy sweetness of the fruit. She swallowed and looked up to find the two of them watching her with concern clearly etched on their faces.

"Better?" Devin asked.

Lena nodded. "I'm still convinced that there's no way I can manage all this, but damn, this is good. Is this one of the desserts you're making for us? Because I think customers will forgive almost anything to do with the dinner if they get this afterward."

Devin laughed and shook her head. "If I was here putting it together at the last minute, we could serve it, but I'll be dropping off the desserts too early in the day. This one gets soggy fairly quickly and wouldn't be at its peak by the time you served it, especially to the second seating." She cut slices for herself and Cheryl, then went back to teaching.

"Your aunt was smart in the way she organized the seatings," she said. "People will arrive at about the same time, four thirty and seven, and they'll all be served around the same time, as well. You won't have orders trickling in all night like you would in a restaurant with staggered reservations."

Lena was skeptical about that. "Are you sure? It sounds easier to get one order out at a time."

"No, trust me," Devin said with a confidence Lena envied. "You'll get focused on one table's food, and three other orders will come in before you're finished, and then you'll be plating everything one at a time."

"She's right, dear," Cheryl added, chasing an errant blueberry around her plate with her fork. "Think of it like an assembly line."

Lena couldn't think of it as anything but a potential disaster. "That might work well if everyone kindly ordered the same dish so I didn't have to make a few of everything. Do I just make one of everything per customer, so I'm prepared for anything?"

"No, and that will be the tricky part," Devin admitted, licking pastry cream off her fork and making everything but her tongue fade into the background for Lena. Her anxiety about the upcoming restaurant opening eased, which was great, but she no longer felt capable of even microwaving a frozen meal. It might be a very good thing that Devin would be bringing her desserts ahead of time and not sitting in the kitchen and distracting Lena every night.

"You'll eventually start to notice patterns, though," she said, and Lena took a moment to regain the thread of their conversation. "In the shop, people will choose all kinds of chocolates, but there are some flavors that are most popular. You'll probably notice that with your dishes, as well, so you'll be able to anticipate approximately how many of each one you might be serving each night."

"All right," said Lena with a sigh. Devin was a nice distraction, but if Lena wanted to meet this challenge—and then be done with it and go home again—she had to pay attention to what Devin was teaching her, not just watch her eat in her tantalizing way. "I need to break each recipe down so I know how long it will take to make, and then fit them all together so I can get everything done at around the same time. That sounds so easy that a child could do it. Provided the child is an adult who has gone to culinary school and apprenticed in restaurants for years. No problem. What else do I need to know?"

Devin pointed at her tart. "Well, I made a double batch of pastry cream instead of just enough for this recipe, so I can use the rest to make mini-trifles for the shop. I also taught Shay, our assistant, how to make it, so after a few more practice runs, she'll be able to handle this on her own. And when I cut up the fruit, I made more than I needed for this one dessert, so I can use the rest in the trifles and for our breakfast tomorrow."

Lena noticed that Cheryl was furiously taking notes, but she wasn't sure how Devin's advice applied to them. "Do you want me to make schnitzel trifle?" she asked.

Devin laughed. "Please don't," she said. "Those specific examples don't apply directly to you, but the theory behind them does. Find ways to do similar tasks at the same time, like chopping the onions for every dish all at once and not one at a time. Boil the potatoes for your potato salad and mashed potatoes all at once, not as two separate tasks. And teach your sous-chefs to make parts of the meal on their own, so everyone has jobs that are their responsibility. That way, when you're in the midst of a busy service, you don't have to worry about giving orders and assigning tasks randomly the entire night."

"You're amazing," Lena said, shaking her head. "I'll bet you'd have the entire menu organized and tasks delegated in no time. You're hired." She turned to her aunt, who was still taking notes. "There, I found you a star chef. I'll be heading back to Portland in the morning."

They laughed as if they thought she was joking. "I'm sure it will go better than you think," Cheryl said. She stood up when they heard the front door open. "That'll be the waitstaff," she said. "They're here for a training session and to go over the menu."

Lena dropped her forehead on the metal surface of the island. "Was I supposed to train them?" she asked, her voice sounding muffled. "That never even occurred to me."

Cheryl patted her on the shoulder. "I've got this. Kirby and Layla will be here later, so they're your responsibility. Devin, why don't you come over for dinner tonight? We can order off the menu and let them prepare the dishes without knowing what we want ahead of time. It'll be good practice for them. Oh, and you might want to cut her another slice of tart. She's looking a little shaky still."

CHAPTER EIGHT

Devin popped another slice of fruit tart in front of Lena, then divided the rest into five pieces to give to the waitstaff when they came through the kitchen during their training. She gave Lena a chance to eat and process what they had talked about so far before continuing on the topic.

"Would you like to try timing out one of your recipes?" she asked gently, not wanting to push Lena too hard since she had been looking more and more fragile as their discussion had gone on. "Maybe the sauerbraten, since that's your signature dish, and it seemed to give you the most trouble last night?"

Lena gave her a weak smile. "You're talking to me like I'm a frightened child that needs to be soothed. Do I look like I'm about to burst into tears or something?"

Devin shrugged but couldn't keep from grinning back at Lena. "Maybe a little," she admitted.

"Good. Because I just might, and I wouldn't want to startle you if you weren't expecting it. And I thought my sauerbraten was spectacular. How many chefs are skilled enough to not only undercook a roast, but also burn the hell out of it?"

Devin laughed. "All of them who have ever panicked because something wasn't cooking fast enough, so they turned the oven as high as it would go."

Lena crossed her arms over her chest. "Are you telling me I'm not special?" she asked in a mockingly haughty tone.

Devin reached over and patted her on the head. "Of course you're special," she said in a patronizing voice before reverting to her normal one, "just not in this way. Every cook since the discovery of fire has burned or undercooked a meal."

She paused, looking at Lena and wondering how honest she could be with her. She decided that hiding her opinions wouldn't do Lena any good, so she might as well share them. "I think you're angry about being here, in this restaurant and with your aunt. You're competitive and driven, so you want to make this work and do a good job, but at the same time you want to keep sulking and hiding behind your claims about how horrible you are at cooking and how badly you're going to fail. If you keep using those excuses, you're going to make them come true, whether subconsciously or not." She hesitated, trying to read Lena's expression. "Do you want to throw something at me right now?"

"A little bit," Lena said, then shook her head. "You're right, though. I guess I want to keep reminding myself and everyone else that I'm not qualified to do this, and I'm going to fail. That way, no one will be able to blame me when I do."

"But you *can* do this," Devin said, giving in to the temptation and trailing her fingers along Lena's jawline, where she could see visible signs of her internal struggle. "It won't be easy, and you might not get glowing reviews in the *Leavenworth Echo*, but you can serve decent food and give diners a nice experience while they're in town. You're smart enough and hardworking enough to do it, as long as you stop wasting time telling all of us that you can't."

Lena laid her palm against Devin's where it rested on her cheek, then turned her head and gave her a quick kiss on the wrist. They both pulled back at the same time. Devin thought she saw the surprise she felt at the intimate moment they had just shared echoed in Lena's expression, but she wasn't sure.

Lena cleared her throat and rested her palms on the island. "Jacquie is going to love you when she comes here to visit." She sighed. "I really need to make some new friends who are perfectly happy humoring me and not calling me out on my weaknesses."

"That's what family is for," Devin said slyly. Even after

knowing Lena for such a short time, she was aware that her family was probably more brutally honest than anyone else would be, and she was rewarded with a burst of genuine laughter from Lena.

"Well, they are the ones I turn to when I'm sad and need some cuddles." She wiped her eyes. "Thank you. I needed that. Both the joke about my parents and the reality check about my negativity. Let me get the recipe, and we can get at least this one dish mapped out."

She was just standing up when Cheryl and the waitstaff burst into the kitchen, bringing with them an energy and noise that helped dissipate the last of the tension from the room.

"Remember to stay to the right when going in or out of the kitchen, so you don't crash into someone going the other way," Cheryl said, herding the kids over to the warming shelf. "You'll find your tables' dishes on this counter, with the order ticket under them. Even-numbered tables on the bottom shelf, and odd ones on the second shelf. Be sure you check the order to make sure it's correct before you take the food into the dining room. Oh, and it looks like Devin has made you a little snack. Why don't you go back out to the tables and eat, and then we'll continue."

They eagerly swarmed the island, thanking Devin and scooping up plates, before disappearing through the door again.

"Was that the waitstaff, or a school of piranhas?" Lena asked, looking forlornly at the tray that now held only a few crumbs and a smear of pastry cream.

Cheryl shrugged. "They don't make a lot, and we can't be sure how much they're going to get in tips, so we need to supplement with food whenever we can to keep them happy."

"I'll be sure to bring a little something extra for the staff when I deliver the desserts," Devin said. "We always have some leftover chocolates and things in the shop at the end of the day."

"Thank you, dear," Cheryl said. "Just add it to our bill. Now, I'd better get back to it."

"I hope she's paying you enough," Lena said when they were alone again. "Is she?"

"More than enough," Devin assured her. She had given Cheryl her estimate for the season, assuming she'd be paid on a weekly basis since there was always a chance the restaurant—and Lena—wouldn't survive the full three months, but Cheryl had prepaid through February, going far over Devin's estimate and refusing to take any back. Devin was more than happy to take up the slack by bringing extra treats for her, Lena, and their staff.

"Good," Lena said, going over to the little desk in the corner of the room and returning with a yellowed and wrinkled piece of paper, handwritten in a lovely, old-fashioned script.

"Your grandmother wrote this?" Devin asked when Lena handed it to her, holding it gingerly by the corner. Lena nodded, and Devin set the paper on the counter, carefully avoiding contact with any buttery pastry crumbs. "You need to copy this down and put the original somewhere safe," she said.

Lena sighed. "I know. I'm not used to being in kitchens where gravy rains from the sky, so I've always been able to have this with me when I cooked it, which I've only done twice before. It's not the most helpful recipe, and I don't even know if she followed it. She used to just add ingredients without really measuring, which I think is why I loved watching her cook so much."

Devin read through the vague instructions. "I'm surprised," she said, with part of her mind on the ingredients list and the rest on Lena's voice. "You seem like someone who would prefer structured, measured cooking, not going by intuition."

"Well, now I do…" Lena's voice faded, and Devin looked up at her. She met Devin's eyes and shrugged. "My aunt probably cooks that way, and I think it would irritate me to watch her, but it didn't bother me back then. I loved how passionate my grandmother was about food, and how she just seemed to know if a sauce needed more seasoning or if it should be cooked a few minutes longer, without using a timer or measuring spoon. I'm not sure what changed."

"Let's at least start by giving this recipe more structure," Devin said. "Maybe in a month or so you'll find yourself going by gut feelings a little more."

Lena opened her mouth as if to respond, then bit her lip and sat down on her stool again. "You should be proud of your student," she said. "I was about to make a joke about people's gut feelings after tasting my food, but I didn't."

"You get a gold star for attitude, then," Devin said with a laugh. She pulled the yellow legal pad Cheryl had been using to take notes in front of her. "Let's start with the type of roast you need to buy."

They spent the next half hour going through the recipe line by line—and occasionally reading between the lines—and piecing together a more professional-kitchen-friendly version, while still keeping the main flavor profiles intact. Lena used her tablet to search for guidelines about marinating and cooking times, while Devin copied down their revised version of the recipe. She had a feeling Lena might want to spend some time thinking back to her experiences in the kitchen with her grandmother, perhaps trying to recapture some of her willingness to metaphorically color outside the lines that she had when she was young, but for now, she needed timelines and solid ingredient lists. Lena seemed to have fun with the process, too, even bookmarking some other recipes she came across while searching, in case she wanted to add them sometime as specials.

Lena leaned over her shoulder to read their final version, her arm lightly pressed against Devin's shoulder. Devin was glad they had finished the main work on the recipe, because her ability to form coherent thoughts was greatly hampered by Lena's touch. She smelled fresh, in a citrusy, woodsy kind of way that made Devin recall the dark chocolate–covered rosemary caramels she'd experimented with a few seasons ago. She was definitely making those for the shop again this year.

Lena leaned her elbows on the counter next to Devin and bumped her shoulder with hers. "I really can't believe how helpful this is," she said. "I'll be able to get the other recipes done the same way. I don't know how it will go once there are actual people waiting for me to get all these steps done, but it makes me feel better to have a game plan."

She turned to Devin and rested her chin in her palm. "You said you went to pastry school. Is that where you learned all this?"

Devin gently placed the original recipe in between two blank pages of the legal pad. "They taught a version of these methods there, but I had already learned it from my parents. Chocolate can be fussy, and you need to know how long to temper it, how much time to let it rest before you use it, and how long to let it set. All the elements from decorations to fillings also need to be timed exactly, as well, and every type of truffle or nougat or caramel has its own characteristics, so I was absorbing all this as soon as I was able to work alongside them. By the time I was twelve, they could have gone on vacation for a week during Christmas season, and I would have been able to prep all the inventory and have the shop ready to open for a crowd of tourists every morning."

Lena nodded. "How long ago did you lose your mom?" she asked quietly.

"Five years ago, last month," Devin said, remembering how difficult that first Christmas season without her had been. She hadn't been certain they could manage the store without her presence, but somehow the routines of tempering chocolates and making fillings had helped them through the worst of their pain. She and her dad had worked like robots at first, making chocolate after chocolate on autopilot, but then they had started talking. About her mom, about past seasons and funny customers, about their ingredients. Just talking. Devin had missed her mom every day since then, but somehow the store had healed them both just a little bit that first Christmas.

"I'm sorry," Lena said. She reached over and tucked Devin's hair behind her ear and then cupped her cheek gently. "It must be hard to let go of the store and all those memories, but you must feel her with you whenever you make one of your creations. You'll always have that."

Devin sniffed and nodded. "Plus Dad won't have the strain of running the business alone. I worry about him when I'm not here."

Lena dropped her hand to the counter again, and Devin felt the loss of contact more sharply than was comfortable. It was too easy to be around Lena. To talk to her, to laugh with her. She was saying good-bye to enough things this year. She didn't need to add another person to miss once the season ended. Unfortunately, she had a feeling she wouldn't be able to resist being around Lena as much as she could, even if she was only adding to the pain her February self was going to experience.

Lena was silent for a moment. "If you don't mind, I'm going to be nosy and pry into your personal life. I feel it's my right, since you lectured me earlier about my bad attitude. We've crossed a boundary now."

Devin laughed at her exaggeratedly miffed tone. "I'm here as a teacher. It's my job to lecture you."

"Fine, but I'm still going to ask." She waved her hand around, generally indicating the counter with its empty Meyer's box and their recipe notes. "You're so good at this. At running the store, making divine desserts, all of it. You come back here for holiday seasons, and you even went to pastry school, although I have a feeling you'd have been better suited to be a teacher than a student there. Even before that, you basically had the equivalent of an advanced degree in running an artisan chocolate shop. So why aren't you doing this for a living?"

Devin shrugged, although she felt anything but casual when she discussed this topic. "It's what I was supposed to do. It was my whole life, ever since I was a baby. Yes, I love the process of making chocolate. The smells of the ingredients, the challenge of creating something really special from scratch, and the feel of a perfectly tempered chocolate. It's wonderful, and I love it. But it also was suffocating, and at times I hated that I was merely the next generation in line to run the store. My decision to go to pastry school was my ticket out."

She sighed and fidgeted with the legal pad, not meeting Lena's gaze, although she could sense her watching and listening carefully to her. "I kind of lied about my reasons for going. I'm not proud of it, but I wasn't fooling anyone. The culinary program I went to in Seattle is really good, and I claimed I wanted to go so I could learn new techniques for the store. Maybe expand into pastries to supplement the confectionary sales. But really, I just wanted to break free. I really did learn some new skills, but I could have taught the classes on chocolate better than the teacher, and I had to keep myself from correcting him sometimes. Anyway, pastry school turned into staying in Seattle to get a business degree because I claimed it would help me run the store. And then I just stayed."

"Were your parents upset?" Lena asked, and Devin could hear a slightly anxious tone in her voice. She was certain that Lena's own parents wouldn't have handled the situation well if it had been Lena breaking free from their expectations.

"They were sad, but I was the one who fell apart when I came back here and told them I had taken a job in Seattle. I had been living with guilt and anxiety for a few years, and telling them I wasn't coming home to stay pushed me over the edge. It wasn't the big surprise for them that I expected it to be, though. They had known from the moment I left for Seattle the first time."

Lena exhaled softly. "It was kind of them to understand. But now you're happy? You're making your own decisions in life?"

Devin looked away again, tapping her fingers on the yellow pad. "Sort of, I suppose. Although I was so focused on getting away from Leavenworth and everyone's expectations, I never really had a sense of what I was working toward. And even though no one forced me to, I always felt like I had to come back and help during the busy season, especially after Mom died. I hate admitting this to you, but it's made me sort of a drifter, career-wise. I've had to quit jobs if I couldn't get a leave of absence. I've had good jobs, and I've done well in all of them, but I haven't advanced the same way I could have if I'd been more dedicated to them than to my family."

"You hate admitting that to me?" Lena asked with enough genuine surprise in her voice that Devin was startled into meeting her eyes again. "Do you honestly believe I would think less of you because your family is your priority? Or because you've changed jobs a few times?"

"Yes," Devin said, without hesitating. "I've heard you criticize your aunt for the exact same thing I've done."

Lena's expression was astonished. "I haven't...I've never... All right, I've been critical of her lifestyle, but that has nothing to do with you and the choices you've made."

"She broke away from your family's expectations, didn't she? Making her own decisions, even though they led her to a less traditional way of life than your family follows? You said your entire family works in the medical field. Well, mine works in chocolate. I left that stable lifestyle, and now I sort of wander through careers. Lena, I'm the Cheryl of my family."

"It's completely different," Lena said, although her brow was furrowed, and she had less conviction in her tone. "For one thing, you're the one coming back to help your family, while Cheryl expects us to bail her out every time."

Devin had to laugh at that. She gestured around the well-appointed kitchen. "Lena, do you really believe you're bailing her out of anything? Do you have any idea what this restaurant is worth? It's in the heart of downtown, this kitchen is gorgeous, and you have access to whatever ingredients you need before you've even opened your door to paying customers. If she needed someone to get her out of a financial bind, would she really be giving you the chance to run this kitchen, or would she hire a professional chef? I could give her the names of five experienced local ones right now, and I'd be willing to bet they already came knocking at the door once they heard she bought this place and moved into town."

"I..." That seemed to be all Lena could manage. She was looking around the kitchen as if she hadn't really seen it before.

Devin was about to ask if she was all right, but then her phone vibrated. "It's my dad," she said. "He never texts, so it must be important." She stood up to leave but laid her hand on Lena's shoulder. "Are you okay? You can come back to the shop with me and get some chocolates if you want."

Lena gave a small laugh and reached up to squeeze Devin's hand. "I'm fine. You've given me quite a lot to process today, between the recipe stuff and...well, everything." She waved her hand vaguely in the air. "You'll be back tonight, though, for dinner? And bring your dad. I could use as much practice as possible, and he looked too kind to be very critical."

"We'll be here," Devin said, hoping she hadn't done irreparable damage to their relationship by convincing Lena that she was more similar to Cheryl than she seemed to have realized. She wanted Lena to appreciate her aunt more, not decide that Devin was worthy of disdain, too, but she'd have to wait and see how the evening went. She wasn't going to give up a chance to spend more time with her, though.

"We'll bring dessert," she said, before heading out of the kitchen and leaving Lena alone at the island.

CHAPTER NINE

Lena answered Jacquie's video call and waved when her friend's face appeared on the screen. Today's glasses were bright red sequined cat's eyes, and Lena felt a pang of homesickness for Portland.

"I was just about to call you," she said, propping up her phone on the counter while she chopped cabbage. She was technically supposed to have made it yesterday so it had time for the flavors to marry, but she couldn't travel back in time, so she figured she'd just use a lighter touch with the vinegar and sugar tonight.

Jacquie leaned over, as if she was trying to see what Lena was doing, so she adjusted the phone to give her a clearer view. "That's better," Jacquie said. "Devin told me you were looking a little pale when she left, and she thought you might want to talk."

Lena's knife slipped, and she barely missed chopping off the tip of her finger. "What? You talked to Devin? Are you here?"

"No, I'm here. In Portland. She texted me."

Lena decided it might be best to set down all sharp objects for this conversation. She traded the knife for the phone so she could see Jacquie. "The two of you are texting now?"

She shrugged. "Just since last night when you gave her my number so she could send me the video she took. Your speech about the food was hilarious, by the way."

"Yeah, I'm expecting a call any minute now, asking me to do a TED talk about my menu." She paused. She had known Jacquie and

Devin would get along well, but it still felt weird for her two worlds to be colliding, and without her involved at all except as peripheral entertainment. "So, she's nice, isn't she."

Jacquie laughed. "Subtle. Yes, she's nice. And smart and kind. All sorts of good things, including a resident of the town you hate. Be careful with her."

"I will be," Lena said, touched by her friend's concern. "She doesn't live here full-time, but we have very different lives, anyway. I wouldn't want to start anything and then deal with the pain when it's time for me to leave."

"I meant be careful that you don't hurt *her*," Jacquie said with a snort. "I've never seen you shed a tear for failed relationships. Your girlfriends don't, either. You won't let yourself get close enough for there to be pain, and you pick women who are the same way. Devin doesn't seem to be like that."

True. Everything Jacquie said was true, but… "*She* could hurt me," Lena said quietly.

"Then be careful for both of you," Jacquie said. "Now, why was she worried about you today?"

Lena sat on one of the stools and picked up a thin strip of red cabbage, chewing thoughtfully before she spoke. "She called me out on my attitude," she admitted. "She said I won't stop saying I'm going to fail, and as a result, I'll be likely to fail."

"Wise," Jacquie said with a nod.

Cheryl came through the kitchen door with one of the fancy steins and set it on the back counter. She was going to be seating diners and serving all the alcohol, so Lena figured the stein had something to do with that. "I'm trying to be more positive," she continued, speaking to Jacquie, "but part of me believes that I could say all the affirmations in the world, and my food will still be shit."

Cheryl walked over and plunked the mug in front of Lena, tapping it with her fingernail. It had a small sign that said *Swear Stein* on it.

Lena fished in her pocket for a dollar bill and stuffed it in the stein. She had remembered Cheryl's threat about the jar, so she'd changed a couple of twenties at a local market today, hoping the stack of ones would last her for the entire season. Unlikely.

"Jesus," she muttered under her breath. Cheryl frowned and tapped the mug again. "That wasn't really...oh, all right," Lena said, adding another dollar. She swiveled her phone and let Jacquie see the stein, which of course sent her into gales of laughter.

"Hello, Lena's friend," Cheryl said with a wave.

"Hello, Lena's aunt," Jacquie answered. Lena figured the two of them would be besties before the night was over. They could group chat with Devin, while she'd be in here chopping vegetables and scrubbing the walls.

"Keep her accountable if she swears," Cheryl said, heading out of the kitchen.

Jacquie was wiping tears of laughter out of her eyes when Lena faced her again. "This is so awesome," she said. "I wish you could install cameras in the kitchen. I'd watch you like a reality TV show."

"I can't afford to. That damned stein is going to eat all my money."

She sighed and added another dollar, letting Jacquie watch as proof. "Say, Jacquie, do you think my aunt is rich?" she asked in a more somber tone. "Not that it matters, but I guess I always thought of her as just managing to scrape by."

Jacquie shrugged casually, as if Lena's worldview wasn't shifting out of her control. "Loaded, I'd guess. She sold that alpaca farm for three million."

"Dollars?" Lena asked, shocked by the news Jacquie so casually mentioned.

"No. Three millions skeins of wool. Yes, dollars, silly. That's probably how she could afford to buy you a restaurant to play in."

"This is not play," Lena said indignantly. "I've been working my ass off because I thought I was the only hope standing between her and bankruptcy—oh, okay, I'm adding a dollar. But what am I even doing here if she could afford real help?"

Jacquie shrugged. "Why don't you ask her? When's the last time the two of you really talked, anyway? You're basing everything you think you know about her on things your mom and dad have said."

Lena had to admit that was true. Both her parents routinely criticized Cheryl for her way of life, but Lena herself was the one who had assumed that meant she was financially irresponsible, when all they might have meant was that she was not settling down to be a doctor.

"I'll talk to her," she said. "Not that it matters, of course, except why am I here now, if she doesn't need me?"

"If her future isn't dependent on your mushroomless schnitzel sauce? I don't know, maybe for some bonding time? Maybe she wants to get to know you, and to give you a chance to learn who she really is, not just what your family thinks of her."

Lena nodded, still attempting to process everything. She sighed and changed the subject. "Enough kitchen drama," she said. "How are you? Have you looked at any more condos?"

They chatted for a few more minutes while Lena finished chopping her cabbage, and then ended the call because the sous-chefs—apparently the fancier term for *teenage kitchen help*—would be arriving soon for their trial dinner and training. And then Devin would be back. Lena found herself missing her, even after such a short time of knowing her. She wanted to talk to Devin about what her dreams were, now that she was soon to be free from the generational weight of the store. To get her opinion on the shifts in perspective Lena was experiencing today. And to maybe find out if she ever dated women who came to Seattle to visit.

Maybe she should omit that last one. Maybe.

Cheryl came in the kitchen again, carrying a tray of wineglasses and interrupting Lena's debate about any possible future with Devin, thank goodness. "Sorry," she said, setting the tray on a side counter. "I'll be right...oh, you're off the phone. Do you need any help with your prep?"

"I don't think so," Lena said, giving the cabbage one last stir and hoping the strong vinegary smell would ease up by the time it was served. "I want the three of us to treat this like a real dinner service, in miniature form. I could use some help with the recipes, though, if you don't mind."

"Oh, I'd be glad to help, dear," Cheryl said. She had seemed resigned when Lena said she didn't need help with the food, but unmasked pleasure replaced resignation at Lena's next words.

Cheryl sat on the stool next to hers, and Lena showed her what Devin had done with the sauerbraten recipe. "I need to do the same thing with all the others," she said. "Although today we can just start with the three we're going to serve tonight. I asked Devin to bring her dad, too."

"Oh, it'll be nice to meet him," Cheryl said. "Where would you like to start?"

They worked through the bratwurst and schnitzel recipes, as well as a chicken dish with mustard cream sauce, which was pretty much the same as the schnitzel but with a variation on its mushroom gravy. Lena searched for cooking time and oil temperatures while her aunt squinted at the handwritten recipes and did her best to decipher them. When they finally finished, they had three recipes with every step sequentially laid out.

Cheryl laid out the recipes side by side with the originals. "This could be the start of a lovely cookbook," she said. "You could have photos of the originals alongside the more detailed variations that offer more help than *cook it until it's done*."

"My favorite was the line about the mustard sauce that said *be sure you don't*...with nothing after it," Lena said with a laugh. She looked at the recipes on the counter and could picture her aunt's suggestion, complete with photos of her grandmother and the region of Germany where her family originated. That was a project for another lifetime, though.

"Why am I here?" Lena asked, her voice dropping to a more serious tone. "It's not because you can't afford a real chef, is it."

Cheryl laughed. "Goodness, no. Who told you that? Oh, never mind, I know." She sighed and set down her pen. "You're here because when I saw this restaurant for sale, I remembered you sitting on the counter watching Mom cook. You were always so earnest, asking questions and just so absorbed in what she was doing. I thought you might like a chance to live out the life of a chef, for a little while, at least. When your dad said you were about to be between jobs, it seemed like perfect timing."

"My job goes through cycles like this all the time. I finish one project, and then immediately start looking for the next one. Until this time, thanks to Dad's interference after he heard about the restaurant," Lena said. She hurried to reassure Cheryl. "Not that I hate being here, of course." Well, she didn't exactly *hate* it. "But it would have been nice to feel like I had some say in the matter."

Cheryl shook her head. "I'd pretend to be shocked, but that does sound like something he'd do. He's such a meddler, always has been." She patted Lena's arm. "No wonder you seemed so angry when you got here," she said.

"So, you bought this place for me? You didn't just end up with it, and needed someone to bail you out?"

"Yes."

"Because you thought I'd have fun being a cook like grandma, but for hundreds of strangers instead of just for family."

Cheryl smiled fondly at her. "You always did like a challenge," she said.

"Yeah, thanks. And the alpaca farm? Did you buy that for Landry because he saw a picture of an alpaca in a book when he was a kid?"

"No, I bought that farm because the widow who had run it for over forty years with her husband desperately wanted to sell and move to Denver to live with her sister. The farm needed a lot of renovation and some new stock to make it profitable again, and Landry happened to have a few months off while he was waiting for his visa to go overseas. I thought it would be good for him to get his hands dirty for once."

"I'm sure he appreciated that," Lena said sarcastically.

Cheryl just shrugged, unaffected by her snarky tone. "Does he talk about his experiences on the farm very often?"

Lena didn't even have to think about that one. "He's brought it up at least once in every conversation I've had with him since," she admitted. "And I get alpaca wool scarves, complete with lectures about how they're sheared, every Christmas."

"There you go," Cheryl said happily. "I had a chance to spend time with him, and he got to live a completely different lifestyle for a short time. The memory of it will last forever for him."

"And all the times Dad has helped you with businesses?"

"I like to spend time with my brother, as annoying and meddlesome as he can be, and to be honest, dear, I've never felt especially welcomed when I came to his home. But he's different when it's just the two of us." She smiled with an evil glint that Lena hadn't seen in her before. "Plus, it's fun to see him struggle to learn new things, especially since he's so accustomed to being the best in everything he does. Damn him, though, that he always picks up any new skill so fast that it's only funny for a little while."

Lena nudged the stein toward her, and her aunt pulled a dollar out of her pocket and tucked it in. Between the two of them, the jar would be full before the weekend was over. They could take the staff on a vacation to Hawaii in March.

"So, this place. Another widow needing to sell?"

Cheryl shook her head. "A young couple who got in way over their heads and couldn't find a buyer that would pay enough to get them on dry land again."

Lena scrunched her nose and thought it through. The family opinion was that Cheryl was irresponsibly changing careers left and right, but Lena had always assumed she was only hurting herself in the process—and maybe annoying her family, too. But this was a different story than the one Lena had known, and she wasn't sure how she felt about it. "So," she repeated, "you flip businesses. Buy them for cheap, put in a little work, and sell for a profit?"

Cheryl laughed. "My accountant would love your version. She's not impressed by the way I do business, although I'm sure I've put her three kids through college. No, Lena, I'm not a vulture. I love the excitement of starting new projects, and the steep learning curve at the beginning of them, but then I get bored quickly. My solution is to buy failing businesses for much more than they're worth, put some work into them, and then sell them for even more.

I help people who can't get out of bad situations, plus I'm helping the economies of the communities they're in. I make a profit, but my main goal has always been to make enough so I can invest in something new and different."

Lena rubbed her eyes. "This is overwhelming," she admitted. She felt as if her parents had been lying to her about Cheryl, but they never had. They had just brought up the way she failed to meet their expectations, which had nothing to do with money.

"If you want to leave, you can," Cheryl said. "You'll still be my beneficiary, whether or not you stay for the season or not."

"Jes—Jeez, I don't want your money," Lena said.

"Well, too bad, because you're getting it. And if you only use it to make prudent investments in stocks, I'm coming back to haunt you."

Lena laughed, but it quickly faded to a more somber mood. "I'm sorry," she said. "I know what my parents are like, and how they impose their beliefs and expectations on everyone else. I should have realized that they were doing the same thing to you, and any…well, negative things I might have heard were results of their biases."

Cheryl smiled, but her eyes looked suspiciously bright. "That's all I want, dear. For you to know who I am. Does this mean you'll stay, for at least a little longer? I'd like to get to know the woman you've become, too."

"I'll stay," Lena said. "For now. If the weekend is a disaster, I might change my mind." She paused. "Do you mind if I check out of the hotel and move in here? It'll probably be easier to be here instead of walking back and forth. Unless, of course, you're worried about being with me in a kitchen full of knives now that I know you're rich and I'm the beneficiary?"

Her aunt laughed and patted her on the cheek. "Oh, Lena, I'm very worried about being near you and the knives, but not because I believe you'll intentionally try to hurt me. I'm afraid I'll just be collateral damage while you're slicing the roast."

Lena tried to look insulted, but ended up laughing along with her. She might actually enjoy this getting-to-know-you part, and she was more willing to stay in Leavenworth than she wanted to admit because Devin was here, too. She wasn't ready to say good-bye to her just yet.

But the kitchen and its contents? Lena could gladly do without those.

CHAPTER TEN

When Devin got back to the shop, her dad was polishing the glass on the display cases while Shay was pulling out the mop bucket from the back storeroom. It didn't look like the site of an emergency, but her father did have a frantic air about him as he cleaned.

"What's happening?" she asked. "And why are we mopping the floors before we've even closed for the day?"

"They're coming," her dad said.

"The British? Aliens? A zombie swarm?" Devin shook her head when he gave her a stern glare. The dread in his voice could only mean one thing. The potential buyers were coming to the shop.

"Shay, please put the mop back," she said briskly. "The last thing we need is for them to slip on a wet spot and sue us for the store. Then check the pantry to make sure the labels on all the couverture boxes are facing the wall. I'll be in the office."

Shay nodded and wheeled the mop bucket back through the swinging door.

"What should I do?" her dad asked.

He normally could handle crises without any problems, but this situation had too much emotion tied to it for him to be his usual calm self. She would step up and take care of this for him. "Keep cleaning the cases," she said. "We want it to look as pretty as possible in here."

Truthfully, she was more concerned with protecting the shop's interests. The ratios in their proprietary blends of couverture—the high-quality chocolate they used—and the names of their vendors would be handed over to the new owners, but not until the contracts were signed. She went into the office and made sure everything was locked away except the packet of financial information that their lawyer had said they could share with prospective purchasers. She didn't really think these people were spies from some other chocolate shop, but she also wasn't willing to gamble their trade secrets on that assumption. Chocolatiers were protective of their secrets, and her family had spent generations honing their craft. She wasn't going to share their results with anybody who walked in off the streets.

Once she knew the office was ready, she walked through the kitchen and pantry, double-checking that everything was okay. She didn't care if they knew what brand of sugar she used, but they damned well weren't learning the percentage of cocoa butter they had in their couverture.

"What should I do when they get here?" Shay whispered to her as they returned to the main room.

"Just take care of customers like you always do," Devin said. "Dad and I will show them around and then probably go in the office to talk finances. Oh, and you can offer them some samples, too. They'd probably like that."

She tried to appear unflustered by this sudden visit, but the two of them looked a little panicky, and it was rubbing off on her. She just hoped they wouldn't scream and run into the back room when the couple came through the door. That wouldn't make a good first impression.

"Remember what Carmen told us, Dad, not to go into specifics about anything, like which wineries buy our chocolates or whose weddings we've catered. Keep it general for now, until we know if they're really serious about making an offer."

He nodded. "I'll leave the talking to you, if it's all right. I'll just stand here and smile."

"Oh, scary smile," Shay said, watching him demonstrate. "Maybe go for the Serious Businessman look instead."

"Is this better?" he asked, apparently trying for a more serious expression, but landing somewhere around serial killer instead.

"Not really," Shay said thoughtfully. "You look kind of stiff. Why don't you lean casually on the counter, like you're about to sell some chocolates to a happy family."

"How's this?"

"The happy parents would grab their children and run," Devin said, rubbing her temples. "You've had decades of practice being the kindly store owner who is definitely not homicidal. Why don't you stick with that."

He managed the death mask version of that. Devin had two options. Snap him out of it, or lock him in the cupboard with the mop until the potential buyers left.

"We've been invited to be lab rats at Haus Bavaria tonight, Dad," she said. "Lena is practicing some of her entrées and asked us to come. We need to bring dessert."

"Dessert," he repeated, his face brightening and returning to some semblance of normalcy. "A Sacher torte would be good, wouldn't it? Come on, Shay, I'll teach you how to make candied apricots. They're not the traditional garnish, but everyone loves them."

Okay, one crisis averted. He'd make a better impression if he was in the kitchen looking industrious than if he continued looming at the counter. She wondered if she should go check her own expression in the mirror, but she figured she was somewhere in the realm of About to Vomit. The buyers were just going to have to take what they got with her. She wished this was over, all of it—the season, the sale of the shop, moving her dad into a new place. They would both feel better once it was finished and they were settled into their new lives. Wouldn't they?

She wished Lena was there to talk to her. Shake her up and help her through the next hour or two. But when all this was over, Lena would be gone, too. She'd be back home, back to her job and her life in Portland. Devin could wish she was around—she couldn't stop herself from doing that if she tried—but it would remain in the realm of fantasy. She couldn't allow herself to rely on Lena for support or comfort because then she'd be lost once she was gone.

The door chimed and Devin looked up to see a couple entering the shop. They looked to be in their early fifties, with friendly, eager smiles. Devin imagined Lena standing behind her, whispering *Here come the evil developers!* and she had to stifle a laugh.

"You must be Devin," the woman said, introducing them as Brent and Natalie Comstock.

She shook hands with both of them, then gestured around the sales floor. "I can give you the grand tour, if you'd like."

"We'd love that," Brent said. "We've been here before, as customers, but always around Christmas when this room was full of people."

Devin nodded. "Weekdays in the offseason are quite different," she said. "Come Saturday, it'll be wall-to-wall in here, and then every day from after Thanksgiving to February. We make enough profit during those three months to cover most of our expenses the rest of the year, but there are plenty of opportunities to do special orders for weddings, restaurants, and other events year-round."

She walked them through the different types of confections they sold, pointing them out in the display cases and handing out occasional samples.

"And the recipes will come with the shop?" Natalie asked.

"Of course," Devin said. She'd have to write them out, though. She and her dad didn't use recipes since they had been making the same chocolates forever. When they wanted to experiment with new flavors, they just created something new. Devin thought of Lena with her grandmother's handwritten recipes, and she decided she wouldn't mind writing her own for the shop's inventory. She'd maybe even get a set of them bound as a present for her dad.

Speaking of her dad, she decided he had been working in the kitchen long enough to be more relaxed and ready to meet the Comstocks. She led them through the swinging door to where her dad was preparing a springform pan and Shay was standing by the stove stirring what Devin assumed were dried apricots in a Cointreau syrup. Shay gave a small yelp when they appeared, and her dad dropped the parchment paper, which unrolled across the floor. But still, it was a less dramatic reaction than she had been expecting from them. She was just glad her dad hadn't been whipping the egg whites for the batter at the time.

She introduced her dad and suggested he explain what he was baking. As soon as he started talking about the torte's Austrian origins and its flavor profile, he was back in his element and seemed to relax. While he was showing them around the kitchen, Devin quickly picked up the parchment paper and got a fresh roll off the shelf, cutting out a round and fitting it into the bottom of the greased pan. By the time they had finished their circuit of the kitchen, she had separated the eggs and measured out the rest of the ingredients for him. She sent Shay out to cover the front of the shop and then moved the apricots off the burner to let them soak in the heated syrup.

"Do either of you have experience working with chocolate?" her dad asked.

"Not really," said Natalie. "But I love to bake, and we're willing to learn."

Her dad looked prepared to launch into a lecture about how difficult that would be, but Devin caught his eye and gave him a quick shake of her head. That would be their problem, if they ended up buying the shop.

"Actually," Brent said, looking at Devin, "we hoped you might stay on for a few months. Your Realtor told us about your experience here in the shop and in Seattle, and we thought you might be able to teach us what we need to know."

"Oh, I couldn't," Devin protested. For so many reasons. She settled on the easy one. "I have a job in Seattle. I need to get back as soon as the season is over."

Brent looked disappointed, but he turned to her dad. "What about you, Ron? Would you be willing to put off your retirement for a little longer?"

"Oh, well...I guess...I mean, I'd..." He looked helplessly at Devin, and she understood how torn he'd be about wanting to help them so they didn't completely ruin his family's legacy. But to work here, with all the memories of his wife and family, but not as the owner? It would be far too painful.

"No," she said firmly, jumping in. "Dad will be coming back to Seattle with me. What I could do, though, is contact a couple of my confectionary professors from culinary school. I'll bet they know of some recent graduates who would love a chance to come work for you, whether it's temporary or on a full-time basis."

Her dad looked relieved, but Natalie sighed. "We really wanted one of you to stay since we've been so impressed by your products in all the years we've come here as a family. We want to keep everything the same as it's been. But I suppose having a qualified chocolatier would be the next best thing."

Devin gently herded them through the rest of the tour, talking up her experiences in pastry school so they'd be more receptive to hiring one of their graduates. They finally returned to the front of the shop, where Devin had Shay pack them a box of candy, and then they were out the door and back on the snowy sidewalk, having promised to contact her soon through their Realtor.

She went back to the kitchen with Shay trailing behind her, and the two of them leaned against the counter and watched her dad finish mixing the cake batter.

"They seemed nice, I guess," Shay said, breaking the silence.

Devin and her dad just nodded. She didn't trust herself to speak just yet and figured he felt the same. The couple *had* seemed nice. And they claimed to want to be true to the store's history and products, although Devin knew that wouldn't last. They'd eventually want to change recipes, make them their own. Or they'd decide to cut corners on couverture, choosing less expensive chocolates instead. Or they simply wouldn't develop the knack for combining flavors and really understanding the nuances of their product, like she and her dad did. Whichever one happened, the result would be the same. In a few years, the shop would be nearly unrecognizable to her. The taste, the look, and the mouthfeel of the candies would be altered. Perhaps only subtly, but changed nonetheless.

She almost wished they were planning to do something radically different, like selling pipes and tobacco instead of chocolates. That would be better than the slow erosion of everything her family had built.

Her dad slid the pan into the oven, then went back to teaching Shay how to make the apricot garnish, so Devin left the kitchen and decided to make another batch of wedding chocolates while she watched the front of the store in case any customers wandered in. She mentally went through the list of confections she still needed to make and settled on pistachio pralines. When she went to get the ingredients, though, she changed her mind and brought out a sealed container of white couverture instead. White chocolate truffles might not be on the list, but they always went well at a wedding.

She put some heavy cream and glucose on the burner to heat and measured out the white chocolate coins. It was only natural that she would feel more emotional about the sale now that she had met the possible buyers, and they were now real people in her mind. Change was always difficult, and this was a major one for both her and her dad. She had felt the same trepidation and melancholy when she first moved to Seattle, and look how well that had gone.

Okay, maybe that wasn't the best comparison to make. She slowly poured the cream mixture over the chocolate and got out her favorite blue spatula, thinking about how she had told Lena that she hadn't really known what she was aiming for when she left Leavenworth behind, only knowing she wanted to get *away*. She never really had found the destination she was seeking. She took jobs just because the opportunities arrived at the right time, and she dated women who were as citified as she could find, avoiding relationships with anyone who might be interested in small town life because she didn't want to be tempted to move back home.

She gently stirred the ganache, keeping her breathing even and focusing on the smoothness of the chocolate rather than the turbulence in her mind. She loved Seattle and didn't regret moving there. She had friends in the city, and she took advantage of all the cultural opportunities that had been lacking in Leavenworth, with its emphasis on Christmas-related plays and concerts.

It would be better when her dad was there. When she wasn't torn between two homes and could finally settle fully into one. As if he knew she was thinking about him, he came out of the kitchen just as she was measuring a small amount of pear brandy into the ganache. He looked at her ingredients, then gave her an understanding smile and a quick hug. He wordlessly got some piping bags out of the drawer and returned to the kitchen, leaving her to make her mother's favorite confections in peace.

CHAPTER ELEVEN

Lena went back to her hotel to pack her belongings and check out before the evening's practice dinner. She decided she was more anxious about moving into the apartment above the restaurant than she was about the meal. She had two assistants, after all, and they were only making three meals. A one-to-one ratio sounded doable. Technically, they were making six meals, but since they'd be the ones eating the other three, they didn't really count. That food would either serve as a reward if they'd done well, or a punishment if they messed up.

She really wished that she had checked out her new living space before telling Cheryl she'd move in, but she had been caught up in the familial moment. Would she have her own room, or would they be sleeping in bunk beds? She had no idea. She hadn't had a roommate since college, preferring to keep living arrangements separate from her dating life. That was probably another reason why her relationships didn't have long shelf lives. Not only did she choose women who were basically too busy to ever see her, but she removed any chance of them spending the edge times together, like they would have if they lived together.

But that was not today's problem. She had enough to worry about without thinking about love and relationships, and how she might be able to give her next one a better chance of making it for the long term.

And on a completely unrelated note, she would be seeing Devin again tonight. She wasn't sure if Devin was part of her anxiety, or the opposite. She was uncomfortably aware of how her attitude toward her aunt had made Devin doubt that Lena would still respect her after knowing that she had changed jobs more frequently than some people. As if Lena would ever think less of her for taking care of her dad and their shop. She still wasn't convinced that Devin was making the best decision for herself by turning her back on her abundant skills as a chocolatier, especially since she seemed very passionate about the subject every time it came up. And her passion shone through the delicious desserts she made. But Devin was making her own choices, and Lena would completely support her no matter what she chose to do—in a platonic, casual sort of friend who had only met her a few days ago kind of way.

Lena left some of her heavier cookbooks in the trunk of her Saab, where she could easily come get them if she decided to branch out in her repertoire. They'd probably end up staying locked away for the rest of her time here, though. She grabbed her messenger bag and wheeled her suitcase through the dining room and into the kitchen, heading toward the staircase leading to the upstairs apartment.

She came through the swinging door and found a playpen tucked in the corner of the kitchen, in the alcove next to the desk. Her sous-chef Layla was sitting in a chair next to it, holding a baby.

She came to a halt, and the two of them stared at each other in silence for a few moments, while Lena tried to process what she was seeing. Had her aunt warned her about this? Of course not.

"Oh, good," she said. "The meat delivery has come early. An unusual choice, but I can work with it."

Layla made a noise somewhere between a shriek and a laugh and clutched the baby more tightly.

Lena propped her suitcase against the wall and walked over to them. "I was kidding. You know I was kidding, right?"

"Yes," Layla said, still giggling.

"Good. You just caught me by surprise. That's a baby you're holding."

"It is," she said. She was barely over five feet and had pale blond hair that was tucked up in a haphazard bun. She looked nearly young enough to sit in the playpen herself.

"It's your baby?"

"Yes. His name is Jack." She shifted him in her arms and waved one of his pudgy fists at her. Lena weakly waved back. "Are you going to tell me I'm too young to have a baby? Everyone does."

Lena might have been thinking it, but she would never have said it out loud. Besides, something in Layla's eyes made her seem much older than she looked. Lena was willing to bet that this girl hadn't had the easiest of lives.

"I'm not. Because clearly you're old enough to have one, since there he is." She pulled over a chair and sat near them, but not close enough that Layla might try to hand him over. After Lena's unfortunate joke, though, she was unlikely to try. "And he's here because…?"

"Cheryl said I could bring him," Layla said, with a defensive edge to her voice. Her glare wasn't very effective, though, when she had to turn away and blink tears out of her eyes. "We'll go if you want us to."

Lena held her hands out, meaning to placate Layla and keep her from crying, but she worried the gesture might be interpreted as her wanting to hold the kid, so she put them back in her lap. "No. Hey, it's all right. Just…kitchens are dangerous places for babies. He'll probably be covered in gravy before the night is through."

Layla smiled a little at that. "I don't have anywhere else for him to be," she admitted, looking at Jack and not meeting Lena's eyes. "I want to work, but I can't afford childcare unless I get a job, which I can't get until I have childcare."

Lena nodded. "I'm sorry to pry, but don't you have someone to help? Jack's father? Your parents?"

Layla looked at her defiantly. "No to all of them. It's just us now. I applied here because no one else would hire me, but since we're so close to the season starting, all the more experienced kids already have jobs."

"So you thought we'd be desperate," Lena finished for her.

That sounded about right, although she had a feeling her aunt would have given her the job even if a hundred other more experienced people had applied. "Well, as long as you don't mind working with a rookie chef who is likely to make a lot of mistakes, then you're welcome here. Both of you."

Layla gave her a rather teary thank-you, and Lena stood up. She wanted to march out the door, find Jack's father, and drag him back here to take responsibility for his child, but she forced her jaw to unclench and limited herself to offering what little help she could provide. "There are people who can help you get the child support that's owed to you and Jack, if his father is refusing to do his share. I have a friend who's a lawyer, and I can ask her for some ideas about people to contact, if you want."

Layla paused, then gave her a small nod. Lena turned to go, but just then her aunt and Kirby came into the kitchen.

"Ah," said Cheryl, "you've met Jack."

"Yes," said Lena, keeping her voice light, but giving her aunt a glare that naturally went unheeded. "At first I thought you had already hired my replacement, but I was relieved to learn that he's only here to observe."

"Can he make a schnitzel that isn't dripping with grease?" Kirby asked. "Because he might just work out."

"Hey!" Lena said indignantly, although she was trying not to laugh. Layla was hiding her face behind Jack, failing completely at hiding her giggles.

Lena was relieved to find out that her two assistants had some sass to them, and she'd much rather have them laugh together about her cooking than have them meekly wandering through the days they'd be sharing together. Kirby was tall and lanky, soft-spoken with a slight stutter, and Lena hadn't shared more than three sentences with him at the staff dinner. She was glad to find out that he had a sense of humor because he was going to need it if he was going to work with her. Layla seemed to be a fighter, and Lena admired her insistence on finding a job and taking care of herself and her child, although Lena was going to be on the phone with Jacquie for her as soon as she left the kitchen.

She had tuned out of the conversation for a moment but started paying attention again when she realized that Layla was sharing her joke about cooking Jack for dinner.

"Lena!" her aunt exclaimed. "That wasn't funny at all."

"They think it was," she said, indicating her two hysterically laughing sous-chefs.

Cheryl shook her head reproachfully. "Come on, let's get your bags upstairs, and then the three of you need to get to work."

"The four of us," Lena corrected her, picking up her suitcase again. "Get to work, Jack. Those potatoes aren't going to peel themselves."

Lena smiled as she followed her aunt up the stairs. If she'd imagined laughter in her kitchen, she would have thought it would be directed at her food and not a sign of a nascent camaraderie. Her smile faded a bit as she thought about Layla's comments. Lena understood why she had found it difficult to get a job since she had Jack to consider, but she wondered what Kirby's story was. Why had he applied at the restaurant that was the job seeker's bottom of the barrel? Maybe he had been slow getting applications in at more established places and was here because they were latecomers to the town, hiring staff right on the cusp of the holiday season. Or maybe he wasn't at his best in interviews. She had a very different impression of him today than she had gotten last night.

Whatever their reasons, both Layla and Kirby needed Haus Bavaria to do well. They needed the work, and they probably could both use the experience. Lena had the relief of knowing that her aunt's livelihood wasn't dependent on her ability to make the restaurant a success—or, at least, not make it an utter failure—but now she had these two kids who needed her to meet this challenge. Two and a half kids.

Cheryl opened a door at the top of the stairs and ushered Lena into a spacious bedroom. It was decorated in a very Northwest style, with light colored knotty pine furniture and accents of red plaid in the bedding and upholstery. Silhouettes of elk and bears marched across the puffy duvet.

"This is your room," Cheryl said. "You have an en suite, and my room is across the hall. There's also a tiny galley kitchen that we share, or you can use the big one downstairs."

"It's really nice," Lena said honestly, setting her suitcase near the bed. "Did you do all this for me, or did it come furnished?"

Cheryl shrugged. "I did some decorating up here and had the second bathroom added." She paused for a moment. "I'm sorry I didn't tell you about Jack earlier, but I wasn't sure how you'd react. I found a babysitter, so he'll be up here when the restaurant is actually open. Layla just needs a hand getting started in life, but she's eager to work."

"I'm glad they're here," Lena said. Cheryl was probably going to open a day care next, providing a place where other young parents could get help with childcare. While she might admire the idea, Lena was going to nominate her dad to be the one who got to help with that project.

❖

Lena gave her gravy another stir, feeling ridiculously proud of the little brown lumps that were visible signs that she had remembered to add the mushrooms this time. The rest of it was beautifully smooth, after having been blended by a fully immersed immersion blender. She let herself appreciate the moment, while the kitchen was quiet as the three of them worked at their various tasks and the smells of paprika and caraway seemed to warm the air, but she knew this wasn't what it would be like when they had a full dining room.

Tonight, she had let each person pick one dish to make—since she assumed that her three guinea pigs would order one each of the three options she would give them. She wanted to give Kirby and Layla a chance to do all the steps on her printed and laminated—thanks to Cheryl—recipe cards. That would allow her to gauge their strengths and interests before she assigned the tasks by type and not recipe during a normal service. She was making the schnitzel because she wanted the chance to redeem herself after last night, while Layla made the chicken with mustard sauce and Kirby tackled her potato salad and bratwursts.

Turned out that the cabbage truly needed a day to rest before the flavors mellowed, so she had scratched it off the menu for tonight.

Lena had been stopping by each of their stations on occasion, to check on their progress and make any necessary corrections, rather than shouting instructions frantically across the kitchen, which she fully intended to do on opening night. Neither of them had any experience outside of home kitchens, and their knife skills weren't refined, but no one in their dining room would expect perfectly diced carrots tonight. She had another couple of weeks with them before they would be open to the public nightly, so she had been making plans to have some mini-lessons with them on weekdays. They both were trying hard, and they followed her instructions as well as they could, so she was hopeful that she could help them develop their skills even more. Or at least bring them up to the standards of someone with a half dozen cooking classes under her belt.

Look at her, running her kitchen so smoothly. She wished she had installed those cameras so Jacquie could see her.

Although she'd like to edit out the part where she dropped the spoon in her gravy and started a teensy fire when it spattered on a lit burner. Or the part where Kirby dropped an entire bowl of potatoes, and they all had to pitch in and quickly peel and cut a new batch. Otherwise, they were doing an impressive job.

Unfortunately, Devin happened to walk in just after Jack had cried out, and Layla, rushing over to check on him, left her two chicken pieces in the fryer too long. Lena rescued them before they got too brown, although that might be a matter of opinion, and she was waving away the smoke with a towel when she heard Devin's laughter and turned to see her in the doorway, holding a now-familiar white box.

Lena was properly conditioned now to start salivating at the sight of royal-blue ribbons. Because of the desserts inside the boxes, of course. Not because of Devin, who was looking beautiful in brown slacks and a silky tan-colored blouse. She even dressed like chocolate, Lena thought. How could she not see how much it mattered to her?

Devin greeted the two kids and returned Jack's Layla-assisted wave before picking up the swear stein, which was now called Jack's College Fund thanks to the new tag Kirby had made for it. "How cute, and—oh my, that's a lot of money. Is this all just from today?"

"I might need you to run to the mini-mart and change a couple more twenties for me," Lena told her.

Devin picked out a bill and held it up. "Do I want to know what word you used that cost five dollars instead of one?"

Lena sighed while her two obnoxious sous-chefs burst into laughter again. "It wasn't a word. It was a small, slightly inappropriate joke about cannibalism."

Devin put the money back in the stein, laughing along with the kids. "You're going to be dipping into your retirement fund before the season is over," she said. She opened the Meyer's box and lifted out a stunning chocolate cake.

"Wow," Lena said before she could catch herself. She laughed and met Devin's deep blue eyes. "To both of you, of course."

Devin grinned and set the dessert on the counter. "It's a Sacher torte," she said when the three of them clustered around the counter to see what she'd brought. "Dad made it. It's a rich dark chocolate cake with ganache and a layer of apricot preserves."

"Ganache?" Layla asked.

"It's basically chocolate mixed with cream," Devin said. "Although you can also make it with other liquids." Kirby wandered back to his station while Devin talked to Layla about the way her dad had changed the ratio of the two ingredients to make both the thinner chocolate glaze on top of the cake and the fluffier piped rosettes that dotted each slice.

Lena loved to watch Devin when she was teaching because her fascination with the subject was contagious. Layla seemed mesmerized by the glossy torte, so Lena quietly took over her mustard sauce while she asked Devin more questions.

"Devin, it's so good to see you again," Cheryl said, emerging from the door that led to their apartment. She walked over and gave her a hug, even though Devin had been gone only a few hours. Lena envied Cheryl's easy ability to connect with people that way. That must have been something she picked up after she left home to pursue her nomadic life, because the rest of Lena's family was nowhere near as demonstrative. Mostly, Lena envied her ability to comfortably hug Devin in particular, not people in general.

"Another work of art," Cheryl exclaimed, letting Devin go and admiring the dessert. "I don't know how you do it."

"This one is from Dad," she said, with obvious pride in her voice. "It's one of his specialties."

"Is he here? Come, introduce me and we can pick our entrées for the night. Will you be ready for our orders soon, Lena?"

She nodded, glad to have the recipe cards with their specific timelines. "Let us know which dishes you pick, and we'll have them out in about ten minutes."

"You sounded so professional when you said that," Devin said, giving her a wink as she stowed a tub of whipped cream in the fridge. Lena hoped *professional* was just another word for *sexy*.

"And not a single swear word," Cheryl added. "Well done, dear."

CHAPTER TWELVE

Devin followed Cheryl out of the kitchen and introduced her to her dad. Cheryl gave him a big hug, which Devin had warned him to expect, and then praised his Sacher torte and started a barrage of questions about its history and how he had made it. She couldn't have picked a conversational opening more designed to put her dad at ease, so Devin was able to just relax and let them carry the conversation while she thought about Lena and mulled anxiously over the visit from the Comstocks. Mostly, though, she thought about Lena.

She had looked adorable in the kitchen, with her short hair clipped off her face and her cheeks flushed from the heat of her simmering sauces. Well, more likely flushed from the smoke wafting off the burnt piece of pork or chicken, whichever one she had pulled out of the oil when Devin had entered the room. Lena had seemed much more at ease than she had last night, and even though the meal might not be perfect, it would be an improvement. That might give her the impetus to maintain an upward trajectory through the rest of the season. She knew it was important to Lena to do well, even though she wasn't entirely sure what made Lena feel such a need to prove herself when she was obviously accomplished in her career.

Devin looked over the short handwritten menu, trying to decide which of the meals to order. She knew they were each expected to order a different one, and not all pick the same one. The burnt meat—well, *darkly browned* might be a more tactful way to describe it—could either have been the schnitzel or the chicken with mustard sauce. Luckily, Devin didn't know which, since she was torn between wanting to take one for the team and order the meal she knew would have some issues, or let either her dad or Cheryl unknowingly get it instead. How self-sacrificing was she feeling? Apparently, ordering the cabbage as a side was no longer an option since it had been vigorously scratched off the list.

She pulled her mind off Lena and back onto the conversation when she heard the subject change to the sale of the shop. She was ready to step in if it seemed too difficult for her dad to talk about it.

"I was so sad to hear that you were selling your shop, and after how many generations have owned it? Three?" She shook her head. "You seem far too young to retire, but I imagine running the store and making all those wonderful chocolates on your own is exhausting. And Devin, how amazing you are to come back and help every season."

He sighed and reached over to pat Devin's hand. "Yes, she is amazing, but she has her own life to live now." He forced a smile, but his acting skills hadn't improved a bit since this afternoon. "And I'll get to use my chocolate-making skills to make new friends in my retirement community. That will be exciting."

Devin sighed. She was going to have to help him find a new hobby or activity, preferably one that gave him a similar sense of purpose and enthusiasm as running the shop had done. It wouldn't be the same, but she wanted him to stay interested in life and not let his passions fade away. Apparently making chocolates for his new neighbors wasn't enough to pique his interest.

He shifted the subject to the buyers' visit today, and soon he and Cheryl were laughing about his failed attempts to look casual, and the acting advice he'd gotten from Shay. Devin settled back again, letting the two of them talk. They seemed comfortable together, even lapsing into seriousness for a moment when Cheryl asked about her mother, then returning to humor when her dad started telling stories about some of Devin's more spectacular chocolate-making mishaps from her childhood.

"I was *five*," she interjected at one point. "I could barely reach the register, so I probably shouldn't have been left alone at the counter. I think we both know whose fault that mistake was."

"I went to the back room for thirty seconds to get another tray of vanilla caramels. I honestly didn't think you'd have time to sell a dozen fancy chocolates for fifty cents."

Lena stuck her head out of the kitchen and interrupted their laughter. "Hello," she called. "Weren't you supposed to come tell us what you were ordering?"

"I thought one of you would come out and take our orders, dear," Cheryl said. "I didn't realize we were meant to come back there and tell you what we wanted."

"Well, it's been longer than ten minutes, and everything is ready, so we're bringing out the plates. Hurry up and decide which dish you want."

"It smells good in here, but the servers seem kind of crabby," Devin said.

They laughed again, then hastily decided who got which meal. She and Cheryl let her dad get the bratwurst since it came with the potato salad, and they knew that would be good. Devin took a gamble with the chicken.

The chefs trooped out of the kitchen as the most bizarre Christmas parade Leavenworth had ever seen, with Lena in the lead pushing a cart full of food, Layla carrying Jack behind her, and Kirby bringing up the rear, wrestling the playpen through the swinging door. Cheryl introduced everyone to Devin's dad once they had all arrived at the table.

"All right, who gets the schnitzel?" Lena asked, sounding more frazzled than she had when Devin had talked to her in the kitchen before. She wondered what had happened in the past fifteen minutes to change her mood.

She put the plate in front of Cheryl when she raised her hand, then gave Devin and her dad their plates.

"These look delicious," he said. "Your plating is very nice."

"He's right," Devin agreed, looking at her carefully arranged meal. She could barely tell that she had lost the darkly browned lottery. "It's much improved over last night."

"That was all Kirby," Lena said, and Devin heard pride in her voice. It surprised her that someone as competitive and driven as Lena claimed to be was always so quick to give credit to others and to recognize their accomplishments. "He has a real eye for this."

Kirby turned shockingly red at her words and stared down at his plate, but Devin thought she detected a hint of a smile on his face. She guessed that he needed someone like Lena in his life, with her easy praise and kindness. She wondered if Lena had wanted for that, too, when she was young.

The three of them joined the group at the table, and Lena sat next to her, close enough that every time Devin shifted in her seat, her leg brushed against Lena's. She fought to keep her attention off that one area of her body and tried a bite of her chicken. She chewed hesitantly at first, but even though there was a hint of charred breadcrumbs, the food was very good.

Layla was watching her eat. "It's burnt," she said. "I'm sorry."

"It's slightly overcooked, but still good," Devin corrected her. "I want the recipe for that sauce because it's wonderful."

Layla took a hesitant bite, then smiled. "It is good, isn't it?"

Devin nodded. "It'll be a very popular dish, I'll bet."

Lena seemed to relax next to Devin as they talked about the food. Cheryl's schnitzel was perfectly fried and not greasy, and her dad raved about the potato salad. The meal was a success, even with the charred bits.

"Now we just need to replicate this for nearly a hundred guests in one night, instead of three," Kirby said morosely. Apparently, he and Lena shared the same pessimistic streak. Or maybe it was a realistic streak. Devin decided that time would tell.

"We'll be faster when we're each doing our own part of all of them, like an assembly line, instead of working on a single complete entrée and side from start to finish," Lena said. She nudged Devin with her elbow. "See? I listened to your lecture."

They continued to eat while the conversation flowed around

the table, mainly handled by Cheryl and Ron since Kirby barely spoke and Layla was distracted by Jack.

Devin leaned closer to Lena. "Is everything okay?" she asked. "You sounded a little cranky when you came out with the food."

Lena scowled. "Let's just say there was an unfortunate incident involving an entire shaker of salt. I'm now eight dollars poorer."

"That's too bad," Devin said, trying not to laugh. "But if you decide to become a chef on television, your swearing might make you a star."

Lena grinned, then assumed a serious expression again. "Tell me truthfully, is the food really better than last night? Am I getting better at this?"

"Truthfully, yes to both," Devin said. "And not only is everything delicious, but you've also taken some positive steps toward building up your team. You're going to be a good influence on these kids. Well, with self-confidence and cooking, anyway. Not language."

"Thank you," Lena said, pressing her leg against Devin's. "Your dad looks like he's doing okay," she said. "I hope today's emergency text wasn't about anything serious?"

"Just the evil developers coming to call," she said, briefly describing the visit.

Lena shook her head. "Do you really think they can learn how to make chocolates like you and your dad? You both grew up in that shop. Plus, it seems more specialized than regular cooking. I mean, I know the basics of making a meal, so I can follow a recipe and figure out how to make enough for a bunch of people, but what do they know about chocolate?"

"I don't know," Devin said with a shrug. Lena was close enough that Devin could feel their shoulders touch. She tried to focus on creating coherent sentences. "Buying some pieces of candy and eating them while you're on vacation is nothing like making hundreds of those pieces, in all different varieties, every day. It's promising that they realize they need someone to be in the shop with them, at least at first, teaching them and helping to make the product, but who knows how long it will seem exciting and fun to them. I think it could be a very tedious job for someone who isn't excited by the flavors and the challenge of coaxing the chocolate into the shape and flavor and texture you want it to be."

She paused, thinking about some of the things the Comstocks had talked about today. "I knew they were empty-nesters, and from what they said, it sounds like family trips to Leavenworth over Christmas were a real highlight for them. I think they're missing their kids, and this is a way to replace them with something that reminds them of happy memories. I'd bet a lot of money that the reality of running the shop won't stand up to that dream, and they'll resell the place before the next Christmas season even arrives. Who knows if the next buyer will want to keep it as a confectionary, or if they'll just want the building for something else."

She shook her head sadly. "I was thinking today that it would be easier for us if the person buying the shop didn't want to sell chocolates anymore, rather than trying to do it but making changes that affected the quality of the product we've developed. I pictured it full of those meerschaum pipes tourists love to buy, and smelling earthy and smoky like tobacco," she admitted with a light laugh. "But I don't know if either option will make us feel less sad. Either way, it's going to change. I just want to get the pain over with because I can't keep living like this, straddling two worlds."

"Are you sure you're picking the right one?" Lena asked quietly. "I'd hate for you to regret your choice after it's too late to change it."

Devin wasn't sure how to answer. "I don't like the thought of selling the shop," she admitted. "But I don't feel a sense of peace if I picture living here and running it, season after season. It makes me feel caged in. I love the beauty of this area, with the mountains and great places to hike or raft in the summer, but I don't think it's enough for me. It never has been." She sighed. "I just don't know what I want."

Her dad cleared his throat, and Devin looked up to see the entire table watching them. She hadn't realized how much she had been leaning toward Lena while she spoke, but at least she didn't think they had heard what she was saying since she was practically in Lena's lap and whispering in her ear.

They both sat up, edging away from each other slightly. "We were just talking about the schnitzel gravy," Lena said smoothly, looking unruffled by their attention. "I think it could use more salt, but Devin disagrees. Thoughts?"

Cheryl shook her head. "As owner of this fine restaurant, I decree that the swear stein is temporarily the lying stein. You owe it a dollar."

Everyone laughed, which startled Jack and made him start to cry. Devin decided she was quite fond of the kid, since he effectively stole all the attention away from her and Lena.

"If I keep changing twenties around town, people are going to get suspicious," she muttered to Devin. "They probably think I'm spending my evenings in a strip club."

Devin laughed. "Unlikely. There are codes to keep those out, too, just like the evil developers."

Jack's squalls were getting louder, slightly lessening Devin's fondness, and Layla was desperately trying to quiet him.

"Let me try," Devin's dad said, and Layla hesitantly shifted the baby into his arms. He held the baby against his shoulder. "This always worked with Devin when she got fussy," he said, and then he started reciting temperatures for different phases of chocolate making while he bounced gently up and down. Jack immediately quieted, staring at him as if fascinated by his words.

"He's not joking, is he," Lena stated.

Devin shook her head. "I knew those temperatures by heart before I learned my times tables. The family myth is that I was some sort of chocolate child prodigy, but I was just repeating things I'd been told over and over."

Layla looked as if she was about to cry from relief. "Does it work with anything, or just chocolate?" she asked earnestly. Devin's heart went out to her since she sounded so alone.

"It's not the words, dear, but the tone of voice and the bouncing," Cheryl said. "Jack doesn't understand or care what he's talking about."

Her dad switched to reciting some statistics for the Seattle Mariners, keeping his voice and his bounce exactly the same. Jack started to cry again, so he returned to chocolate.

"Well, I'll be damned," Cheryl said before clapping her hand over her mouth. "Fine, I owe a dollar. Looks like we have a future chocolatier in our midst."

Devin's dad carefully laid a now-dozing Jack in his playpen and came back to his seat. "Chocolate is loved nearly universally. It melts at our body temperature. It responds to us, offering better health and happiness, and we respond to it."

"Speaking of which, I think it's time we tried your creation," Cheryl said.

"I'll get it ready to serve," he said, getting up from the table.

Devin was going to go with him to help, but Lena put a hand on her shoulder. "Let me," she said, and Devin stayed in her chair, ceding kitchen rights to Lena. She was glad to see her stepping up to the challenge of being in charge of it.

The two of them were back in no time, each plate holding a generous serving of torte and lightly sweetened whipped cream. Devin picked the garnish off hers and ate it first since it was her favorite part. The dried apricot half had been stewed in syrup until it was soft and dense, and then it was enrobed in dark chocolate.

"I could eat a hundred of these," Lena said, biting into hers.

Everyone devoured the cake, and then Kirby and Layla went into the kitchen to get seconds. The adults stayed at the table, saying it was delicious but too rich to eat more, and then they gave in and followed the kids. They ended up eating seconds gathered around the island, with the door propped open so they could hear if Jack cried. They all seemed to relax, and even Kirby joined in a conversation with Lena and Devin about the best places to white water raft on the Yakima River.

Devin looked over at her dad, eating his second piece of torte while he talked to Cheryl and Layla. This was part of his passion. Part of his heritage. Bringing people together and making them happy. He was unfailingly humble about it, though, always saying that his beloved chocolate did the work while he merely gave it some shape and offered it to others.

Devin sighed. Was Lena right? Were they making a decision they would regret, or would selling the store allow both of them to move on to new, even better opportunities? She didn't know the answer, but she hoped she'd be able to figure it out before the season ended.

CHAPTER THIRTEEN

Lena went through the swinging door into the chocolate shop's kitchen on Friday and saw Devin leaning over her kitchen counter, surrounded by trays and trays filled with candies for today's wedding. She was putting the finishing touches on what looked like a few dozen chocolates, piping a dollop of ganache in one corner of the little squares and then switching her piping bag for a pair of tweezers to press a tiny curl of candied orange peel onto each drop.

She set down the tweezers and stood upright, arching her back in a stretch that pulled her lavender T-shirt, leaving a hint of skin visible above the apron she wore tied around her hips. The move made Lena start to reconsider her presence here today. She had come as a chum, a good pal, ready to help. Instead, her body seemed to be planning some things that were definitely beyond the friend zone.

"Can you please hand me the other piping bag?" Devin asked, holding out her hand in Lena's direction.

Lena took the bag off the counter and walked over to Devin, standing perhaps closer than she should have when she handed it to her. "Here you go," she said, making Devin startle and nearly drop the ganache.

"Lena," she said. "I thought you were Dad or Shay. I wasn't expecting to see you."

For a brief moment, Devin's expression was unguarded. In that small bridge of time, Devin looked genuinely happy to see her, in a way Lena didn't think she had ever been regarded by anyone before. It was something beyond friendship in the same way Lena's earlier thoughts had crossed that boundary, and she knew she wasn't alone in feeling a connection growing between them. If her reaction to seeing a mere inch of Devin's skin wasn't enough to make her run back through the swinging doors, out of the shop, and back home to Portland, then the way Devin had looked at her just now should have set her in motion, the equivalent of a starting gun.

Lena could list all the reasons why staying was a bad idea, starting with their temporary status as fixtures in each other's lives and ending with the external stressors each of them was coping with right now.

So, of course, she stayed. She leaned her hip against the counter and picked up the discarded piping bag, managing to squeeze the last drop of ganache onto her finger and licking it off. Devin watched her for a moment and then exhaled in a breathy sort of way and went back to piping ganache with the fresh bag.

Lena grinned at her reaction. "This tastes amazing," she said, when the coffee-flavored chocolate exploded on her taste buds. She might have been tempted to tease Devin a little more, but she had work to do. Lena was here to help, not to distract her. For the moment, at least.

"Thank you," Devin said, giving her a smile before returning her attention to the chocolates. "These are Grand Marnier and espresso truffles." She sighed and shook out her right wrist before continuing to pipe. "I always manage to leave the fiddliest decorations until the last minute, when I'm nervous and my hands get tight, but the peel has the most flavor when it's really fresh."

Lena looked around the kitchen at the multicolored, intricately shaped and decorated confections. The squares Devin was finishing were glossy and looked as if they had been airbrushed with striations of brown, red, and orange. "What could you possibly have to be nervous about?" she asked. "These all look perfect."

"I worry because even though this is just another job for me, it's one of the most important days in their lives. And the chocolate table is going to be the centerpiece of the reception, where everyone can see it, and if something goes wrong, or they taste awful, it'll completely ruin the entire wedding."

"Well, okay, then," Lena said, smothering a laugh. "As long as you're not putting any excessive pressure on yourself…"

Devin laughed a little. Not much, but it seemed to loosen her up a bit, and she quickly finished the last of the chocolates. "So, maybe not the entire wedding, but most of the reception would be ruined."

"Are these chocolates the only dessert, or is there cake, too?"

"Dad made a mini–red velvet cake for the couple to cut and share, but otherwise it's just these."

Lena nodded. "Yep, you're right. If they're disgusting, then the reception will be ruined."

Devin playfully pushed her shoulder. "Thank you. I feel much better now." She snapped a plastic cover over the tray of candy and tidied away the bowl of orange peels and the piping bags. "You didn't say why you were here. Do you need help with something for the restaurant? Are you ready for opening night tomorrow?"

Lena put a hand on her stomach, where some hippos were currently rampaging. "I am definitely not ready. Luckily, though, it will just be normal diners and not any couples celebrating their wedding. I can handle ruining a random dinner for a bunch of strangers, although I'd rather not. I'm here, though, because your dad mentioned that you were catering this wedding on your own, and I want to help. I can carry trays with the best of them, you know."

"Really?" Devin asked, clearly surprised by the offer. Lena decided it said a lot about Devin that her first instinct on seeing Lena was to offer to help her, even though she was in the middle of a massive job of her own. "I appreciate the thought, but don't you need to practice, or something?" She paused and bit her lip. "Not that I think you need lots of practice or anything, but maybe your assistants do?"

Lena laughed at her belated attempt at tact. "We spent a few hours together this morning, running through each dish and handing out assignments. We'll all be there well before opening tomorrow, so the only thing I'd have on my agenda if I stayed at the restaurant today is obsessively worrying about my food. I'd much rather spend the afternoon with you, watching you obsessively worry about your chocolates. That way, I can eat any that you decide aren't utterly perfect." She leaned over the clear plastic lid of the tray and pointed at one of the truffles. "Like that one. It looks a bit more like a rhombus than a square."

"It does not," Devin said, although she did sneak a peek at the potentially offensive chocolate. "Come on. If you honestly don't mind helping, we need to get these into the van. I'm going to change tops, but my work one is just in the office, so I'll be right back."

Lena was about to offer to help with that, too, but Ron came through the kitchen door at that moment, carrying a delicate little cake on a pearly white stand. It was covered in thick green frosting, with lacy white icing piped along the sides in an intricate design. The whole thing was dusted with sparkly silver sugar.

"That's stunning," Lena said. "And it's the greenest red velvet cake I've ever seen."

"Green and silver are the wedding colors," Devin told her, appearing in the kitchen again, wearing a black top with her black pants. Lena had taken a guess and was wearing all black, too. Devin took off her white apron and tossed it in a hamper near the door. "The bridesmaids will probably all look nauseated in the reflection of their green satin."

Lena laughed as she held a white cake box steady while Ron carefully set the cake inside. "You can carry this on your lap once we get the rest of the trays loaded," he said. He patted her hand where she was still holding the side of the box. "Thank you for coming today," he added. "I'll feel better knowing that Devin has some help. We've been too busy with the early weekend tourists today for us to leave Shay all alone."

"I'm happy to help," Lena assured him and Devin. "It's really getting busy out there, isn't it? I knew it would get more crowded, but I wasn't expecting it to happen so fast."

He and Devin laughed. "This is nothing," she said. "By the time we get to December, you won't be able to see the sidewalk for the crowds."

Great. Lena had been hoping for an uncharacteristically slow tourist season, with only a few tables full each night. Based on the number of tourists she'd seen today, and given the number of restaurants in town, her aunt would have no trouble filling every single chair in the damned place.

Today, though, she was focused on Devin. She couldn't get distracted by her personal concerns, slip on a snowy sidewalk, and accidentally drop a tray full of truffles, or anything equally devastating. She carefully picked up one of the heavy trays and followed them out to the minivan, where they snapped each one into place in a built-in metal rack.

"Dad designed it," Devin said proudly. "The trays and the rack."

"Ingenious," Lena said, leaning down to look at the locking mechanism. "How did you get this made?"

"I have a friend who teaches engineering at Wenatchee Valley College," Ron said as they went inside for another load of trays. "He and some of his students made it as a special project."

"Well, it's brilliant, and you should patent it," Lena said, making a note to ask Jacquie if she knew any patent lawyers. She would hopefully be here in a couple of weeks, which made Lena feel excited and homesick at the same time. And very nervous, since Jacquie would no doubt actually want to eat at the restaurant.

She got in the van, and Ron handed her the cake box, which she held gingerly on her lap.

"How did I get put in charge of the one item that really could ruin the wedding if something happened to it?" she asked as Devin navigated along the busy streets.

"We're only going about two miles from the shop," Devin said, turning off Front Street and looking more relaxed once there were fewer pedestrians and cars surrounding them. "You might want to loosen your grip a little, though. You might crush the box."

Devin pulled into a parking spot in the back lot of the community center, and she came around to Lena's side of the van and took the cake box from her. Lena grabbed a tray from the back and followed her inside.

They entered through the kitchen, and Devin greeted the

caterers as they walked through. There were a dozen of them, all efficiently unpacking plates and foil-covered pans of food. Lena wondered what they were doing for the rest of the weekend. If she could cram even half of them in her kitchen tomorrow night, they'd be able to get all the meals out, no problem. She was idly wondering whether it would be cheaper to hire all of them, or just order takeout from another restaurant to feed her customers, when they left the brightly lit kitchen and entered the reception room.

"Ow, my eyes," she said. The room looked as if someone had taken Ron's cake, blown it up to massive proportions, and shoved even more glitter on it.

Devin laughed. "Winter Wonderland. The theme of every wedding in Leavenworth between November and March. Your retinas will eventually adjust to all the sparkle."

"I'm going to be seeing spots for days," Lena said. They had stopped in front of a large table covered with a green velvet cloth edged in silver lace, directly to one side of the dance floor. The table had three tiers, each with a row of fancy silver platters.

Lena looked around. The table was front and center in the room, bigger than everything else except the bar, and ringed with flower arrangements. "You were right," she admitted. "If you messed this up, you really might ruin the wedding. You're the main attraction here, and your truffles are going to get more attention than the bride and groom."

"Chocolate," Devin said, fastidiously centering her dad's cake on the topmost center platter. "It's always the star of the show."

Lena handed the tray to Devin once she had finished placing the cake to her satisfaction. "I'm going to be the pack mule and carry the trays," she said. "I'll let you do the arranging."

Devin smiled somewhat sheepishly. "Thank you," she said. "I can be a little fussy about how they're arranged."

"No, really?" Lena said. "I am completely surprised by that revelation."

She rolled her eyes at Devin and headed back out to the van, satisfied by the sound of Devin's laughter behind her. She was determined to help Devin stay calm and relaxed today, which would be more helpful to her than having Lena handle the chocolates and leave smudged fingerprints on them.

Lena watched the display come to life with every trip back to the reception room. Velvety hearts, white chocolate truffles that looked like snowballs with their textured domes, faceted pink candies with delicate shaved-chocolate roses on each one. The lower tier held dozens of green candies with a curved line of silver running across the middle. They might not be as garishly sparkly as the rest of the room, but Devin was right—they were going to be the center of attention.

She got out her phone and took a few pictures, then sent them to Jacquie and Cheryl. She hesitated, then sent one to Layla, too. She had seemed interested in talking to Devin about the desserts she made, so she might like to see them. Lena put her phone in her back pocket and walked over to Devin, who had just added the final empty tray to the stack. They stood in silence for a moment, looking at the display, and Lena put her arm around Devin's waist and leaned over to kiss her cheek.

"You astound me," she said. Part of her wanted to scream that Devin couldn't possibly waste this talent by doing anything else with her life, but it wasn't her place. It wasn't her choice to make.

Devin leaned into her for a moment, then pulled away and went over to the trays. "Here," she said, coming back to Lena's side. She handed her a royal-blue Meyer's apron and one of the white truffles. "White chocolate and pear brandy," she said. "They were my mom's favorites."

Lena draped the apron over her neck and then took a bite of the truffle. Devin could have saved her one of any of these masterpieces, and Lena would have appreciated it as a tasty gift. But this one? She was surprised by how touched she felt by the gesture, by the way Devin managed to speak through her creations.

"This is wonderful," she said, finishing the truffle. She could have eaten a dozen of them. "It's so delicate."

Devin nodded. "White chocolate can be cloyingly sweet, but the pear mellows it."

She stepped behind Lena and tied the strings of her apron,

letting her hands rest momentarily on her waist when she finished. Then she moved away yet again, picking up an armload of the trays. Lena took the rest, and when they got back to the van, they could see the wedding guests starting to arrive for the reception. They sat on the edge of the van's cargo area, leaning back against the racks of trays while they waited until dinner was over and it would be time for them to check and refill the dessert trays. The slowly darkening night and quiet, softly falling snow made them seem cocooned in their own world, protected by the overhang of the van's roof.

"He's selling because of me, isn't he?" Devin said eventually, speaking quietly. "My dad. I keep trying to convince myself that he wants to retire, but it's not really true, is it?"

Lena sighed and shifted closer. "I couldn't say for sure," she said. "But I can tell that he loves you very much. And maybe part of the reason he agreed to sell the shop was because it will allow you to move forward in your own life, but that doesn't mean it's not the right move for him."

"You think I should keep it," Devin said, resting her head on Lena's shoulder.

"What? No, of course not," Lena said. If she hadn't been surprised by the sudden contact with Devin, filling her senses with the lingering scent of oranges and chocolate, she might have been able to mask her true feelings better.

Devin made a sound somewhere between a laugh and a sigh. "That was very convincing."

Lena shifted, freeing her arm from between them and settling it over Devin's shoulders, holding her closer. "Sorry. I'm not a good liar in the first place, and you distracted me with your intoxicating truffle perfume. I don't necessarily think you should stay in Leavenworth and run the shop, not that it's any of my business in the first place, but you really seem to love what you're doing here." She waved her free hand to encompass the wedding, the store, and the entire town. "You're gifted and knowledgeable. You claim your dad is the one who's passionate about chocolate making, but I see it in you, too. When you talk about chocolate, when you're making candy, and when you put so much care into how you present what you've made. It seems like a waste to give it up and just make the occasional caramel as a hobby."

Devin was quiet long enough that Lena wondered if she had overstepped, but she didn't pull away.

"I can't separate any of it right now," she said. "I'm sad about losing the store and the memories, but does that mean I should stay? I've spent my life trying to break free. If I do take over the shop, will I regret it in a year when I'm stuck here? Or will I regret it if I sell? I tried working in a couple of chocolate stores in Seattle, while I was in school, but it wasn't the same. The level of quality wasn't there, and I had to make the same basic candies every day. I didn't have the autonomy to experiment and create. But I can't afford to open a place of my own, and Dad will need most of the money from this sale for retirement."

She sat up again and looked at Lena. "You said that your family had expectations about you going into the medical field. I know you sort of chose your own path by combining it with coding, but still, you didn't turn your back on what your parents wanted for you. Are you glad you did? It must be better than feeling ripped in two by your choices."

"Well, I…" Lena was caught off guard by the question. She had always seen herself as the rebel in her family—second to Cheryl, of course. Health care was familiar to her, but she wasn't actually sticking people with needles or scanning parts of them. She was surprised to realize that Devin saw her in nearly the opposite way, as someone who had followed her family's wishes, just in a slightly veering path. "I mean, EHRs are my specialty. I guess it makes family dinners a little easier since I'm still in their sphere, in a sense, but I really love…well, love is a strong word. I get excited when I'm working in complex systems and designing elements that will bring all the groups and departments together."

Devin nodded. "Don't punch me when I say this, but you remind me of your aunt that way. You both seem excited about learning, and eager to be challenged."

Lena laughed. "No punching. Aunt Cheryl and I are on better terms now, at least. I suppose we share that trait a little, but in very different ways. She moves to a new challenge every few months, but I've been doing the same thing since I graduated, just on a different level now. That makes it sound depressing, I suppose, but I don't mean it that way," Lena continued. "Every job is different, so I really…I just…"

She faltered to a stop. Most of her jobs were similar enough that she could take the bones of her previously created systems and just make a few changes to help them fit her new clients. And when she did have exciting or innovative ideas, her customers often preferred a more familiar and basic system rather than taking a chance on something too new or different. It sounded like Devin's experiences in the chocolate industry in Seattle.

Devin put her hand briefly on Lena's cheek. "I didn't mean to insult your work," she said. "I was feeling jealous because you're settled. You found your niche. I wish I felt that way."

Lena wasn't sure if she'd wish her position on anyone, especially Devin. She had been on the same career trajectory for years, following the same patterns. Finish a job, and then find a new one, always in the same industry. She'd been focused on growth, aiming for bigger and more varied health care systems, but she hadn't ever considered a lateral move. Until now.

"Niche, or rut?" She sighed. "I couldn't honestly say if I like the medical side of my work. The coding, definitely, but I could do almost anything with that. But I had contacts through my parents in the health care industry, and it was a way to appease them when I didn't choose medicine as my career."

She was a freelancer, though. She could go in any direction she wanted, follow any intriguing opportunity that arose, without needing to give up on developing EHRs if a good gig came along.

"I blame Aunt Cheryl," she said. "It never even occurred to me to widen my net when I was looking for jobs. I hate the in-between times, but I still wait until another health care company wants to hire me, rather than being open to finding something new. This damned restaurant has made me realize that I can do other things. I know for certain I don't want to be a chef, but I could be one. Or I could design databases for food supply companies, or chocolate shops, or apron manufacturers. That's what she wanted me to learn here, isn't it? And I'm not putting a dollar in that stein because I'm really angry that she was right."

She shook her head. "You say you're jealous that I found my niche, but now I'm not sure I want to stay in it. And you have a niche that you love, and that seems to be creatively fulfilling for you, but your opportunities for working in it are stifling for you."

Devin laughed and bumped Lena with her shoulder. "We're both messy right now," she said, meeting Lena's gaze. They were only inches apart.

Lena nodded, leaning slightly closer. "Chaos personified, times two."

Devin lightly brushed her nose against Lena's, a mere hint of contact. "Definitely not in any position to start a relationship."

"No way," Lena agreed. "That would be irresponsible and—"

And something else, but Devin closed the distance between them and kissed her, and Lena forgot what she had been about to say. She forgot the restaurant and her aunt and her family, and all that existed were Devin's lips pressed against hers. And when Devin teasingly bit her lower lip before sliding her tongue against Lena's, she forgot her name and birthdate, too. Nothing existed but the two of them. Devin's hand threading through her hair. The feel of Devin's cheek under her palm, and then her shoulder, and then her hip as Lena slid her hand down Devin's side and then pulled her closer on the edge of the van. Nothing but the sweet taste of her and the smell of chocolate and—

And a damned phone that wouldn't stop beeping.

They broke apart, and Devin swore when she checked her phone screen. "It's Kyle. The caterer. I asked him to let me know when they were about to cut the cake."

"We're back on duty?" Lena asked. Devin sighed and nodded. "Good thing, too," Lena said sarcastically, running a hand through Devin's mussed hair to tidy it. "We might have been about to do something irresponsible and..." She snapped her fingers. "And foolish. That's what I was about to say when you kissed all the words out of my brain."

"Rescued just in time," Devin agreed as they picked up trays full of chocolates that would replenish the dessert table. "Or, I suppose, about five minutes too late."

CHAPTER FOURTEEN

Devin felt like she had about ten minutes to relax after her wedding responsibilities were over before she was caught up in the preparations for the first weekend of the holiday preseason. For the next couple of weeks, until Thanksgiving, there would be heavier crowds from Friday through Sunday, and even when their cases and pantry shelves were full of truffles and pralines, they often sold out and closed the shop by late afternoon. During the high season, they'd usually close even earlier. There were only so many chocolates that they could make and store in the shop.

The wedding had been...well, Devin was having trouble coming up with words to describe it. The kiss had been exhilarating. One touch of Lena's tongue had utterly destroyed Devin's belief that there was something wrong with her because she never felt much emotional response to the women she dated. Her body and soul had apparently been waiting for Lena's arrival, saving up all the warmth and connection and desire she thought had been lacking in her, and releasing the entirety at once. And that was just one relatively short and tame kiss in a parking lot. What would dating her be like? Having sex? Spending days and nights in her company? Devin wasn't sure she could handle it and still function in her everyday life, but a rogue part of her kept thinking *What the hell—let's give it a go*.

Aside from the kiss, the night had been more fun than Devin ever would have expected. They had refilled platter after platter of chocolates, making bets about which ones would disappear the quickest, and having brief but vigorous snowball fights every time they went back to the van for more trays. Devin won them all, of course. Portland's handful of inches of annual snowfall hadn't given Lena the experience needed to beat a Leavenworth native, and she made the rookie mistake of spending far too long carefully forming her snowballs into perfect rounds, leaving her back open for ambush.

All in all, Devin had to admit it had been a Winter Wonderland of a night. The chocolates had vanished rapidly, especially at the end of the evening when Devin put out a bunch of tiny boxes so the guests could each take a couple of pieces home with them. The bride and groom had been thrilled with the entire event, and especially her dad's special cake, and even though the bridesmaids had looked a bit sickly in lime green, there had been nothing but smiles all around.

And then it was over. By the time they were packing up the last of the empty trays, the snow was falling in wet, heavy flakes. They were both damp and shivering when they got back to the shop, and Devin's dad had shooed them both off to get dry and warm while he unloaded the van. There hadn't been time for more than a hug, a thank you, and a last lingering glance before she and Lena separated for the night.

Although she had been tempted to sneak over to the restaurant and find Lena, Devin knew it was probably for the best that they didn't even have a chance to revisit the kiss. Devin had hours of work ahead of her before she could go to sleep, and she'd be up only a few hours later to get back to her chocolate making. And Lena had her first dinner service coming up. Plus, they were both facing change and decisions and choices. For Devin, the change was full of sadness and difficult emotions. But Lena, too, was letting go of some things. Old, limiting beliefs, her ties to her family's expectations. Neither one of them was in a good place for starting a relationship.

Or did that even matter? Couldn't she struggle with her career choices and regrets in Portland? Or couldn't Lena explore other ways to use her coding expertise in Seattle? Did they really need to wait until life was perfectly wrapped up with a neat bow before they explored what they could mean to each other? Devin wasn't sure, but they didn't need to make a choice right now. They could wait until the end of the season, unless Lena decided to leave earlier than that.

Devin stood at the counter behind the display cases and measured out the ingredients for the shop's staple salted caramel truffles without needing to pay much attention to what she was doing. She had already made dozens of her new chestnut and cranberry truffle stockings, but most of the items they stocked this weekend would be standard customer favorites, as they welcomed the tourists back to Leavenworth for the holidays. For now, the store was closed, and the snow fell silently and steadily outside the window.

Her dad came through from the kitchen with a slender tray full of lemon cream truffles, and he slid it into place in one of the cases. He set a slightly misshapen one next to her on the counter.

She laughed and popped it in her mouth, where it melted immediately into a pool of tart creaminess. "I know you do that on purpose," she said. "You always make one a little too lumpy since you know they're one of my favorites."

"Never," he said, pretending to be shocked by her assertion. "That one just fell on the floor and got slightly squished."

He leaned against the counter and watched her for a moment. "I forgot to mention, Lena's aunt came by while you were at the wedding. She's invited us to the second seating tomorrow night as a surprise for Lena, to show our support." He looked at his watch. "I guess it's tonight, not tomorrow."

Devin wasn't sure if their presence would be a good surprise or a stressful one for Lena, but her dad looked like he wanted to go, so she agreed to it. Besides, by the end of the day, she and her dad would both be so exhausted that they wouldn't want to do more than poke holes in a plastic cover and microwave a frozen meal. A good, home-cooked...well, they would be there to support Lena, no matter how the food tasted.

She sighed. The shop always felt safe and comforting on these late nights, when it was just the two of them working together. She wouldn't have a better chance to really talk to him than this.

"Dad, if you really don't want to sell the shop, we don't have to," she started, hesitantly. "I know you've agreed to this for me, not necessarily because it's what you want. You've always done that. You've taken care of me, and you've supported me when I wanted to make my own way, but I don't want to be the reason you give up the store. I can come back more often, or just move back and work here. It's not like I have a great job waiting for me in Seattle, and I—"

He held up a hand to stop her. "It's all right, Devin. I'll admit, I was thinking of you at first. This shop is the reason why you don't have a fulfilling job in Seattle. I wanted to give you the opportunity to fully commit to being there, to finding a career, and hopefully a woman, that you truly love, without feeling like you're living two part-time lives."

He shrugged, spinning a metal whisk on the counter. "But, if I'm being honest, it hasn't been the same here with your mom gone. At first it was because I was sad, with so many reminders of her everywhere. But for the past couple of years…well, I think I've come to understand how you felt before you moved. Sometimes I feel trapped. Stuck. It's hard to let the store go, but I'm ready to try something new. Go somewhere else."

He put his hand on her shoulder. "But not Seattle. That's your dream, and I'm not ready to settle there and make candy for the neighbors in my retirement community. I'll be there to visit you, though."

"What if *I* don't want to sell the shop?" she asked, her voice sounding small when her throat was tight with tears.

He smiled fondly at her. "You do. You wouldn't be any happier living here than you were when you were young. You moved away, but you never really let go, and it' s been holding you back. Some of that is my fault, but when you let go, you'll finally see a way forward." He shrugged. "Or a way to Portland, which is probably the same thing."

She laughed and threw a piece of chocolate at him. He caught it and tossed it in his mouth before giving her a tight hug and heading back to the kitchen, leaving her with her tears and the knowledge that he was right.

❖

Devin wasn't sure what to expect when they arrived at Haus Bavaria for the second dinner seating. An angry riot? A shell of a burned-down restaurant? At first glance, the place looked intact and calm. A few stragglers from the earlier seating were leaving as they came in, and they seemed normal. At least they weren't clutching their stomachs and calling for ambulances.

Devin smiled. That must mean that Lena had managed the entire service just fine. She was proud of her for taking on this challenge and impressed by how well she was handling it.

Cheryl hurried over as soon as they walked in the door. She looked much less composed and nonchalant than usual, with her apron askew and her hands full of dirty wineglasses. Devin saw the waitstaff rushing around the dining room, tossing dishes into plastic tubs and ferrying them back to the kitchen. She wondered if they had bussed tables as diners left, or if they had left them all until the room was emptied. She suspected the latter.

"Thank goodness you're here," she said to them, her words pouring out in a rush. "Devin, can you please go in the kitchen and give Lena a pep talk? I have to get the bar cleaned and ready for the next service, and get people seated as soon as the tables are clean. I had no idea how hard it would be to help on the floor and handle all the alcohol. No wonder the other restaurants didn't want to hire underage waitstaff."

"I'll talk to her, don't worry," Devin assured her. "Dad, do you mind sitting without me for a few minutes?"

He reached for the glasses Cheryl was holding. "Actually, I might take a turn as bartender, if you don't mind. At least to help get the first drink orders out. I always thought the job looked like fun."

"It's not fun in the least," Cheryl said. "But thank you. You're wonderful, both of you, and your desserts were a hit, Devin. If you two can manage Lena and the bar, I can help get these tables set."

Devin's dad grinned. "This will be exciting," he said.

"Just don't try juggling the bottles," Devin warned him as he walked away. He chatted with the waitstaff as he passed them, and she wondered if he was already planning his new career.

She shook her head and went into the kitchen, carefully avoiding a server with a tub full of clean dishes who was coming out on the wrong side of the door. Lena and her assistants were huddled together on one side of the island, either making a game plan for the next service or blockading themselves away from the customers. They were dressed like the waitstaff, in matching tan canvas aprons with blue and red Bavarian-inspired flowers embroidered around the edges, and Tyrolean hats. She was sure the hats had been Lena's idea. Most likely, everyone else wanted to burn them.

Lena smiled with unfiltered relief when she looked up and saw Devin. "You're here," she said, coming around the island to give Devin a strangling sort of hug. "How did you know I needed you?"

"I didn't," Devin wheezed, when she was released. "Your aunt invited me and Dad to dinner to surprise you, and now he's the new bartender, and I was sent in here to talk you down off the top of the fridge."

"Good luck with that," Lena said with a groan that was echoed by Kirby and Layla.

"What happened at the first seating?" she asked. She didn't see any signs of burned food or any other obvious disaster. Actually, she didn't see signs of much meal prep going on, which didn't bode well for the second seating.

"Do you want the dramatic version, or the more realistic one?"

"Dramatic, please," said Devin. "Get it out of your system."

Lena took a deep breath. "It was a total failure. I ruined the reputation of the restaurant, and no one will ever come here again. I *told* her I wasn't qualified to do this, and now we'll have to close, and all these kids will be out of jobs, and it's my fault. And I'm sure most of the diners will come down with food poisoning, but we won't know about that until tomorrow or the next day."

"Well, you weren't kidding about it being dramatic. So, what really happened?"

Lena slumped against the counter, as if worn out from her cathartic story, and Devin came and stood next to her. "The fryer has an automatic shutoff," Lena said. "I didn't know, until it had cooled so much while we were still cooking that the last few chicken pieces were just kind of soaking in there like they were in a sauna. We tossed those ones, of course, but a couple others were sent back because they were too greasy. All the waitstaff were working the tables, and we didn't think to assign anyone to the dishwasher, so we got behind on getting anything clean."

"*Way* behind," the boy who was currently running trays through the dishwasher clarified unhelpfully.

"And no one ate the cabbage," Kirby added. "That recipe has got to go."

Lena nodded. "It's awful. The ratios are all wrong, even if it sits overnight."

"That doesn't sound so bad for your first night," Devin said cautiously, in case there was more to come. "Did you bankrupt yourself with the swear stein?"

Lena shrugged. "Three dollars. I'm improving in that area, at least."

Devin smiled at that. "Did anything go well? Any compliments or plates that came back with everything eaten?"

"People loved the sauerbraten," Layla said. "We had a little taste, and it was really good."

"It was cooked all the way through," Kirby said.

"Yay," Lena said, waving her hands in a weak celebratory gesture, although Devin saw the smile she was trying to hide. "Your desserts were praised to the heavens, of course," she said. "Annoyingly so."

She bumped Devin with her shoulder and grinned at her, but the smile faded quickly. "And now we have to do it all over again, and I'm not sure I can."

Kirby and Layla looked defeated, too, taking their cue from Lena. Devin wanted to step in and get them moving again. Do some organizing and give some directions and fix this for Lena. Judging by her somber mood, Lena would probably welcome the intervention, but Devin fought her natural urge to fix it and instead walked over to a rack of aprons and put one on before washing her hands.

"Since Dad is probably out there having the time of his life serving beer, I can be an extra pair of hands for a while. What do you need me to do?"

She looked at Lena, and so did Kirby and Layla. It took a few moments, but Lena sighed and pulled herself together. "Can you help Kirby make another batch of potato salad? We'll swap that out for the cabbage, and no one is likely to complain about that. Layla, we're running low on the mushroom gravy, so why don't you get another pan going. I'll check the oil temperature and make sure it's ready to go."

Kirby and Layla headed to their stations, but Lena caught Devin's hand as she was starting to follow Kirby. She pulled her into another hug, less despairing than the earlier one, and just held her for a moment. "Thank you," she said when she let go and stepped back.

"You're welcome, but I really didn't do anything. You're the one who's doing a great job," Devin said. "You've had a few opening night glitches, but you're back on track now. This is impressive for someone who's never run a professional kitchen."

Lena touched her cheek, and then they got back to work. Devin checked the dining room occasionally as the evening wore on, but her dad seemed to be enjoying himself, bringing wine to tables and chatting with the patrons, so she stayed in the kitchen and lent a hand wherever needed. Eventually she found herself with Layla, pouring sauces and gravy before plates were sent out to the tables.

"Lena sent me a photo of your wedding table," she said shyly. "It was the most beautiful thing I've ever seen."

"Thank you, Layla," she said, remembering how interested she had been when Devin was explaining how to make ganache. "Do you like making desserts?"

Layla shrugged. "I don't really know how. I used to make cupcakes for my friends' birthdays, and I liked decorating them."

Devin wondered at the use of past tense but didn't ask what

had happened to those friends. Whatever the reason, Layla seemed to be lonely.

"You know, I've been starting to teach our shop assistant how to make some of our chocolates and the tarts you serve here," she said. "You're welcome to come join us sometime, if you'd like to learn. You can bring Jack," she hastened to add, since Layla's expression had shifted from excitement to despondency when Devin had made the offer. "We can set up his playpen in the office and prop the door open so you can see him. Dad will pitch in, too."

"I'd love to…I mean, if you're sure it won't be a bother."

"It'll be fun," Devin assured her. They talked about schedules and settled on a couple of days the following week when Shay would be done with school and in the shop. Layla went back to the stove to get another pan of sauce, and Lena stepped beside Devin, startling her since she hadn't realized she was nearby.

She leaned over and kissed Devin on the cheek. "That's the best I can do when we're in a room full of people, but imagine that it was a much better, much longer kiss. That was very kind of you to do for her."

Devin shrugged casually, although her imagination was quite happily following Lena's directive and expanding on the brief kiss. "It'll be good for her to learn some new skills if she's interested in working in restaurants as a possible career, and she seems drawn to pastries and desserts. Plus, I like sharing what I've learned from Dad and school."

Layla came back with the sauerbraten sauce, and Kirby plated the final two orders and handed them to one of the waitstaff. And then they were done. It still hadn't been perfect, since Lena was struggling to master the finicky fryer, and they'd had to do some creative plating to stretch the potato salad on double the orders, but Devin thought Lena and her staff seemed justifiably proud of themselves. Hopefully they could do the same next time, when they wouldn't have her as an extra helper.

Her dad and Cheryl came back to the kitchen while they were cleaning up, once the dining room was empty, bearing glasses of wine for the adults and sparkling cider for the kids. They toasted the only slightly qualified success of the night, and when talk turned to some of the challenges they had faced and how to fix them, Devin and her dad left them to it. She would have loved to stay and hang out with Lena. Maybe get that promised kiss. But they had their own shop to run, and there were several empty trays they'd need to fill before they were done for the night. She waved good-bye to everyone, smiled in what she guessed was a longing way at Lena, and left the restaurant.

CHAPTER FIFTEEN

Lena joined the crowds on Front Street on Sunday morning. She hadn't seen much of Leavenworth besides the markets, Haus Bavaria, and Devin's shop since she had been in town, and she wanted to experience it like a tourist. Devin had told her that the light displays, the sleigh rides, and the wall-to-wall crush of people wouldn't happen until the season officially started. Lena went into her first shop—one filled with home decorations and kitchen gadgets—and she couldn't imagine that the place could get any busier. She shuffled along, following a line of people as they made a circuit of the store. She figured that if she saw something she wanted to buy, she'd better grab it in the first pass, unless she wanted to force her way back to something, like a salmon swimming upstream to spawn.

She'd had enough of kitchen gadgets to last her a very long time, so she didn't mind when she found herself back on the sidewalk. She trooped along with the rest of the mass of humanity until they reached the next shop. This one was a more jarring experience, with walls covered floor to ceiling with intricately carved cuckoo clocks, all ticking and chiming seemingly at random. She figured they had been intentionally set that way, to keep the tourists from feeling like they were trapped in a massive metronome. She was glad to get back outside again.

She picked up a few Christmas gifts for her family, including a bottle of local wine for her parents, a beautiful imported sweater for her sister, and a felted Christmas tree ornament shaped like an alpaca for Landry, because it was too perfect to pass up. Mostly, though, she let herself be swept along with the current of people, finding it surprisingly restful to just be pushed along with no decisions to make. They were all going this way? Okay, she was, too.

The comforting mindlessness of it made her realize how stressful this past week had been. Last night had gone much better than she would ever have anticipated, even though it had been nowhere near perfect. It had been all right. Good enough, which, given the circumstances, seemed like a major triumph. She had taken a long time to wind down and get to sleep, though, and she jolted awake several times because she dreamt she was tripping and dropping an entire roast. After the third time with the same damned roast, she had turned on her light and read for a couple of hours before trying again. She had managed to get to sleep this time, but her dreams were endless loops of searching for ingredients and repeating recipes.

Even her most complicated and important jobs hadn't made her this tense. She assumed that some of the worry would ease after she had gone through the routine of a dinner service a few more times, but the thought of doing it all again tonight was almost too much to bear, let alone repeating the experience nightly for the next few months.

She broke from the crowd and crossed the street, merging with another line of people. This one took her past Devin's shop, and Lena managed to pause for a moment outside the window. The small room was jammed with people, and Devin, Ron, and Shay were weaving around each other behind the display cases as they filled boxes with chocolates. She didn't go inside, not wanting to distract Devin while she was so busy, but somehow she seemed to sense Lena's presence, anyway. She paused on her way to the register and looked up, meeting Lena's eyes. Lena smiled and waved, and Devin grinned back, nodding at her before getting back to work.

Lena let the crowd carry her forward again, feeling unaccountably buoyed in spirit by the brief, nearly nonexistent encounter. Last night had been the same, but in much greater proportions, when Devin had walked into the kitchen between seatings. Her presence and support had been enough to break Lena out of her downward spiral, and she, in turn, had gotten her team back into motion. For a moment, she had wanted Devin to take over and run the rest of the dinner service, but she hadn't. She had offered help but hadn't stepped in to rescue Lena or to take over. Lena realized that she wasn't accustomed to that kind of relationship, where support and encouragement were combined with respect and boundaries. Devin had been there for her, but the night's success—what there was of it—was Lena's and her team's.

Still, was it too much to ask for Devin to come keep her company in the restaurant every night? She'd be more convinced of her ability to survive the season if she knew Devin would always be there to cheer her on. They could even set up a small station where she could make candy for her store, and Ron had seemed to enjoy playing bartender, so, really, why not hang out at Haus Bavaria in the evenings?

Lena smiled at the ridiculousness of her suggestion. Devin and Ron would be working nearly around the clock to fill their cases with amazing goodies, and spending the rest of their time sleeping or eating. A night here and there, though, in exchange for all the schnitzel they wanted—which admittedly, probably wasn't much— might be doable. She'd offer to help them make chocolates in exchange, but Lena was much more qualified to eat their chocolate than to…well, than to do whatever magical things one did to chocolate to turn it into those amazing finished candies.

She was jostled from behind, and when she looked up, she realized she was back at the restaurant. She sighed and went in, hurriedly shutting and locking the door behind her in case the crowd tried to sneak in with her. Kirby and Layla would be here soon to get started on the meal prep for the night, and Lena wanted to research some new cabbage recipes before that. She'd share what she found with them, and they could choose a couple as experiments for the upcoming week. That full, glorious week with no customers, before the next weekend descended upon them.

She sighed and climbed the stairs to her room. She just needed to get through tonight first. And she'd probably spend the entire evening watching the swinging door and hoping for Devin to walk through it.

❖

Three hours later, Lena opened the oven door and peered inside, checking on her roasts. They were browning nicely and smelled delicious. She still expected to look in the oven and find them either completely raw or burning like sauerbraten flambe. Or both at once.

She shut the door again and glanced around the kitchen. She had spent some time over the past week working with Kirby and Layla on knife skills and how to coordinate their prep work, but it hadn't taken long before she ran out of knowledge to share with them. They had listened, though, and were managing their own tasks without needing much help from her. Part of it might be due to the limited menu. Once they had figured out how to make the few sauces and sides, they could just repeat those steps over and over during a dinner service. Mostly, though, they were hard workers and genuinely seemed to like being in the restaurant. They had come in today, said hi to her and Cheryl, and immediately started getting out ingredients and putting pans on the stove. Kirby had one section of the counter filled with little tubs of garnishes, and Layla already had two of her sauces simmering and filling the kitchen with an earthy, mustardy scent.

Maybe Lena could just go take a nap. Let the two of them handle everything tonight. But then who would stare at the swinging door, wondering if Devin might come by this evening to pep them up?

Yes, she played a vital role on this team.

She was still feeling nervous about tonight, but in a slightly more controlled way. She pounded and breaded chicken and pork slices, watched the sauces while Layla ran upstairs to nurse Jack, and opened the oven door more than a dozen times to look at the roasts, even though she knew she shouldn't keep doing that.

Eventually, they heard the raised voices and bustle of patrons entering the dining room. The three of them exchanged glances, all looking slightly sick, and waited for the first orders to come in.

Lena was lowering the first schnitzels into the fryer when her aunt came into the kitchen and stood on the opposite side of the island from her.

"Lena dear, now don't freak out about this."

Lena turned toward her and spread her hands wide. "Who the hell says something like that?" she asked, digging a dollar out of her apron pocket and stuffing it in the stein. It was habit by now. "It just makes the other person freak out even more. We haven't even served one entrée yet, so what could possibly have happened?"

Cheryl put out her hands, palms down, and patted the air. "Just calm down, dear. Oh, I suppose that's not a helpful thing to say, either, is it? Anyway, your dad is here."

Her dad. Lena had been thinking it was something minor like a bomb threat, or Mount Rainier erupting. He'd said he and her mom might try to come to Leavenworth while she was here, but she hadn't expected it to really happen. And not so fucking soon, when she still was trying to figure out what the hell she was doing...

"Are you freaking out?" Kirby asked.

"A little bit," Lena said, leaning against the counter.

"Okay." He moved behind her and took over at the fryer.

"Should I get her a piece of one of Devin's tarts?" Layla asked.

"Not yet," Cheryl said. "But be ready. Now, Lena dear, it's going to be fine. He's just here for dinner and to see you, and everything smells delicious. He's going to be so proud."

"Apparently you haven't met my dad before. I'll have to introduce you." Really, didn't she know her brother at all? Lena rubbed her forehead. "What did he order?"

Cheryl crossed her arms over her chest. "I'm not telling you."

"You're not...what?" Lena looked at her incredulously. She couldn't make every dish perfect tonight, but she could maybe manage one.

"You'll just fuss and bother over it until it ends up ruined."

"I will not," Lena said indignantly.

"You'd totally do that," Kirby said, and Layla nodded in agreement.

"This is mutiny," Lena told them. She looked back at her aunt, but suddenly she could see her aunt's resemblance to her father, when he had made a decision and wouldn't be swayed out of it.

She threw her hands in the air. "Fine," she said, ungraciously.

Cheryl nodded. "Good. And well done with the stein. I expected that little interchange to cost you at least five dollars." She went back into the dining room, leaving Lena to pace along the counter.

She decided to check every dish and make sure it was perfect, but after two of them, she gave up. She had decided one had too much sauce and scraped some off, only to add more again. Kirby had needed to replate the dish, and Lena wasn't about to double his work for the evening because of her own neuroses. She sighed and got back to her regular jobs.

Maybe because she was so focused on her dad that she didn't stress about anything else, but the service went more smoothly than last night's. There were a couple of complaints about singed bratwursts, and the mashed potatoes were a little lumpy, but for the most part, they served edible food to people who didn't run screaming out of the restaurant after eating.

Cheryl brought her dad into the kitchen while they were cleaning up before the next seating. He was looking impeccable as usual, in a camel-colored knit turtleneck and brown cords. He came over to her and gave her one of his awkward half hug, half pat on the back kind of greetings usually reserved for special occasions.

"Lena, what a wonderful meal," he said. "It tasted just like I remember Mom making. A culinary trip down memory lane. And are these your sous-chefs? You're both so young to be this talented. Tell me, what parts of my dinner were you responsible for?"

They both got a little flushed and stammered under his focused attention, but he complimented the sauce and the plating so profusely that it glossed over their awkwardness. Lena was accustomed to her dad in the role of social whirlwind, but he could be overwhelming to people who weren't prepared for him. He turned back to her abruptly.

"And that chestnut tart. Which one of you made that delight? I could have eaten the entire thing, but your aunt only let me have one piece."

He frowned at Cheryl in a playful way, and she shoved him on the shoulder. They looked like a typical brother and sister in that moment, and Lena knew she'd never seen them interact in that way before. She maybe understood a little more why Cheryl preferred to be around him outside their natural family habitat.

"Devin Meyer makes all our desserts," Lena said. "We could go to her shop tomorrow and you can meet her. She makes unbelievable chocolates."

"Ah, I'd love to, but I have to drive back tonight because I have to be at the hospital in the morning."

"You came all this way for one meal?" Cheryl asked, sounding disappointed. Lena expected to feel relieved, but her emotions echoed what she heard in Cheryl's voice. She had felt a flare of anticipation at the thought of introducing him to Devin. Her chestnut tart had won him over, and she had a feeling he'd like her as a person, as well.

"I couldn't miss opening weekend, could I? But Lena, your mom and I will be back for a weekend at the end of January. I had to call in a favor, but I managed to book us a rental house just outside of town. We'll have dinner, get some of those chocolates, and hopefully do some skiing, if there's enough snow. Now, I should get going."

He gave her another partial hug. "You did a good job, but I didn't doubt that you would. You're my daughter, after all."

Lena wasn't sure if that was a compliment for her or for himself, but she was going to take it. She knew that if her food had been subpar, he would have told her, even with other people in the room. Praise from him wasn't frequent, but it was honest.

Cheryl handed him a foil-wrapped package. "Another piece of Devin's tart, for the road," she said, pulling him into one of her more generous hugs. He didn't pull away or lecture her or do any of the usual critical things he did when she visited their home.

"You did it again, Cheryl," he said with a shake of his head.

He looked at Lena, too. "How two people with zero restaurant experience could pull this off, I don't know, but you did it."

He said good-bye to Kirby and Layla, then headed to the door. "Third weekend in January," he said before he left. "Oh, and Lena, a friend of a friend knows a woman who is opening a chain of mental health clinics, and she's interested in hiring you to put together an EHR for them. The group's called Heartwork, I think. I'll email you the details."

And with that, he was gone. The room seemed to lose some of its oxygen when he left, as if he'd been breathing extra life into it.

"He seemed nice," Layla said, still watching Lena with concern, as if she might collapse into a puddle on the floor.

"He's very nice," Cheryl said with a sigh. "But he can be overwhelming." She clapped her hands. "Well done so far, all of you, but we'll have another full dining room in just a few minutes. Let's all get back to work."

Lena managed to get through the rest of the evening with minimal mishaps, but she was relieved when everyone—diners and staff—had gone and she was alone in her room. She pulled out her phone and called Devin.

"Hey," she said when she answered. "How did it go?"

Lena toyed with the edge of the comforter. "Oh, the usual. The potato salad and desserts were big hits, a few of the bratwursts were overcooked, and my dad drove up from Portland for dinner."

Devin made a shocked sort of laugh. "What? Is that a joke?"

Lena shrugged even though Devin couldn't see her. She still wasn't sure his visit had been real. It had happened so fast—maybe she had slipped and hit her head on one of the metal counters and just imagined the whole thing.

"I'm fairly sure it really happened," she said. "He said my sauerbraten tasted like Grandma's."

"Oh, Lena, that's a wonderful compliment," Devin said, her voice warm. "I don't know him except from your descriptions, but he doesn't strike me as the type to say things he doesn't mean."

"You've got that right," Lena said, resting back against her pillows. "He thought your chestnut tart was divine. Oh, and he found me a job."

Devin laughed again. "Well, he owes you, doesn't he? For sending you here and keeping you from looking for a new one?"

"He does, and he probably found this for me because he felt guilty about that. It's exhausting having him playing God with my career, though. And I kind of wanted some time to think before jumping into another EHR project. To decide if maybe I want to try something else?"

Her comment sounded more like a question since she still wasn't certain if she wanted to change, or expand, her career trajectory. She felt as if he'd stuffed her back into that box, which wasn't really fair to him since that's the kind of work she'd been doing for ages. She had been complaining about not having the chance to look for a new project after finishing the last one, but there was nothing to keep her from researching prospects while she was here. She had spent her evenings searching for recipes and cooking tips—not jobs.

"Well, you're not leaving yet, are you?" Devin asked, her voice hesitant.

"No, not yet. I promised to stay through the season, plus I can't just leave Kirby and Layla like that." And she didn't want to leave Devin. Not yet. Not until they had more time to decide what they might mean to each other, if they managed to find time for anything but work in the coming weeks.

"Good," Devin said. "I don't want you to go. You can take your time, then, and decide if this job is the right move."

Lena smiled at Devin's words, and the easy honesty behind them. "I'll do that. Leave it to him to manage to come up here for two hours and complicate my life even more. I don't want to think about what he'll say if I turn down the job."

Devin was silent for a moment. "I don't doubt that your relationship with him and the rest of your family is complex, and that I've heard about only a small fraction of it. But, Lena, your dad just made a nine-hour round trip in winter just to have dinner on your opening weekend. If he'd just come to criticize, he could have made up some nitpicky issue about the food, but he didn't. Maybe he loves you and wouldn't care as much as you think if you made some career changes."

Lena opened her mouth to speak, and then closed it again. What Devin had just said was obvious, but Lena had been focused on other aspects of his visit and the discomfort she felt rather than on the simple fact that he had made a big effort to come see her and Cheryl. He might not be good at showing affection, but that didn't necessarily mean that he never felt it.

"You're right," she said, ready to change the subject. "Are you making chocolate right now? I think I hear bowls clinking every once in a while."

"I just finished a batch of gingerbread-spice truffles with chopped crystallized ginger and a white chocolate shell," Devin said, as if making such a magnificent-sounding confection was nothing special. "We sold out of almost everything today, so I need to get more ready for tomorrow. It should be a quieter day, at least."

"Well, I'll keep you company until I fall asleep," Lena said. "What are you making next?"

Her sleepless night and stressful day finally caught up with her, and Lena felt herself relaxing as she listened to Devin's voice. She fell asleep while Devin was making rosemary caramels and didn't drop a single roast in her dreams.

CHAPTER SIXTEEN

A week later, Devin used a piping bag to add decorative dark chocolate bows to a tray of white chocolate coated pistachio candies while simultaneously watching Layla and Shay as they rolled out pastry dough on the opposite side of the counter. She had deliberately chosen a task she could do in her sleep because she wanted to be ready to step in and help, but she also didn't want to lurk over their shoulders and make them nervous. Working alongside them seemed the best option.

She set down her piping bag and walked over to Layla. "You'll want to start in the center and roll outward so you don't end up with a bump in the middle," she said. Layla's dough resembled a small hill, with the sides tapering to a paper-thin layer.

She used a bench scraper and quickly gathered the dough into a ball before adding more flour to the surface and rolling it out again with short strokes. She rotated the dough a few times. "See how the extra flour keeps it from sticking?"

She gathered the pastry dough again, and placed the newly formed disc in front of Layla.

"You make it look so easy," Layla said, with a hint of despair in her voice. "I don't think I'll ever be able to do that."

Devin laughed. "I've been rolling out dough, marzipan, fondant, you name it since I was just a little older than Jack. This is your second day. Give yourself at least a week before you give up. Or maybe a few years, before it's second nature."

Layla and Shay laughed, then refocused on their work. Devin

walked over to Shay and found an evenly rolled circle. "Very nice," she said. She scraped up the dough, making Shay yelp, and moved the untouched disc in front of her. She had had each of them make two batches of dough the day before.

"If that one was good, why couldn't I use it?" Shay asked, picking up her rolling pin again.

"We've worked this one too long by now," Devin said. Because the practice batch had to be rolled, gathered back up, and rolled out numerous times, it wouldn't have a great texture in the final tart. "The gluten will be overdeveloped, and the tart shells wouldn't be very tender if we used those. This way, you get lots of practice, but your end product won't suffer for it."

Layla needed three more tries before she got over her timidity with the dough and rolled it quickly and surely into a decent circle. They were just putting the tart shells in the oven, covered with parchment paper and dried beans to keep them from puffing up, when Lena came into the kitchen.

"Am I in time to be a taste tester?" she asked. She walked around the counter, managing to *accidentally* bump their hips together as she walked behind Devin. She paused there for a brief moment, her hand on Devin's waist, before continuing her circuit of the kitchen, as if looking for handouts. "I generously let everyone sample my wonderful meals before I served them, so I think it's only fair that you repay the favor. Are these extras? I can get rid of them for you," she said, pointing at the pistachio confections.

"Everyone can have just one," Devin said. She had barely finished the sentence before the three of them converged on the tray and selected their chocolates.

Her dad came through the swinging door. "Are we eating something?" he asked, following his usual instinct for knowing when food was available.

"You two," Devin said, trying to look stern and clearly failing since no one appeared afraid of her. She pointed at Shay and Layla. "Come read these recipes for your mousse filling, and then gather your ingredients. And you two, stop eating those. We won't have any left for the display case."

"Rude," Lena said to Devin's dad. "I've never limited the number of bratwursts she can have in my restaurant."

"We'll make our own dessert," he said. "Come on."

Devin looked up from where she was huddled over the recipe cards with Layla and Shay, going over each of the steps they'd have to take. "Is anyone minding the store, or are we switching to self-serve today?"

He waved her off. "We'll listen for the door chime. Are these up for grabs?" he asked, pointing at the two practice dough discs that had been abandoned on the counter.

"Yes, but they're overworked. Should be fine for scrap pies, though, if that's what you're doing."

She helped her students melt bittersweet chocolate, then stumble through the tricky process of making a sabayon flavored with a fresh raspberry puree that she had made the night before. Part of her attention was on them, and the rest was focused on Lena. She was leaning over the counter, concentrating on her task of using a scalloped cookie cutter on the dough Devin's dad had deftly rolled out.

In the past week, they had become fixtures in each other's kitchens, going back and forth across the street with samples of trial cabbage recipes or unusual chocolates. Or just to hang out for a few minutes and watch the other person cook, lending a hand with ingredients or cleaning up. And since last Sunday night, when Lena had fallen asleep during their phone call, they had ended each night together. Just on the phone, and one or the other usually fell asleep sometime during the conversation since their days were full and neither seemed to want to end their calls.

It was something tentative, but tangible, and Devin had never experienced anything like it. Just having someone *there*, with no expectations or requirements. Lena listened when Devin worked through her emotional reactions to selling the shop, sometimes offering advice or commentary, but usually just letting her talk it out. And Devin did the same for Lena, with her struggles about accepting the job her father had found for her, and listening to her hilarious stories about her second weekend as a chef. Nothing had gone seriously wrong, but Lena managed to make the evenings sound entertaining anyway, and Devin found herself wishing she had been able to come up with a good enough excuse to go to the restaurant. Most of the time, though, they talked about their days, and about books or movies or favorite hikes. Just...sharing.

Lena glanced up, either searching Devin out or sensing her attention. Lena gave her a wink, then returned to helping Devin's dad transfer the cutouts onto a parchment-covered baking sheet, where they brushed them with butter and topped half with raspberry jam and half with cinnamon sugar. Devin watched Lena's hands as she worked, admiring the dexterous way in which she always seemed to pick up new skills. And she watched Lena's hair, her skin, the curves of her body. Their relationship was growing in the midst of daily life, but the physical side of it—although not fully explored—was always present between them. Devin loved the little touches, and how they each went out of their way to be close to, and to reach out for, each other.

Brief kisses, subtle contact. It was wonderful, but now she wanted more. She had a feeling she always would with Lena, that she would never tire of being with her. She thought Lena felt the same way, and she had noticed Lena watching her at times with the same intensity that Devin felt, but they both were cautious. They each had decisions to make and futures to plan before they could fully commit to something more permanent and serious between them.

That didn't keep her from wanting to take Lena up to her room and rip her clothes off, though.

She shook her head, mentally resetting herself and focusing on the lesson she was meant to be teaching. She supervised Shay and Layla as they whipped their sabayons, then some cream, eventually folding them together with melted chocolate and butter. She only stepped in once or twice, to rescue the mousses before they were overwhipped or about to separate. They took a break while the tart shells were cooling and polished off the entire tray of jam and sugar covered dough scraps when they came out of the oven.

Devin's dad and Shay went out to the main room to help some

customers who had come in, and Layla went back to the office to check on Jack, and Devin and Lena were finally alone. There always seemed to be other people in their kitchens, and Devin relished these moments when it was just the two of them.

Lena was sitting on a stool next to her, and as soon as they were alone, she put her hands on Devin's hips and drew her closer. Devin went willingly, stepping between Lena's thighs and putting her hands on her shoulders. From there, it was only too easy to slide her hands into Lena's hair and bend down to kiss her. This stolen moment felt different somehow. More urgent. Devin wasn't sure if it was because they were both tired of dancing around their relationship and wanted more, but whatever the reason, Lena seemed to feel it, too. Her mouth opened under Devin's lips, her tongue seeking Devin's. Lena's hands moved up to Devin's waist and slipped under the hem of her shirt, leaving a trail of heat everywhere those talented fingers touched her skin. Devin closed the last millimeter of distance between them, pressing her hips between Lena's legs and arching toward the heat she felt there.

Devin wasn't sure which of them broke the contact first, but sanity slowly seeped in to replace lust, and she stepped to the side as she remembered that while they might be alone for a moment, there were other people only a few yards away. Still, she didn't move far, but rested her back against the counter next to Lena, with her leg close against the outside of Lena's thigh.

"That was your fault," Lena said, her voice sounding slightly husky. "You're very sexy when you teach."

Devin laughed. "I'll gladly take the blame," she said. "That was…" She exhaled, unsure what words to use.

Lena nodded. "Yes, it was," she agreed. "I've wanted to touch you like that, and more, all week," she admitted. "I wasn't sure if you felt the same way."

"Yes," Devin said simply, not wanting Lena to doubt how she felt about her. She skimmed her finger along the rounded neckline of Lena's shirt, dipping under the fabric and trailing along her collarbone. She smiled at Lena's sharp intake of breath. "I absolutely feel the same way."

Lena captured Devin's roving fingers and kissed them, her touch gentle, but with a frown creasing her brow. "I want to be closer to you," she said. "But I don't want...I just have so much to figure out about my career, my life, before I can...well, before I can start something new."

Devin sighed and rested her forehead against Lena's. Her words were sensible, and Devin appreciated Lena's honesty, but her body wanted to shout *Screw caution. Take off your clothes!*

"It's not good timing for either of us," she admitted, after a brief struggle with her increasingly insistent body. "I don't even know where I'll be living in the next few months, let alone what career I'll have."

"Right," Lena said with a nod. "So we agree. We'll protect ourselves and each other, but maybe someday...maybe once we're more settled..."

Devin laughed, leaning back and meeting Lena's gaze. "So, when do you think you'll have your life and work and future plans all sorted?"

Lena shrugged, and Devin was standing close enough that even such a small movement added heat to the friction between them. "I think I'll have my entire life figured out and on the right track by the twelfth of December," she said. "About fifty years from now."

Devin widened her eyes in mock surprise. "That's my anticipated timeline, too. What a coincidence." She tried to laugh and keep her tone light, but she wasn't sure she succeeded. She wanted to get them back to merely brushing against each other and not leaving a mark, but she knew it was too late for her. Still, she was saying good-bye to so much this year, she wasn't prepared to add Lena to the list. She nudged Lena's leg with her hip. "So maybe that's the way we should stay, just for now. As friends."

"With a little smooching on the side?" Lena asked, her voice playful again, an exaggeratedly hopeful expression on her face.

Devin laughed, her tension easing. She had hoped Lena wouldn't think she was pushing her too far away. Not yet, at least. Lena seemed to feel the same—not ready to commit to anything, but not quite ready to walk away.

"There should definitely be a little smooching," she agreed, moving away from Lena as she heard her dad and Shay approaching. Layla joined them after a few minutes, and Devin went back to her teaching, unsure whether she was glad that they had been interrupted or not. Lena seemed determined to be sensible, while Devin's own resolve felt more tenuous. She turned away from the nagging question of why they were fighting so hard for the right to handle life and their problems completely on their own and returned to her teaching.

CHAPTER SEVENTEEN

Lena pulled a sheet pan full of cooked bacon out of the oven and set it aside to cool while she finished chopping her onions. With each thunk of the knife on the cutting board, she felt her tension ease just a little. Considering that today's tension was brought to her courtesy of sexy Devin and her enticing lips, Lena might have to chop a few dozen onions before she was fully calm.

She finished the onions and slid the small chunks into a hot sauté pan, where they hit the melted butter and sizzled with an explosion of fragrance. She added some pieces of uncooked bacon and gave the contents of the pan a quick toss before turning back to her cutting board.

She peeled and diced two green apples, wondering how the hell cooking had turned into a relaxing activity for her. She had enjoyed the classes she took in the past, and of course her time watching her grandmother, but beyond that she had somehow relegated cooking to special events when she had company. Most nights, on her own, she settled for easy meals like pasta dishes or takeout. Even though the restaurant was a source of turmoil, and she was still half convinced that she was going to fail as its chef—and she wasn't about to admit that to Devin—she found herself looking forward to working in the kitchen when it was quiet and empty. The gentle sounds of preparing and cooking ingredients, the aromas that filled her senses as she added each layer of components to a dish, and the methodical process of following recipes brought an unfamiliar sense of peace to her. She had no expectation that she would ever feel the same zen-like serenity when the dining room was full of strangers pounding on the tables with their knives and forks and demanding food—or, admittedly, just quietly ordering items off the menu—but she was hopeful that she would be able to make her own kitchen at home a sort of oasis once she got back to it.

Which, of course, made her remember that once she was back in her own kitchen, Devin wouldn't be right across the street anymore. There would be no more quick visits to run ideas by each other or just to chat about their days. They could still talk on the phone, but they wouldn't be close enough to touch. Or to kiss.

Lena set down her knife before she chopped off her thumb and turned back to the stove. She added a little sugar to the onions, and once they had caramelized, she added the apples and some red wine. Sliced red cabbage and spices followed, and then she lowered the heat so the mixture could simmer. She had been hoping for a good recipe to replace the horrible cabbage experiments she had tried over the past week, and judging by the smell, this was going to be a winner. Tenth time's the charm.

She sat on her usual stool at the island and poured the leftover wine into two glasses. She rested her chin in her palm and stared at the far wall, letting her mind wander back over this afternoon's kiss. Devin had felt so warm and perfect between Lena's thighs, with her exploring tongue sweetened by a hint of raspberry and cinnamon. And even beyond the physical, they were a good fit. They were in similar situations, with too much going on in their lives to be able to fully commit, but both ready to accept what the other was willing to give, and not demand more. Lena had said she needed space, and Devin had agreed. Lena should be ecstatic.

She took a drink of her pinot and sighed. She didn't feel ecstatic. She had during the kiss, but after was another story. She could get back to Devin's side in less than five minutes, but she somehow felt worlds away.

Lena had too much space. And she had more than enough thoughts rambling through her mind, vying to fill the void left after she had dashed the hope of a relationship with Devin—at least, one that went deeper than just a holiday fling with no strings attached.

A selfish part of her wanted Devin around while Lena sorted out her future. She wanted Devin's input and support. Her methodical way of tackling problems, her honesty, and her kindness. And an equal part of her wanted to be there for Devin just as much. She hated the thought of her going back to Seattle alone, leaving behind her dad and her family legacy. Or staying in Leavenworth and running the store on her own, giving up her dream of breaking free from the town and its expectations of her.

They were right not to rush into another big change by starting a more serious relationship with each other when they were already facing so much uncertainty. Weren't they? When the timer went off, Lena placed her palms on the counter and pushed herself upright, feeling as if her scattered thoughts were physically weighing her down. She turned off the burner and added some grated potato to the cabbage mixture, and then took a fork and tasted it.

Damn. It was wonderful, but instead of making her feel better, the accomplishment only made her want to take the pan over to Devin's and have her try it. Even this tiny victory felt hollow without her.

"Oh, is it another cabbage failure?" Cheryl asked. Lena had been so focused on her internal musings that she hadn't heard her come down the stairs. "It smells much better than the last attempts, at least."

"No, it's really good," Lena said. She handed Cheryl a clean fork and watched as she took a delicate bite. She couldn't blame her for not taking a big mouthful, especially given the dubious quality of her previous trials.

Cheryl's expression brightened. "This is delicious, Lena. Plus it will add a nice pop of color to the plates. What are those spices I'm tasting?"

"Caraway and cloves," Lena said with a sigh, setting the pan aside to cool. "Festive."

She sat down again and pushed the second wineglass in front of Cheryl before sliding a plate piled with apple slices and crispy bacon between them. "Leftovers from the recipe," she said, waving at the unconventional snack plate.

"Thank you," Cheryl said, sitting on the stool next to her and picking up an apple slice. "So, your cooking isn't the cause of your hangdog expression—for once, thank goodness—so I'd make a guess that you're moping about Devin? Did the two of you have an argument?"

"I don't mope," Lena said, in such a gloomy sounding tone that she couldn't help but join in Cheryl's laughter. "Okay, maybe I do, a little. But no, Devin and I aren't fighting. We're getting along great. Better than ever. We both want exactly the same thing out of our relationship."

Cheryl hesitated. "I want to say congratulations, but your expression tells me this might be a trap. Doesn't this make you happy?"

Lena shrugged. "We both have a lot going on. I'm having doubts about the career path I thought I'd follow until I retired, and she and her dad are dealing with the sale of their family store. We like each other, but neither of us is in the right place for a serious relationship. It's what we both want, but it makes me feel…sad, I guess."

Cheryl took a drink of her wine, then reached out and patted Lena's hand. "Devin and Ron are facing some tough decisions right now, but they have each other to help them through. And she knows you're here for her, too. She's not going through this alone, and you don't have to, either. If you want to talk through some of your doubts, I'd be happy to listen."

Lena could sense Cheryl's hesitation as she made the offer. Her voice grew quiet, as if she didn't have confidence in Lena's response, and she uncharacteristically wouldn't meet Lena's eyes. Lena understood why she might fear Lena's rejection of her overture. Their familial relationship was still new and fragile, although they both were trying to get past their differences and the years they had spent without seeing each other. Lena had to admit that she often used the restaurant and her cooking as convenient excuses to avoid spending too much time with Cheryl, but right now she really wanted to talk to someone.

"I suppose it's only fair, since all of this is your fault," she said, smiling to let Cheryl know she was joking. Mostly. "Coming here"—she waved her hand vaguely, encompassing the town and the restaurant with her gesture—"it's made me start to question the life I left behind. Not that I have any plans to become a chef, but I guess the experience has reminded me of parts of myself that I've been ignoring. I love my job…well, I like it, and it's fulfilling… Well, maybe fulfilling isn't the right word. I'm good at it, and I feel a sense of accomplishment when I've done quality work for the people and companies that hire me."

She hesitated and thought that through. "Yes," she said. "The last sentence is true, with no qualifiers. It's a decent career, and I never really imagined doing anything else." She sighed, finding it difficult to express what she wanted to say. Cheryl sat quietly, eating a piece of bacon and giving Lena the chance to think and talk. She listened as well as she hugged.

"I always believed I was the rebel of the family," Lena finally admitted, then laughed. "Aside from you, of course. I was the middle-of-the-road rebel."

"And I was your safety net?" Cheryl guessed.

Lena nodded. "You were. I could break from family tradition and not go to medical school because compared to someone who changed careers regularly, being a coder was practically *acceptable*. But I was talking to Devin the other day, and she saw me in a completely different way. She saw me as someone who had followed her family's expectations by staying in health care. She didn't judge me for it or anything, but her words made my perspective shift. I used to see myself as someone who was forging her own path, and as long as I didn't go as far afield as you had, I could get away with it. But what I was really doing was just walking on the shoulder of the family road."

"That's a perfectly fine place to be," Cheryl said. "As long as it's *where* you want to be."

"I thought it was," Lena said, frowning as she struggled to explain. "I thought I had made my own choices, but now I'm not sure. Am I staying in this job because it's what I want, or because I subconsciously chose a career that was nothing more than a compromise? Something that was close enough to what they wanted me to do so it didn't cause too much trouble? Did I cave, even though I thought I was being defiant?"

"You might be overthinking this, Lena," Cheryl said gently. "Your career choice probably had a number of influences, from the way your mind processes information to classes you enjoyed in school to your familiarity with the medical field since your entire family works within it. There's nothing wrong with that. But if you're truly questioning whether this is a fulfilling line of work for you, then why not try something else for a while?"

Lena shook her head. "You make it sound easy, but I don't think I'm cut out to live like you do, switching jobs every few months and not having any sort of stability in my work."

Cheryl laughed. "It's not a choice between one or the other, dear. I enjoy the early stages of a challenge, so my lifestyle works for me. Your dad is single-minded and focused, so his career choices have worked for him. I have a feeling you're somewhere in the middle. You want to focus on your work. Dive deeply into it and improve. I've seen that in this kitchen, where you've narrowed your focus on a few dishes and you're working to perfect them. But you also like to try new things every once in a while. You have a little of me in you, and you thrive on taking on challenges and learning new things. Why not shake things up now and again? Take some new skills you've learned, like the ones in this restaurant, and use them in your coding work?"

Most of what Cheryl was saying made sense to Lena, giving her even more to have to untangle and ponder, but she wasn't ready to admit that, so she focused on the one thing that seemed too flippant. "How exactly do you expect me to combine my cooking skills with programming? Should I make meals for prospective clients? Or databases for restaurants? That's just...oh, wait."

Lena tapped her fingers on the metal counter as the idea unfolded in her mind. Again, Cheryl sat in silence while Lena's thoughts unspooled.

"A lot of the variables are predictable," Lena said thoughtfully. "The number of seats, the dishes that are most popular. I could create a database that would analyze patterns and predict supply needs. Reports that would show how much revenue each dish generated. And I could apply the method Devin taught me to the recipes, creating workflow schedules that would help coordinate staff and meal services. It would be adaptable, too, so new recipes or seasonal ingredients could be plugged in as necessary, and supply lists and service timing would automatically adapt."

Lena heard herself speaking faster and in a more animated way as the idea took shape in her mind. She had always intellectually known that she could apply her skills to businesses beyond health care, but working directly in the restaurant had given her the real-world tools she needed to design a product that might work. Might. She needed to calm down and think this through more carefully, but the germ of the idea excited her.

"I'd need to interview chefs and restaurant owners to find out what I could add that would make this more useful than a more piecemeal method of tracking data," she said, voicing her internal caution. "But it might work. Wow. Thank you, Aunt Cheryl."

Cheryl shrugged, but she smiled with obvious pleasure. "See? You don't need to throw away everything you worked so hard to achieve if you're feeling in a rut. You can find new ways to use your talents. Explore your personal interests more often and see what ideas they open up professionally."

Lena smiled and poured the rest of the wine into their glasses. "You need to be more careful about coming up with sensible ideas. You might ruin your image."

Cheryl laughed. "I hate to completely destroy the reputation your parents have built for me, but I'm just as practical as your dad. We get that from your grandfather. I might change industries often, and I might have a less linear approach to work than he does, but I'm the practical one in my business ventures. I see what needs to be done to make a store or restaurant more fiscally viable, and then I hire creative people like you to make it happen."

Lena paused with an apple slice partway to her mouth. Cheryl casually took a sip of her wine as if she hadn't completely shifted Lena's worldview in a handful of sentences. She had slowly been coming on her own to the realization that Cheryl was nowhere near the scatterbrained picture her mom and dad had painted of her. She had handled the majority of the details of running a restaurant and managing a staff, compensating for Lena's lack of experience and allowing her to focus solely on cooking and her two assistants. But years of subliminally getting the message *Don't be like Aunt Cheryl* couldn't be overcome in a matter of weeks. She was trying, though, so instead of commenting on that part of her aunt's speech, she focused on the less believable part of it.

"I'm not creative," she said, setting the apple slice on her napkin. "I'm analytical. Numbers, codes, that sort of thing."

Cheryl shook her head. "You're believing the reputation people have built for you, too. You might understand the basic theory underlying your codes and numbers in an analytical way, but what you do with it, the way you adapt and manipulate it to solve problems and meet your customers' needs, that's nothing but creative. You're not just duplicating what other coders have done, but you're creating something new. You get that from your grandmother."

Lena made a scoffing sound. Ridiculous. She was more robotic than creative. Although—and she wasn't about to admit that her aunt was right—she *had* been merely duplicating her own programs, with minor variations, for the past few years, which might explain why her work had felt less fulfilling lately. And why the idea of a new restaurant database had her feeling inspired again. She sighed. This entire trip to Leavenworth had shaken up her life, shifting her perspective on what she thought she knew about her family and herself. And about love.

"You're lucky with your career in another way, too. You aren't tied to any one location," Cheryl added, as if sensing where Lena's thoughts had gone. "I understand that they have computers and internet service in Seattle these days, if you were ever interested in moving to a new city."

Lena rolled her eyes, as if her own mind hadn't been traveling westward, in Devin's future direction. The thought of being close to her, with unlimited time to get to know each other instead of a brief holiday season, was even more enticing than her new career ideas.

"Apparently meddling runs in the family, too," she said.

Cheryl got up and leaned over to give Lena a kiss on her cheek. "Your dad and I are more alike than he cares to admit. That's why we squabble so much. And also why, no matter how much he complains, he'll always drop everything and come help me if I offer him an interesting opportunity. He claims he's rescuing me, but he once admitted these new experiences gave him a fresh approach to his own work, no matter how different they were."

She added her empty wineglass to the tub next to the dishwasher and headed toward the door to the dining room.

"Aunt Cheryl," Lena said, making her pause and turn back to face her, "I'm glad we've had a chance to talk."

Cheryl nodded, her eyes suddenly bright. "Me, too, dear."

Lena sat at the counter for a few moments after she left, but her already full mind was now overflowing with new ideas added to the mix. She put the bowl of cooled cabbage in the fridge, then went over to the alcove's desk. She rummaged for a spare piece of paper, finding a receipt for an order of beer, and scribbled down her latest cabbage experience, focusing on her aunt's tentative expression when she tried it. She tossed the paper in the top drawer and then got out her tablet. She might as well start working on the idea for a restaurant database now, while it was still fresh in her mind. She tapped her fingers on the desk for a moment, then opened up a search screen instead. It wouldn't hurt to just glance at apartments in Seattle first, would it?

CHAPTER EIGHTEEN

Lena managed to stay away from Devin until the next day, but she barely made it until noon. They talked on the phone at night, as usual, but they kept the conversation on casual topics like chocolate and cabbage. Even though her mind was suddenly turning toward the possibility of starting a real relationship before their lives were perfect, she wasn't sure how Devin would respond to her newfound enthusiasm. She had to respect Devin's wishes in this case, but at least she knew that she wasn't the only one with deepening feelings.

With any other woman, she might have been uncertain, given their talk the day before, but, well, this was Devin. If she wasn't interested in Lena, she would have told her exactly how she felt—or didn't feel—and then would have given her the perfect chocolate to heal a broken heart. Definitely something with caramel in it. But Lena had no doubt that Devin was feeling the same attraction she was. The same pull toward another body, another soul, that kept them up late on the phone or spending hours going from one kitchen to the other just to talk and help each other work.

Lena wasn't going to avoid Devin, but she was going to honor her need to remain friends for now. While Lena might be considering some changes to her career—and that mattered to her, and was challenging—for Devin, selling a generational family shop and losing her connection to her mother and her own passion for making chocolate was an entirely different type of transition. Lena was going to be there for Devin and not push, but she also wasn't planning to hide how she felt. They would be stronger if they went through this together. It wouldn't make solutions any easier to find, or remove the pain of loss, but it would make that pain more bearable. And maybe they would come up with solutions the other person hadn't expected. Or their careers and lives would always be messy, but they'd be messy together.

Devin's dad was spraying some candy molds, but he looked up when she walked in and gave her a warm smile, nodding toward the kitchen.

Lena held up the lidded plastic bowl she was carrying. "Come try some soup when you're at a good stopping point," she said before using her hip to open the swinging door. She hadn't meant to sneak in without Devin noticing, but Devin was intent on both what she was doing and on the phone next to her, so Lena had a chance to watch her work unobserved.

Devin poured some melted chocolate on a marble slab and started to scrape it across the surface with one thin metal spatula, using a second triangular one to clean the first after every stroke. It was a mesmerizingly rhythmic action, and the click-click of metal and marble was soothing and constant. Devin seemed relaxed as she worked, with some of the tension in the usual way she carried her back and shoulders seeming to release. She returned the chocolate from the slab to a mixing bowl, stirred it, then poured some back onto the marble and started scraping again. Weird, but it was probably her version of meditation.

Devin reached toward her phone, and Lena stepped back, unsure if she was interrupting her or not, and hit the swinging door hard enough for Devin to notice and look up.

"I can go," Lena offered, but Devin shook her head before she finished her sentence.

"Stay, please," she said. "And when I'm done with this call, you can tell me if I'm overstepping and being intrusive."

Lena shrugged. "Okay," she said. Now she was intrigued. She pulled a stool up to the counter and sat down, placing her bowl next to her.

Devin touched the call button, then went back to her chocolate scraping while the phone rang. She had it on speaker so Lena heard the somewhat hesitant *Hello?* when a man answered.

"Chef Dunham? It's Devin Meyer," she said. "I'm not sure if you remember me, but—"

He laughingly interrupted her. "Devin! How could I not remember the most gifted chocolatier to come through our school? Call me Ben. How have you been?"

"Oh, fine," Devin said vaguely. "And you?"

"Good, good. Still teaching, of course. So, what can I do for you, Devin?" Ben asked.

Lena could see Devin take a deep breath before she started speaking. "I was hoping you could let me know about scholarship opportunities at the school. I remember that you helped one of my classmates with some lesser known ones, and I'd appreciate some suggestions, if you have any. I know a couple of young women here in Leavenworth who have been coming to me for informal lessons in pastry and chocolate making. They're both talented and enthusiastic about learning, but neither would be able to afford to move to Seattle and put themselves through school without some help. They're willing to work hard, though. One is our assistant here in the shop, and the other would have glowing recommendations from the German restaurant where she works as a sous-chef."

She glanced at Lena as if to gauge her reaction to the call. Lena raised her eyebrows in surprise but then grinned at Devin. Leave it to Devin, who was currently buried up to her eyeballs with stress, to make the effort to help other people. And not just a simple gesture of assistance or support, but a major, life-changing one.

"Hmm," Ben said. "Sounds like they'd need a housing stipend, as well?"

"Yes," Devin agreed. "Shay's parents would probably help as much as they can, but she has four siblings, so I don't know how much they can afford. Layla is supporting herself and her baby, so she'd definitely need housing and money for expenses. They both would be assets to any kitchen, so they could easily supplement a scholarship by working, but they need help getting started."

"Let me talk to some of my sources here, and I'll put together some information for them. Just give me a few days." He paused. "You mentioned the shop. Are you back there permanently now?"

"No, just for the holidays," Devin said. She scraped the chocolate off the slab and into the bowl, setting it aside as she talked. "We're selling the store. This will be our last season."

"Oh, I'm sorry to hear that," he said. "My wife and I used to love coming to Leavenworth during the holidays, and we always had to get a big box of Meyer's chocolates to bring home. It's a special place."

Lena got up and went to stand behind her, loosely wrapping her arms around Devin's waist, sighing when Devin leaned into her support. "I'm glad to know that you have good memories of the shop," she said, her voice steady, even though Lena could feel a slight tremor run through her. "I do, as well."

"Yes, I'd imagine you do. So, do you have a buyer yet?"

Lena rested her chin on Devin's shoulder and said "Hmmm," softly in her ear. His voice had changed when he started talking about the store. He sounded more…thoughtful.

"One couple seems interested, but we haven't had an offer yet."

"Ah. And you're planning to sell the name? Your recipes, supplier lists, all proprietary information?"

"We are. Dad is going to retire, and I'll be moving back to Seattle to do…to go back to work."

"Maybe we'll get a chance to catch up when you're in town, then. It was good to talk to you, Devin, and I'll get back to you soon with information for your students."

She thanked him and ended the call, turning in Lena's arms to face her. "Do you think I'm being intrusive, calling about Shay and Layla?" she asked. "I didn't want to talk to them about it before finding out if the idea was even feasible. Right now, I don't think either of them expects to have an opportunity like this, and I'd hate to suggest it and get their hopes up, only to dash them again." She put her arms around Lena's neck, moving closer. "They ask me so many questions about the school, and what it was like, what I learned to make. And they've both learned a lot, even in just a few days. Layla's planning to make another chocolate raspberry tart for your staff treat on Saturday, but it won't be long before she can make some of the desserts you serve to your customers. And Shay can make a few of our chocolates on her own, well enough that neither Dad nor I can find any mistakes."

Lena leaned forward and gave her a kiss. "I think it's a great idea, and you're wonderful to have come up with it. What a gift for them to have a career opportunity like that. But let's come back to how amazing this is later. The question for now is, does this guy want to buy your store?"

"Who's buying the shop?" Devin's dad asked, coming into the kitchen and taking a bag of sugar off one of the shelves. "Did those people make an offer?"

"No," Devin answered him. "But I just talked to my old advisor from pastry school, Ben Dunham, and he sounded very interested."

"He's a chocolatier?" Ron asked, sounding hopeful.

"His specialty is Viennese pastry. But he's the one who taught me to make those raspberry cream cheese whirls you love."

Lena stepped away from Devin while they talked, getting some bowls out of a cupboard, nearly as comfortable in this kitchen as Devin now was in hers.

"You have to try this while we talk, before it gets too cold," she said, locating a ladle in an overstuffed drawer and doling out three bowls of soup. "So, does it make a difference if Pastry Man buys the shop instead of the other couple?"

Devin shrugged. "At least there'd be a better chance that he could keep the store going. He'd appreciate the high-quality ingredients we use and would be less likely to cut corners. I don't know if it really makes a difference in how it's going to feel to say good-bye, but I think it might help a little to have someone more proficient take over."

Her dad nodded. "I love those pastries. I'd be okay with him selling those, too, and not just chocolate."

Lena had to smile at that. She was tempted to have her aunt buy the shop as her next project, just so these two could come back and visit it whenever they wanted.

"We'll see, I guess," Devin said, taking a bite of the soup Lena had given her. "This is delicious," she said. "Chestnut soup? I love it."

"It's so silky," Ron added. "And I taste a hint of nutmeg. Are you going to serve this in the restaurant?"

Lena sighed, taking a bite. She hadn't been able to resist buying the bag of chestnuts when she found them in the store, and she had spent hours searching for the perfect recipe for them. "That was the plan, but after I made it this morning, Aunt Cheryl vetoed the idea. She said we'd have to charge twenty dollars a bowl to cover the cost of the chestnuts and the time it took me to roast and peel them, which was way harder to do than it looked in the video I found online."

Devin laughed. "I'm happy we get to share the trial batch, at least."

Ron rinsed out his empty bowl and put it in the dishwasher's tray. He pointed at the bowl of chocolate next to Devin. "Did you temper that to use it, or just as stress relief?"

"Stress relief. Do you need it?"

"Yes, thank you," he said, picking up the bowl and the bag of sugar. "There's actually a little sunshine outside today. Why don't the two of you walk down to the park? I'll be out front if anyone comes by."

Lena smiled. "That sounds perfect," she said. Devin nodded, too, without protesting that she had too much to do. She looked like she needed a break, and Lena was happy to share it with her. They put their coats on and went out into the chilly afternoon. Lena reached for Devin's hand, lacing their fingers together as they walked.

The air felt clean and bright after the morning snowfall, and there were patches of blue sky mingling with the clouds that promised more snow later. For now, though, the weak sunlight felt good on Lena's face, and it reflected off the snow on the surrounding hills, which lay more thickly than it had on Lena's first day here.

She hadn't spent much time in the town since her brief walk with the herds of tourists over the weekend since she was usually either in the restaurant or in Devin's shop, aside from brief trips to the grocery store. She felt as if she had blinked and the town had transformed from the sleepy, Christmasy village it had been on her arrival to full-on North Pole. The colors seemed brighter now, with more lights and decorations than she had noticed before. The melting top layer of snow crunched under their feet as they walked, joining with the muted sounds of various carols wafting from each shop they passed. Even the smell on the street was different, with competing scents of spices, oranges, and pine boughs making her suspicious that someone had sprinkled potpourri on the sidewalks.

Devin nudged her with her shoulder. "Some of the shops spritz essential oils along their storefronts to draw in customers and get them in the holiday spirit," she said, apparently noticing the way Lena was sniffing the air.

"By holiday spirit, do you mean the spending spirit?" Lena asked.

Devin laughed. "They're one and the same in Leavenworth."

"What about you and your dad? Do you spray eau de chocolat on the snow outside your shop?"

"We wouldn't stoop so low. Our chocolates speak for themselves," Devin said haughtily, before giving her a grin. "Although we have been known to prop the door open and steep peppermint or citrus tea on the burner, depending on which type of candy isn't selling fast enough. Works every time."

They came to Front Street Park and walked over to one of the wrought iron benches, brushing off the powdery snow and sitting down, hips touching and hands still entwined.

"Are you ready for the weekend?" Devin asked, leaning into her.

Lena sighed. Another busy weekend until Thanksgiving came and thrust them into the season, and then the season would begin, with no more days of semifreedom until March. "I made it through our opening night, two other services, and a dinner with my dad as one of the guests. It should be a cakewalk from here on out." She laughed. "Not that I'm expecting perfection, of course, but we know we can do it, so I feel less anxious. The good thing is, we won't ever be any busier than we were last weekend. The place was full, and there are only so many seats, so we know what to expect."

She rested her head on Devin's shoulder. "My worry is that the kids will get burned out. Or I will, which is more likely. I'm planning to start training one of our waitstaff, Ruben, as a replacement sous-chef so Layla and Kirby can have an occasional day off if they want. He's been coming early on the weekends and lending a hand, just on his own, so I think he'd be interested. Still, a three-month season with hardly a break will be tough."

"It is," Devin agreed, rubbing her cheek gently against Lena's hair. "But it also speeds by since you're so busy. Try to shake things up every once in a while. Add a new special to the menu, or let Kirby or Layla pick a new dish to make. That's what we've always done. At least once a week we add a new specialty chocolate with unusual flavor combinations. They're not always the best sellers, and we often don't ever make them again, but it keeps us interested."

"That's a good idea," Lena said. "I worry about the monotony. I just hope Aunt Cheryl doesn't get bored and move on to her next project, leaving us stranded without her."

"If she does, give Dad a call. He'll be excited to tend bar for you again."

Lena sat up again, thinking about Ron's reaction to the news about another potential buyer. He had seemed earnest in a charming way about allowing Ben to add pastries to the shop's offerings, but he hadn't slipped into the melancholy expression she had seen before when the subject of the sale came up. "I've noticed that he seems happier lately. Do you think it's because of the talk you had? About him making his peace with selling and moving on to something new?"

"He does seem more cheerful," Devin agreed with a thoughtful expression. "It must be that. Now I seem to be the one having trouble letting go. I fought so hard to get away from all this, and now I'm considering staying. I just don't know if I'll be satisfied either way."

"At least you have some time before you have to decide, although Ben did seem really interested. I'd be surprised if he didn't make you and your dad an offer before next week is over, especially since you told him that there were others interested in the place. You know…" Lena started, and then she hesitated. She was determined to give Devin the space she needed, but she also wanted to keep their options out in the open, so Devin might start to believe in them, too. "I was kidding about Aunt Cheryl stranding us. Those types of jokes are so common in my family that I don't always think before I make them. We had a really good talk yesterday, and I've been learning that I have a lot of misconceptions about her, and about myself."

She gave Devin a quick rundown of their conversation, leaving out—for now—the parts that related to Devin and Seattle.

"You're exceptionally creative," Devin said with a shrug, as if this wasn't news to her. "I'm sure everyone who knows you realizes it, even if you haven't thought of yourself in that way before. This database idea is unexpected, though, but I can see how much potential it has. Dad and I know these details about our shop since we've been doing the same things for decades, but most stores and restaurants would have more turnover in staff and product. This could be a very marketable new pursuit for you."

Devin sighed and seemed to deflate a little. "Dad and I might not need this, but I'll bet the Comstocks would appreciate your help if they decide to buy the shop. I was going to leave them our recipes and vendor contacts, but I'll bet they'd love working with you to learn how to manage the shop better."

Lena frowned. She hadn't even met the Comstocks, and they might not be evil developers, but she still saw them as the enemy. Her loyalty was fierce, and she wasn't about to take their side over Devin and Ron's.

She kissed Devin's temple. "If it would set your mind and Ron's at ease about them buying your store, then I'd gladly help them, no charge. But if it would bother you to have me working with them on operating *your* store, then they can muddle through on their own."

Devin nodded. "I'll let you know," she said, which told Lena volumes. Her lack of immediate denial was all Lena needed as proof that Devin was feeling the pain of loss before she'd even signed the sale papers. Lena wasn't about to add to that, and she decided to finally shift to the subject weighing more heavily on her mind.

"You know," she started slowly, staring across from them at

some kids who were sledding down a small hill in the park. After even the small sun break, the snow was more slush than powder, but their delighted screeches indicated that they didn't care. Lena wished she felt as carefree as they did, unconcerned about her future and whether the person she wanted most to share it with could ever feel the same.

"Most of my work is remote, whether I try something new or continue working on EHRs, or both," she finally continued. "All of it, sometimes. I mean…if you decided to keep the shop, I could maybe stay here for a while longer. Keep you company. Or I could work from Seattle just as easily." Lena shrugged, trying to appear calm, although her heart was beating so hard it must be visible. "Or maybe you'd prefer Portland, as a change of pace. Whichever you choose, I could make it work. We could be together and give ourselves a chance to see where this goes when we're not consumed by work or facing a deadline at the end of the season," she said, almost surprised by her own words. She had always used busyness as a way to maintain her distance in relationships, avoiding the need or opportunity to explore them fully.

"Oh," Devin said when Lena fell silent, a noncommittal sound that didn't give Lena much information to use to gauge her reaction.

Lena glanced at her, but Devin was looking at the children, too, and hopefully not wondering how to extricate herself from Lena's embrace. She sighed and continued, even without any encouragement that she would meet with success.

"I guess lately I've been thinking of a career change like it would change who I am. But it won't. It's what I do, and I can see opportunities to bring it more in alignment with my personality, but no matter what, I'm still me. And the person I am really…really likes you, Devin. I don't need to have everything else figured out to know that much. I don't want this to be a season, with us trying to fit in time together, and maybe someday when we're sorted we'll give us a chance. I want us to make these decisions together."

Devin shifted on the bench until she was facing Lena. "I want that, too, but I don't know if I'm ready. Maybe after we get an offer, and I know for sure whether or not I'll be moving away? You might be right that we don't need everything mapped out before we decide for certain, but I think I need this part resolved. I need more time to figure out what my future might hold before I can add another person to the equation."

She rested her hands on Lena's cheeks and pulled her close for a slow, soft kiss. "I'm not saying no," she assured Lena when she pulled away. "And the thought of having you close, no matter what I decide to do, is very tempting, but I don't want to use you as a security blanket because I'm hurting or because I feel lonely. If I can just get a few answers about the shop, maybe I'll feel like I'm ready to be more of a partner for someone. For you." She gave Lena a somewhat strained smile, obviously attempting a lightness she didn't completely feel. "We have until February, at least. Nothing needs to be decided for certain before then."

Until February. There were a lot of schnitzels to fry between now and then, but Lena felt more hopeful now, knowing that her time with Devin might not have to end when her responsibility to the restaurant did. She wanted to make promises now, but she'd keep them inside her heart until Devin was ready to hear them.

She sighed and fell silent, and Devin picked up the conversation by pointing out the gazebo where period-costumed carolers would sing every evening in December. Lena followed her lead and let go of the serious topics for the moment, and they just sat together, talking about Jacquie's upcoming visit and how the park would look when it was filled with Christmas lights.

Eventually, the sun went behind some threatening-looking clouds and it got too cold to comfortably sit on the bench any longer, so they got up and headed back to the shop. Lena kissed Devin good-bye, then left with her empty soup container and a package from Ron of spicy chili chocolates covered with a shimmery red coating for her and her aunt.

Thick flakes of snow were starting to fall as she walked back to Haus Bavaria, but Lena barely noticed. She felt warmed by the whole afternoon, from her talk with Devin, to the possibility of a new future for Layla and Shay, to the kind way Ron had hugged her before giving her the beautifully wrapped box of candy to take home. This town had changed her in unexpected ways, drawing her into the lives of these people and opening her mind to new possibilities. And that was in just a few weeks. She doubted she'd recognize herself once February came.

CHAPTER NINETEEN

Devin sat on her usual stool next to the kitchen's island and spread a thin layer of milk chocolate on a marble slab. She dragged a fine-toothed decorating comb over it, and then slid the marble to one side before pulling a second in front of her. This one already had a layer of white chocolate spread over the combed base layer, and she used a knife to shave strips off the rectangle, forming a bunch of uniform, marbled chocolate straws.

She worked quickly, using three slabs in various stages of the process, allowing each layer time to set while she worked on one of the others. She already had several parchment-covered sheet pans filled with the little tubes, ready to be stored in the cooler for the upcoming week.

This task had been one of the first entrusted to her when she was a child, and she had somehow never tired of the monotonous activity. They kept these rolled confections in mugs on the counter, free for customers to sample, and they went through hundreds a day during the holiday season. She knew she'd have to repeat this exact task several times a week, just as she had every Christmas she had worked in the shop, but she never got bored with it. Maybe because she could remember her mother bending over her shoulder, helping her awkward fingers through the process until it became second nature. She would have been sitting at this exact spot—though on a taller stool to let her reach the counter—and even now she could smell her mother's vanilla and lavender perfume, mingling with the scent of chocolate.

Devin sighed and moved the next slab in front of her, switching to a white chocolate that she had tinted red, but going through the same ritual. Another reason she loved this job was because it kept her hands busy, but let her mind wander free. When she had been young, her daydreams carried her around the world. Now—unsurprisingly—she was preoccupied with thoughts of Lena.

Lena's words at the park had been so full of promise that Devin had been tempted to say yes. Yes, she wanted Lena here with her, or in Seattle, or anywhere. But she had forced herself to take a step back. Listen, but not accept. Not just yet. She was sad about the store and worried about her father. Afraid that even if she wasn't being torn between her life in Seattle and her family's shop anymore, she *still* wouldn't be able to find any true calling. She hadn't been able to for over ten years—what made her think she'd suddenly find her purpose just because the shop was sold? Maybe she never would.

She was proud of Lena's self-discoveries since she had come to Leavenworth and was excited about Lena's new ideas. She wanted nothing more than to be part of them—to cheer Lena on as she developed them and even to offer some suggestions based on her years of working in this industry. But how long would it be before Lena got tired of being with someone who just coasted along in dead-end jobs, feeling bored and unfulfilled while Lena flourished?

Devin sighed and pulled the first slab in front of her again. She knew that was unfair to Lena. She wasn't interested in Devin because of what she did for a living, and she'd be just as supportive if Devin was making chocolate or fast-food burgers. It was her own insecurities causing her doubts. She had given herself yesterday to think about Lena's suggestion, but she hadn't gotten any closer to a decision. Putting more space between them wasn't helping. If nothing else, Devin had these next couple of months to be with Lena. Why was she trying to isolate herself and go through even this part all alone, when there was someone so willing to share it with her?

She rolled a few more straws while she thought, but she couldn't come up with a satisfying reason. She reached over and picked up her phone, smearing chocolate on the screen as she called Lena.

"Hey, sexy," Lena said when she answered. Her sultry voice shifted as she laughed. "Oh, I hope I'm not on speaker with your dad in the room. Sorry, Ron!"

Devin grinned. Why had she wasted even a day away from Lena? "He's not here, so you don't need to worry that he'll leap to defend the virtue of his darling daughter. Not that he'd mind, anyway. He likes you."

"The feeling is very mutual," Lena said.

"He went to Peshastin tonight," Devin continued. "I thought you might want to come over and keep me company?"

"Sure," Lena said. "I just have a few things to do in the kitchen, but then I'm free. I have a reprieve for Thanksgiving, so there's no prep work to be done, for once. Will there be anything for me to sample? Any chocolate, I mean, of course."

"I'm making chocolate straws, so you can have as many of those as you want," Devin said, feeling her cheeks flush at Lena's suggestive comment, and her laughing retraction of it. *And anything else you want*, she added to herself.

She settled in to chat with Lena while she finished her tasks, tucking the phone under her chin and returning to her own work. "Do you have any idea what's on the menu for tomorrow night?"

"Not a clue. I'm just happy not to be cooking, so I don't care what we're served. A bag of frozen meatballs and some spaghetti will be just fine, as long as I don't have to even boil the water."

"I doubt it will be—Damn. Someone's knocking on the door because they apparently can't read the Closed sign. Hold on."

"Wait," Lena called. "Take me with you in case it's a robber."

"A robber who knocks?" Devin asked, but she gathered up a handful of straws and kept her phone as she went through the door to the main showroom. She came up short when she saw Lena standing outside the door. "It's you," she said unnecessarily.

"It is," Lena said, still speaking into her phone. "I started walking when you asked me to come over."

Devin smiled and put her phone on the counter, going over to unlock the door and let Lena in. She pointed at Devin's hand with a laugh.

"You brought chocolate. Someone knocks on your door after hours, and you bring them chocolate?"

Devin shrugged sheepishly. "I didn't want to send them away empty-handed," she admitted. "Here, you can have them. I didn't expect you so soon. I thought you still had work to do."

Lena shook her head, letting her fingers linger on Devin's wrist as she took the handful of straws from her. "You called and asked me to come over because your dad is out of town. Did you really think I was going to say *Okay, but let me chop these onions first*?"

"Maybe," Devin said with a smile as she led them back into the kitchen. "But I'm glad you didn't."

She sat at the counter again, returning to her work, while Lena pulled up a stool and sat next to her, munching on the delicate straws. Devin felt slightly awkward, now that she had lured Lena into her kitchen, but getting back to her task helped settle her again.

Lena seemed perfectly at ease, though. "These are really good," she said, waving one of the straws. "I don't think I realized before how much better high-quality chocolate is than what I usually get at the store."

"It's worlds apart," Devin said, relaxing with this topic of conversation. She thought briefly of how she would often distract her dad from sad or anxious moods by bringing up anything chocolate related, and she wondered if Lena noticed that she was a little nervous and was doing the same thing with her. Whatever the reason for her comment, it worked.

"This isn't even our good product," she added, rolling more straws. "These are free samples that we give away all season, so we use a standard, relatively inexpensive chocolate for them. Still, it's worlds apart from mass-produced candy bars. We have different grades we use for our confections, depending on the fillings and flavorings. Sometimes the chocolate needs to be more complex and better quality, and other times we can use a less expensive product because it's being paired with something like peppermint that will overwhelm the more subtle flavor profiles of the expensive couvertures."

"And you can really tell the difference in taste?" Lena asked, finishing her straws and going over to the sink. She returned with a damp paper towel and put her hand under Devin's chin. "You have chocolate on your ear."

"It was on my phone." Devin laughed, but the sound faded as Lena gently wiped her cheek, her other hand trailing down Devin's neck before resting on her collarbone. Her touch managed to erase Devin's remaining nervousness, leaving nothing but desire in its place.

Lena stepped away, and Devin cleared her throat. "You can," she said, picking up the thread of the conversation again with some difficulty and switching into teaching mode to give herself a chance to regain her composure. "Think of chocolate like wine or loose leaf tea. A lot of factors can affect the flavor profile, like the variety of cacao, the soil conditions where it was grown, how it's roasted and blended, and so on. We have very specific requirements for our couvertures, and we guard those trade secrets." Devin shrugged. "Of course, there aren't a lot of small-scale, artisanal chocolatiers in the area, so it's a fairly relaxed form of guarding, but we can become fierce at a moment's notice, if necessary."

Lena grinned. "I can picture you and your dad taking down an industrial spy with nothing but a couple of whisks and a pastry bag. Is that why Ben was asking if you were planning to sell your vendor information along with the store?"

Devin nodded. "Someone could make the exact same chocolates, but without access to our ratios and suppliers, it would take a lot of trial and error before they got the same results, if ever. Not that different couvertures would be bad, but they wouldn't be the same. Here, I'll show you."

Devin went into the pantry and pulled several boxes off the shelves, taking a couple of chocolate coins out of each one and arranging them in order on a tray. "Close your eyes," she said to Lena as she came back through the door, shielding the tray from Lena's sight.

Lena laughed, but did as Devin instructed. "Do you honestly think I could identify anything about those chocolates just by looking at them?"

Devin stood in front of Lena's stool and set the tray on the counter next to them. "No, but this will make you focus on the flavors. Now, open your mouth."

Lena opened her mouth and stuck out her tongue. Devin stared at her, knowing all too well how Lena's tongue felt when it rasped against her own. Knowing the taste of her, and the way her touch penetrated Devin's skin and grazed across her soul. And how her—

Lena squinted one eye partially open. "Aren't I supposed to be tasting chocolate?"

"Oh, right," Devin said, her voice sounding rough. She cleared her throat. "I got distracted."

Lena smirked at her and closed her eyes again. Devin picked up one of the chocolate coins and placed it on Lena's tongue, drawing her thumb across Lena's lower lip as she pulled her hand back. Lena shifted forward, as if seeking her touch again.

Lena swallowed. "Mm. Sweet," she said. Devin leaned forward and kissed her along her jawline before straightening up again.

"Very," she agreed. "That's a middle-of-the-road chocolate. We'd use it for peanut butter cups or peanut clusters. Fancy candy bars, really. Now try this one, but let it melt on your tongue."

Lena made a small sound at that and shifted slightly on her stool. Devin smiled, glad she wasn't the only one who was getting distracted. She placed another coin in Lena's mouth, laughing with a slight gasp as Lena gently bit down, capturing her fingers for a brief moment.

"Tastes like chocolate," Lena said, her voice muffled as she held the chocolate on her tongue. "I don't think I…oh, wait." She opened her eyes in surprise and then quickly closed them again. "Sorry. I wasn't expecting to notice any difference, but I think I taste something fruity. It's more layered than the last one."

Devin popped one of the same coins in her own mouth. "That's right. Almost an apple-like flavor. And a hint of almond. This particular one pairs well with fruits or anything spicy, like chilis or ginger. Okay, one more."

She put the next chocolate on her own tongue and pressed her lips against Lena's, transferring the coin to Lena's tongue with a languid stroke. She lingered for a long moment, their breath mingling, and Lena's fingers reached up to grasp the fabric of Devin's shirt, keeping her close.

Lena uncurled her fingers from Devin's shirt and slid her hands down until they were resting on Devin's hips. "Wine," she said. "And a hint of smoke. This is my favorite." She opened her eyes. "Although that might be because I especially enjoyed the delivery system."

Devin grinned. "You're good at this game. This is our most expensive couverture, and we usually only use it when there won't be many competing flavors, so its complexity shines through."

Lena slipped her hands under Devin's T-shirt until they reached her rib cage. She made slow circles with her thumbs until Devin felt as if she had an electric charge running across her skin. "So," Lena said, drawing out the word. "I noticed that you never once mentioned what variety of cacao these samples were, or any details about those percentages you've talked about. Don't you trust me?"

Devin laughed at her teasing tone. "I'd trust you with my life," she said in a husky voice. "With my body and soul." She switched back to a normal tone. "But with Meyer's chocolate secrets? No way. But maybe after the background check..."

Devin raised her hands to Lena's cheeks and leaned forward to kiss her, sucking gently on the tongue that had been tantalizing her since they started this game. Lena laughed in surprise before pressing deeper against Devin's mouth, pulling her between her thighs until their hips were flush against each other. Devin tangled her fingers in Lena's hair, reveling in the heat of her. The kiss mirrored the one they had shared only days before, just a few feet away, but now there was no one else in the shop. No one to interrupt them. No reason to stop.

Lena's fingers splayed across Devin's lower back, barely

skimming below the waistband of her jeans and leaving a trail of fire along her already sensitive skin. Lena pulled away from the kiss and moved her lips to Devin's throat, trailing kisses along her neck with a combination of tongue and teeth that had Devin so aroused she wasn't sure how long her legs would continue to hold her upright. She gasped as she felt Lena unbuttoning her jeans, with the sound shifting to a low moan as Lena's fingers slipped lower, gliding through her wetness, her other hand on Devin's back, supporting her as her hips pressed against Lena's questing touch.

Lena sucked on Devin's earlobe. "Mmm. Complex and a little sweet," she murmured against Devin's ear. "Definitely superior quality."

Her lips met Devin's again, her tongue thrusting in time with the movement of her fingers until Devin's world was filled with Lena's touch, her tongue, her insistent fingers. She came with a sharp cry, bracing her hands on the counter on either side of Lena.

Lena wrapped her arms around Devin's waist, holding her close. "So," she asked, "*now* are you willing to share those trade secrets?"

Devin laughed as she leaned back slightly and started to unbutton Lena's shirt. "Not a chance," she said.

❖

Lena lay in Devin's bed, unable to sleep, but not minding at all since she was able to enjoy having Devin's weight against her side, with Devin's head pillowed on her chest. Lena sifted her fingers softly through Devin's hair, hoping her deep and rhythmic breathing meant she was sleeping more restfully than she probably had since they had started the process of selling the store.

The night had been wonderful, and Lena still felt the echoes of Devin's touch everywhere on her body. Heat and excitement had mingled with openness and trust. There hadn't been any discussions of their future together, and no plans made for anything beyond February, but Lena had grown to know Devin well enough to understand what tonight meant. To be here, in her family home, sharing her bed and her chocolate…Devin had invited her in, and for now, it was enough for Lena. She hoped for more—more time, more life spent together—but she was willing to accept the gift of this one night and to cherish it.

She heard Ron come home in the early hours of the morning and had a moment of panic that he might peek in to check on his daughter, like he had probably done countless times during her childhood, but his steps continued without pause down the creaking hall. Lena sighed and settled deeper in the bed. She hadn't paid much attention to the decor of the room when she and Devin had first stumbled into it, tumbling in a tangled heap onto the bed, but now she took the time to look around her. The icicle lights that adorned every building on Front Street—and that apparently were on all night—cast enough of a glow through Devin's curtains for her to see the room.

Not that there was much to see. The walls, rug, and comforter were all in shades of purple, with bright tones and bold prints likely chosen by teenage Devin, and not the adult one Lena knew. Aside from the colors, though, there weren't any signs of Devin's past. No dolls or teddy bears or baking trophies. No posters on the wall of heartthrob chocolatiers. Lena doubted that Ron or Devin's mom would have packed her things away, so Lena assumed that choice had been Devin's. Maybe an attempt to distance herself from her past, or maybe she had taken everything with her to Seattle. Either way, the room must constantly add to Devin's uncomfortable sensation of being between worlds. Soon, though, she'd be able to get past that, either by staying and turning this into a home for herself as an adult or by leaving the purple room behind forever.

Lena felt a prick of tears at the awareness that whatever choice Devin made, she might not be asked to share it with her. She unintentionally tightened her hold on Devin, who sighed in her sleep, shifting her leg across Lena's thigh and nestling closer. Lena reminded herself to accept what she had now, even if it was temporary, and even if she didn't get the forever that she was hoping for. She closed her eyes and finally allowed herself to fall asleep.

CHAPTER TWENTY

Lena sat in the dining room at Haus Bavaria on Thanksgiving afternoon, fidgeting with her napkin and bouncing her leg up and down under the table. She figured the nervous tic would have bugged the hell out of Devin if she had been paying attention, but she was staring into space, lost in thought. Layla sat near them on a quilt on the floor, handing Jack blocks to throw. Luckily, his little arms couldn't get them far, so she only needed to reach over to retrieve them for him to throw again. She had accepted the invitation to dinner, but now she looked as awkward as Lena would have felt at her age if she had gone to a holiday dinner with a bunch of people she barely knew.

It didn't help that Lena and Devin were both so distracted. Lena wasn't sure why she felt ready to jump out of her skin. She was waiting for Jacquie to arrive. She should be here soon, ready to spend the weekend and celebrate the restaurant's grand opening with Lena. Lena wasn't nervous about her friend coming, though. She had already been in regular communication with Devin, and everyone else was sure to love her, too, so she wasn't the cause of Lena's anxious mood.

Devin wasn't, either, even though she didn't currently seem aware of Lena's presence. If she didn't know better, she might have been concerned that Devin had second thoughts after they had spent last night together. The kiss Devin had given her when they had met at the door today had gone a long way to prove that no matter what the future held for them, Devin didn't regret what was happening right now. She was likely fretting over the shop in some form or another. Lena herself was delighted with their new arrangement and didn't have any cause for stress where Devin was concerned.

Lena watched Layla patiently play the repetitive block game with Jack, who didn't seem inclined to tire of it anytime soon. Lena's heart went out to her, since she obviously wasn't welcome at her family's home tonight, but she wasn't making Lena nervous, either. She seemed uncomfortable right now, but once they were all gathered at the table and eating she would relax. Ron and Cheryl would make sure she did. Jacquie would help, too, and part of the reason Lena had wanted Layla here was so that the two of them could discuss her legal rights regarding child support and maybe come up with a game plan for her.

She leaned over and poked Devin in the arm, making her startle as if she had forgotten anyone else was around.

"I'm nervous," she said. "And I don't know why."

"You're the chef, but they're not letting you be the chef," Devin said without hesitation.

Lena frowned. "I'm someone who is pretending to be a chef, not a real one. Besides, it's a relief that your dad and Cheryl volunteered to cook tonight since I haven't had a break from it for weeks. The kitchen makes me stressed. Being kicked out of it certainly doesn't."

Devin rolled her eyes. "It's bothering Layla, too," she said, basically ignoring the rest of Lena's little speech.

"Really?" She raised her voice slightly. "Layla, does it bother you that you're not in there cooking?"

"Yes. I keep thinking one of them is going to come out here and ask me why the wine sauce isn't ready yet."

"Well, I'm fine with them cooking. Thrilled. And if I wanted to cook so badly, I'd just go in there and help."

Layla shook her head. "I tried. They won't let you."

Lena decided the best way to show them they were wrong was to go into the kitchen and help and be miserable about it. That would prove that her tension had nothing to do with being on the other side of the kitchen door than usual.

She walked resolutely across the dining room and through the swinging door.

"Get out," Cheryl said, not even bothering to look up from the casserole dish in front of her. She was arranging tiny marshmallows across the surface of some mashed sweet potatoes.

"I just thought I'd—"

"You heard your aunt," Ron said, coming across the kitchen and gently pushing her toward the door with hands covered with oven mitts. "You're on holiday tonight. Enjoy it, because you won't have another until March."

He gave her a small shove, and she emerged in the dining room again. She stomped back to the table and sat down.

"Told you so," Devin and Layla said at the same time. They grinned at each other, but Lena ignored them.

"They kicked me out of my own kitchen," she said. "Can you believe it?" She paused. "Hey, when the hell did that become *my* kitchen?"

"Stein," Layla said, pointing at the table where her aunt had placed the stupid mug. She always managed to keep it within Lena's reach.

She shoved in a dollar while she tried to figure out exactly when she had become so possessive of the kitchen, and why it bothered her that Ron and Cheryl were in there using *her* pans and cooking in *her* oven, and...

Lena sighed. "They'd better put everything back the way it was," she said. "They're going to hear about it if we spend all day Saturday trying to find where they put the saucepans. But why are you acting tense?" Lena asked Devin. "They're not messing around in your kitchen."

"No, and neither am I." She sighed and tapped her fingers against the side of her glass beer mug. "Ever since I can remember, we'd get premade turkey dinners from the market and spend Thanksgiving night prepping the store for the weekend. Do you know how many chocolates I need to make tonight? A billion. I'm mentally making a game plan for getting them all done in time."

"We're a cheerful group," Lena said. The other two gave her half-hearted smiles and then relapsed into their respective activities of staring at the wall and handing blocks to Jack, leaving her to fidget with her now mutilated napkin.

She was preparing herself to make an attempt to liven up the depressing party when Jacquie burst in the door, bringing with her a swirl of snow and an almost tangible energy. She set down her suitcase and stood by the door in her purple caftan with her hands on her hips, surveying the room.

"This is the cutest place I have ever seen. I feel like I've gone skiing in the Alps and I'm back at the chalet for spiced wine and caviar. Lena, I have to get one of those steins. Or a T-shirt? Both. Yes, definitely both." She came across the room, bypassing Lena and aiming for Devin, pulling her into a hug. "Look how beautiful you are! My tiny phone screen did not do you justice. And is that a baby? Can I hold him?"

Layla looked at Lena, then back at Jacquie, seeming a little overwhelmed by the rapid sentences. "Um, sure," she said, hesitantly, as if she wasn't sure if Jacquie was an invited guest or someone who had wandered in off the street.

"Layla, this is my friend from Portland. Jacquie, this is Layla and her son Jack," Lena said.

"What a great name," Jacquie said, picking him up. "I was a Jack once, too," she said to Layla. "Not anymore, but I still love the name."

Layla smiled. "I was sure he was going to be a girl, so I picked the name Jackie. We went the other way."

"That's the universe for you, always trying to balance itself out. What do you think of that, Jack?" He answered by reaching for her purple-rimmed glasses and trying to pull them off.

Cheryl and Ron came out of the kitchen with trays of appetizers, and with those two and Jacquie in the room, Lena, Devin, and Layla didn't have a chance of remaining morose. Jack was happy being passed back and forth between Jacquie and Ron, so Layla was able to relax and join the others at the table. She still remained shyly on the periphery, but once Jacquie asked about her baking lessons with Devin, she grew more animated, telling everyone about the caramel apple pie she had helped Ron make for their dessert.

Lena couldn't help but compare their small party to her family's version of Thanksgiving, which usually turned into a grown-up, competitive version of show and tell, with everyone sharing their success stories and trying to one-up each other. Lena was proud of the work she did, but it never had a chance of winning those tournaments. She might have designed a useful interface that saved a clinic's staff a few hours a week, but Landry had made a dead heart beat again, and her mom had stitched together some severed arteries and so on and so on.

She reveled in this Thanksgiving, where the successes these people were interested in were other people's and not their own.

She relaxed back in her seat, with one foot propped on the rung of Devin's chair so their legs were touching, and listened to Ron give Jacquie advice on bartending for the restaurant, in case she was roped in to help over the weekend—which, Lena knew, was very likely to happen.

Devin leaned toward her. "Feeling better?" she asked quietly.

"Now that they're out of my kitchen? Yes," Lena said. "But I have a feeling they'll be going back in there soon to get dinner. And this doesn't mean I like cooking or working here or anything. We just have everything set up the way we like it, and I don't want stuff moved around."

"Right," Devin said, patting her knee. "Whatever you need to tell yourself."

Lena laughed and took hold of her hand. "What about you? Any news today from Ben about the shop or…anything else?"

Devin shook her head. "Not a word. I thought he sounded interested, but it might have been a whim, and then he thought better of it the next day. I hope he gets back to me about the other thing, though."

Lena gave her hand a squeeze. She wished either Ben or the Comstocks would make Devin and her dad an offer soon. She thought it would be easier for Devin if she had to make a decision about the shop instead of being stuck in limbo with some interest, but no real offers.

As she had feared, her aunt and Ron eventually went back into the kitchen to get the meal, refusing offers of help from both Lena and Layla. Fortunately, they had opted for a more traditional turkey dinner, rather than stealing Lena's recipes, too.

Naturally, no one refused Lena's help when she offered to clean up after the meal. Jacquie and Devin offered to stay and help.

"Are you sure?" Lena asked Devin, wanting her to stay, but knowing how much work she had ahead of her.

"Positive," she said. "Dad can get started when he gets home, and I'll pitch in when I get there."

Layla was renting a room in town, not far from the restaurant and above one of the stores—Lena hoped it wasn't the cuckoo clock store—and Ron left when she did so he could walk her and Jack home. Cheryl helped clear the table, and then she went upstairs, leaving the three of them to tackle the mess in the kitchen. Admittedly, it was nowhere near as bad as the disaster zone Lena had created on her first night, but there were still plenty of leftovers to pack up and pans to clean.

Jacquie wanted to hear stories about Lena's experiences as a rookie chef, so she shared them while they worked. For someone who had only worked two weekends so far, she had enough material to entertain them through cleaning several kitchens, let alone this one. Of course, her story about her dad had to include the job offer, which she was still considering.

"I'm really excited about the idea for restaurant databases, but I'll need time to develop it. It would be smart to take this job while I do that, but I'm worried that I'm only saying yes because I'm anxious about how my parents will react if I shift the focus of my work. And then I get anxious because I don't want to live my life based on their requirements. And then I realize that I need to make money, so it would be best to take the job…" She paused and laughed at her own dramatic rendering of a simple problem. "It's a never-ending circle in my head."

Devin watched her for a moment. "I'm going to suggest something, but you're going to gripe when you hear it."

"I don't gripe," Lena said. "Stop laughing, you two. Okay, maybe I gripe a little, but only when it's warranted. For example, by this conversation."

Devin wiped her eyes as her laughter faded. "I think what you need to do is be more like your aunt."

"If certain people are going to complain about my griping, they probably shouldn't say things like that," Lena muttered, stacking dirty dishes in the next tray and sliding it into the cavernous dishwasher. "But go on. I'm listening."

"She's made her own way in life," Devin said. "She loves her brother, and she invites him into her life sometimes. Not to run it or change it, but to share it for a while. I think she has a healthy approach to dealing with him."

"Well," Lena said, then paused. Devin always seemed able to look at situations and discover what really mattered in them. "Well," she continued. "That sort of makes sense, maybe a little."

Devin came over and put her arm around Lena, giving her a kiss on the cheek. "Just something to think about. Now, tell us more stories. You never did explain about the unfortunate incident involving a saltshaker when Dad and I came for your trial dinner."

"Oh, that's a good one," Lena said, starting to wipe down the counters. "At least, it is now, looking back. It wasn't funny at the time."

"Lena, you have got to write these down," Jacquie said. She was perched on a stool and wiping her eyes after laughing so hard.

"I have," Lena said. "I've heard so many stories from Landry about those ridiculous alpacas that I owe him a few hundred restaurant ones. I've been keeping a sort of journal every day, so I don't forget all the things that have happened."

"Really?" Devin asked. "Can we read it?"

Lena shrugged and pointed at the desk in the corner, near where Devin was standing. She went over and opened the top drawer, revealing wads of napkins and receipts, all with Lena's handwriting scrawled on them.

"Are they in any sort of order?" Jacquie asked, joining Devin at the desk and pulling out a random piece of ripped paper.

"They're dated, so they could be put in order. I'm always in here when these things happen, so I just grab whatever's handy and scribble it down."

They read through some of the papers while Lena finished tidying the kitchen, double-checking her drawers and shelves to make sure everything was in order.

Jacquie was laughing while she read. "You're funny when you tell the stories, but they're even better on paper. This is…Lena! Did you threaten to eat sweet little Jack?"

"It was a joke," she said, tossing the dirty towels in the hamper. "It's not like I was sprinkling seasonings on his head or anything."

Devin was sorting through the papers, laying them out in order and adding the ones Jacquie handed her.

"I'm taking these with me," Jacquie said firmly, stacking the sorted papers and tucking them into a grocery bag Devin handed her. "Lena, you wrote a book. A very funny and charming memoir. Or at least it will be, after you finish the season and add more to it. I have a friend who works in publishing, and I'll send her some samples once I get this mess transcribed."

"I jotted down some stories so I could remember them next time I'm around my brother," Lena said. "It's not a book."

Devin turned to her. "Oh, Lena. You told me what your aunt said about your grandmother's recipes when you first got here. About putting photos of the originals in a book alongside your updated versions? Jacquie, wouldn't the two ideas work well together, the humor and the nostalgia?"

"I love it. I'm calling Amy right now. What time is it where she is? Oh well, I'm waking her up."

She took the bag with her into the dining room. Lena watched her go, then turned back to Devin. "What just happened?" she asked. She must have looked as confused as she felt because Devin hurried over and wrapped her in a tight hug.

She stepped back, keeping her hands on either side of Lena's face, with her thumbs brushing Lena's cheekbones. "I have a feeling you're getting a book deal. Does anyone say no to Jacquie?"

Lena shook her head numbly. "I can't write a book," she said.

Devin laughed. "You said the same thing about running a restaurant, and look where you are now."

Where she was now? She had cooked for a whopping four nights so far. She didn't think that made her a qualified chef any more than jotting a few notes made her an author. Yes, she had been intrigued when her aunt had mentioned a book that included her grandmother's recipes, but that didn't mean...

She wasn't sure what it meant. "Do you honestly think this is a good idea?" she asked Devin.

Her response was a big smile and a kiss that made Lena believe she could do anything, as long as she had Devin by her side. She sighed as they pulled apart.

"Come on, I'll walk you home," Lena said, taking Devin by the hand and leading her toward the door to the dining room. Devin hadn't acted anxious to leave, helping Lena clean and also come to terms with this new opportunity, but Lena knew Devin had an exhausting night ahead of her. They would have a lot of tomorrows before March came around, and Lena planned to take full advantage of all of them. Just not at the expense of Devin's store and her peace of mind.

They waved at Jacquie, who was laughing on the phone and apparently reading some of Lena's anecdotes to her friend. Lena hurried them out the front door, finding it oddly uncomfortable to have a stranger hearing her stories. She might have to get used to it, though, if Jacquie had her way. And she always did.

They walked through the snow in silence for a few moments. There were some people still out on the streets, and most of the stores were closed but still festively lit up. There was a sense of peaceful expectancy in the town, as if Leavenworth had inhaled and would exhale with a vengeance tomorrow.

Devin interlaced her fingers with Lena's and pulled her to a stop under the sheltering awning of an art gallery, turning to face her. It seemed to be the perfect place for a kiss, and Lena was more than happy to oblige, but something in Devin's expression made her remain still and wait.

"I don't have anything figured out," Devin finally said. Lena just nodded. They had been over this, but maybe Devin thought Lena needed a reminder, especially after last night.

"I quit my job in Seattle, and my things are in storage because I let my apartment lease lapse," Devin continued. "I've come up with a bunch of next steps I can take after this season, but none of them feel exactly right. I have savings, and I'll be able to get a new job, but I'm…I'm unsettled."

Lena nodded again, reaching up to brush a loose curl off Devin's temple. Devin still wouldn't meet her gaze, looking over her shoulder and toward the dark shapes of the mountains instead. Please don't push me away, she thought, knowing there would be nothing she could do if that's what Devin was doing.

"And if no one offers to buy the store," Devin continued, "I'll need to stay and keep it running. It might be another season or even more before we find the right person. Nothing has changed since we last talked about this."

"No," Lena guessed, dreading what was coming next, "something has changed."

Devin nodded, finally meeting her gaze. "I don't know any of the answers, but I would very much like it…I would love it if we're asking the questions together. That is, if you don't mind that—"

As soon as the first statement sank into her brain, Lena didn't let Devin finish the last one, the one asking if Lena would possibly mind whether Devin had her life completely under control. She swooped in and kissed her, making Devin take a startled step backward and laugh in surprise against Lena's lips, but then she was kissing Lena back, with just as much hope and love as Lena felt.

They broke apart, and Lena knew her cheeks were as flushed as Devin's looked after that kiss.

"Was that a yes?" Devin asked with a grin. "It sure felt like a yes."

Lena rested her forehead against Devin's. "It's always yes for you. Anything you ask."

Lena kissed her again, then draped her arm across Devin's shoulders as they continued walking. "We'll figure it out together, wherever we are," she said. "I've always liked Seattle, and Leavenworth seems like a great place to be in the summer. As long as we're together, I don't care where we go." She stopped and turned them to face each other again, putting her hands on Devin's shoulders. "Even if you decide your career ambition is to be an alpaca rancher, I'll support you. We can hire Landry to clean their paddocks."

Devin laughed, and Lena heard a lightness to the sound that had been missing before. "That wasn't on my radar, but I'll let you know if I get an urge to explore it as an option," she said as they continued on their way.

Lena bumped her with her elbow. "What changed your mind?" she asked. "A couple days ago you were adamant about solving all your problems on your own, so what changed?" She puffed out her chest. "Was it my lovemaking prowess?"

"Yes," Devin agreed with a laugh. "That's exactly what it was."

"Liar," Lena said, hearing the evasiveness in Devin's voice. They stopped outside Devin's shop. "What was it, really?"

Devin leaned her shoulder against the door. "It was because of last night," she admitted. "The sex was great, and I want more of you. Forever. But it was…"

Lena raised her eyebrows inquisitively, waiting for Devin to continue.

"It was after," she said. "Or, rather, in between. You offered to help me clean the kitchen before we went upstairs."

Lena burst out laughing. "So it was my dishwashing prowess that lured you in?"

Devin swatted her lightly on the arm. "No, but it's hard to explain. I guess I knew you offered to help because you understood that it would bother me to leave a mess in the kitchen."

Lena nodded, starting to see what Devin meant. "I did," she

admitted. "I figured you'd sneak out of bed in the middle of the night to do it yourself, and I wanted us to take care of it together instead."

"That's exactly what I mean," Devin said. She shrugged. "We have a wonderful friendship, and I have fun talking to you and laughing with you. And the sex really was amazing. But knowing you were thinking about me, I guess it gave me a small glimpse into what normal daily life would be like with you...and, well, that felt like love."

"Oh," Lena said in a small voice, suddenly able to see that hint of the future, too, where she and Devin would live side by side, tackling not just the major career decisions together, but just plain sharing their lives with each other. "I do love you, Devin," she said when she felt able to speak steadily again.

"I love you, too." Devin gave her another long, slow kiss and then slipped out of Lena's arms and went into her shop, turning to wave at Lena through the window.

Lena wavered for a moment, wanting their life together to start *right now*, but she eventually turned back toward the restaurant. She had company waiting for her, and she wouldn't be much help to Devin and Ron if she stayed—more likely being in their way than helping them—but she would see Devin tomorrow. Suddenly, those tomorrows stretched beyond March, and Lena couldn't wait to greet them.

CHAPTER TWENTY-ONE

Devin hurried to the pantry for a new tray of diamond-shaped lemon and thyme flavored candies. They were an unpredictable offering, but today's customers couldn't seem to get enough of them. Every spare ounce of space in the kitchen, the office, and the pantry was covered with chocolates, and she knew they'd all disappear by the end of the day.

She was running on caffeine and sheer force of habit today, after being up all night enrobing and molding chocolates of all shapes and colors. She had wanted to stay longer with Lena last night—and Lena had clearly not wanted her to go—but they both knew Devin had to get back to the shop to help her dad. While they tempered chocolate and mixed ganache, she had told him about Lena's collection of scribbled stories, and Jacquie's plan for Lena to turn them into a book. She even talked a little about a future where the two of them were in the same place, and the dream of it seemed more real once she spoke it out loud to someone else.

She felt herself grinning with pride every time she thought about Lena and her book during the day. Aside from being happy for her to have a new challenge in her life, she liked that Lena had options now. Even more, she liked that those options, whether Lena worked on the book, or the EHR, her new databases, or all three, would still give her the flexibility to be where Devin was.

Wherever that happened to be. She still wasn't sure what she wanted to do, although her decision about whether or not to keep the shop might be made for her if they didn't get any offers. Then what? They could sell the building as it was, and let the Meyer's Fine Chocolates name disappear, or she could stay in Leavenworth and run the store. That option would be better if Lena was here with her, but she wasn't sure either of them would be happy here for the long term.

For today, though, her responsibilities were simple. Sell chocolates. She and her dad and Shay maneuvered around each other behind the display cases, filling box after box with dazzling confections, and trying not to look impatient when customers took ages to debate whether they wanted lemon or raspberry, milk chocolate or dark.

She practically had to force Shay to go in the back and take a break, but she and her dad weren't any better. She had a stack of sandwiches in the fridge, cut in easy-to-eat quarters, and they'd grab one or two whenever they went back to replenish their chocolate supply.

About an hour from their normal closing time, Devin started to notice gaps in the cases as they sold out of certain flavors. She was in the pantry hunting for more nougats on the lowest shelves when her dad came back with a concerned look on his face.

"Your advisor's here," he said. "Ben. He's out there talking to Shay, but he was asking for you."

She sighed and stood up. She didn't want to deal with this right now, but she supposed it was the best time for him to see the shop, if he really was interested in buying it. Big crowds, emptying cases. This was their most profitable-looking moment of the day.

He was standing off to one side, pointing out various selections while Shay added them to a box. From their gestures, she guessed that he might be sneakily grilling her on the different types of chocolates and the techniques involved in making them, which gave her hope that he might have good news for Shay and Layla, at least. He had never missed an opportunity to question his students and make them think, whether on quizzes and exams or just during informal conversations. She had been on the receiving end enough times to recognize his intensity. Shay, at least, didn't seem to be buckling under pressure, and she smiled and chatted with a confidence that had been growing since her first day as their assistant.

Devin walked over to stand next to Shay. "Hello, Ben," she said. "Shay, this is Chef Dunham. He was my advisor at culinary school."

"Oh…" Shay looked at him as if he had transformed from average customer to demigod status right before her eyes. "Devin's told us all about the school. It sounds like a wonderful place."

"It is," he said with a smile. "It's a great place for students who are eager to learn and grow. Now, I need to talk to Devin for a moment, but I hope we get a chance to chat again soon. Thank you for helping me make my selections from all these tempting choices."

Devin gave Shay's arm an encouraging squeeze, and then she gestured for Ben to come around to the back. She introduced him to her dad on the way through the kitchen, and he complimented him on the shop and the thorough training he'd done with Devin and now with Shay, and then they were sitting in the office. Devin felt a clenching in her stomach, and she figured her expression mirrored the one she'd seen on her dad's face just now. Anticipation warring with dread. She decided the odds of her collapsing into a faint were about fifty-fifty. Well, seventy-thirty, given how little sleep she'd had in the past twenty-four hours. At least if she fainted, she wouldn't be forced into this decision-making moment.

She wished Lena was there with her, but it might have sounded strange for her to ask him not to talk until her girlfriend arrived for moral support. Girlfriend? Yes, Devin decided. When all you could think about during the big moments in life was how much you wanted that other person to be with you, then the word and the meaning behind it definitely applied.

"Did Shay pass your test?" she asked, delaying the inevitable by a few minutes.

He laughed. "You know me well. Yes, she did. She told me which truffles she had made, which I'm sure were done up to your standards and your dad's or they wouldn't have been in that case. She also clearly has a good grounding in the basic theories of chocolate making, even though she's only been working with you for a short time."

He paused, looking at her slyly. "Chef Gilby thought so, too, when she was here Wednesday." He correctly interpreted Devin's confused expression, as she tried to place the name and failed. "She's been the director of the pastry school for about four years now, so you wouldn't have known her. She was here to meet Shay and sample some of your confectionary, but she didn't introduce herself. She wanted to be just another customer."

Devin frowned, wondering why the school was sending secret shoppers to spy on them. It couldn't all be about Shay, since being an expert chocolatier wasn't an entrance requirement for students. "Why do I feel like I'm the one being tested now?"

"Because you're perceptive. And you're also a talented teacher, which is what we really wanted to find out." He drummed his fingers on his knee. "Ian retired last year, which was about damned time, if you ask me. And don't you dare tell anyone I said that," he added, wagging his finger at her. "But it's true. You were one of his casualties, I'm afraid. You needed a talented and innovative teacher to inspire you and help you grow, but instead I fear that you were bored and left to your own devices in his classes because you had already surpassed him in skill before you arrived. A good teacher wouldn't care about that but would seek out ways to challenge someone like you. I think you could be a teacher like that, Devin. We want you to come back to the school as an instructor. You'd be in charge of all aspects of chocolate making. What do you think?"

What did she think? She had no idea. Somehow the conversation had gone in a different direction than she was expecting, and she was jogging mentally to catch up. She thought of her times in the kitchen with Shay and Layla, and even with Lena when she had first started at the restaurant. She also thought about the few teachers, like Ben, who had truly inspired her to improve her skills and creativity.

"I enjoy teaching," she said hesitantly. This wouldn't be the same as her other jobs in the chocolate industry in Seattle, making the same product over and over and working for other people.

She'd be able to plan the curriculum for her classes. Encourage the students who were struggling and challenge the ones who needed to be pushed beyond their limits. "I've only worked with one or two people at a time, mainly with our assistants, but...wow. Yes, I could do that. Wait," she said, "does this mean you aren't interested in buying the shop?"

He laughed. "I thought my questions during our phone call might make you suspicious about that. Yes, I want the shop, but it would come with you as a package deal. My wife asked me to bring her back some chocolates while I was here, but I don't know how pleased she'd be if I told her I bought the entire shop instead. You remember A Pastry a Day?"

Devin nodded, still unsure where he was going with this. She had made pastries and desserts for the student-run bakery for practicums, and some of her friends had worked there. It was one of the storefronts in the campus food court, but people came from all around the area to buy their baked goods.

"There's a small space available next to it that has been vacant for some time. We had thought about expanding the bakery, but now we want it to be Meyer's. You'd lease it from the school, so it would still be yours, but part of the contract would include offering practicums and work-study opportunities." He hesitated, then gestured around them, as if taking in the entire shop. "The name, your vendors and ingredients, your furnishings, those would all be yours. But part of the proceeds would go to the school. It wouldn't be as profitable for you as it would be if you opened a store on your own, but we'd provide you with plenty of assistants, and start-up costs would be minimal. You'd also have a steady supply of customers with all the students on campus and the people who come to the bakery."

Devin nodded slowly, afraid to make any sudden moves in case this was a dream and she woke herself up. She was really tired after her late night, so it wasn't inconceivable that she was actually asleep on the tile floor behind the counters.

"I couldn't afford to move the store on my own," she said tentatively, already thinking ahead to how simple it would be to find a buyer for the empty storefront here, if they didn't need to wait for the right person to come along who wanted to keep it as a chocolate shop. "But it's in Dad's name, too. I can't make a decision like this without him."

Ben clapped his hands together. "Of course. Let's talk to him. Marcia, Chef Gilby that is, wanted me to discuss having him come to the school as a guest speaker sometime. We figured that if you were there teaching, we'd have a good chance of snagging him, too. I know he's retiring, but he has too much knowledge to let it go to waste."

She got up and opened the door, expecting to see her dad hovering outside it. He was, but Lena, Jacquie, and Shay were there, too, all clustered around the island and looking nervous. Well, except Jacquie, who looked like she was having a grand adventure watching all this chocolate-shop drama unfold. Devin hoped they had closed the store a little early, but she wouldn't be surprised if they all had just come back here, leaving the shop to run itself.

Devin glanced at Lena, giving her a smile she hoped would ease the obvious concern on her face. Apparently, her expression revealed some of her growing excitement about the prospect of teaching, and even more, of not losing the store, because Lena grinned back at her. Already celebrating with Devin even though she didn't yet know why. It seemed it was enough for her to see Devin happy.

Her dad glanced from Ben to her, tugging at his apron in a nervous gesture. "Do we have a buyer?" he asked.

"Yes," Devin said. "Me, possibly." She quickly outlined the proposal Ben had offered. Halfway through, Lena came up behind her and stood close, her hand on Devin's lower back.

"What do you think, Dad?" Devin asked when she was done.

He just nodded, speechless for a moment, and then he came over and gave her a tight hug. "You'll be a brilliant teacher. And Meyer's…it'll still be in the family." He turned to Ben and shook his hand, clasping Ben's in both of his. "Thank you," he said simply, but his expression more than made up for the phrase's simplicity.

Jacquie cleared her throat. "That handshake was in no way binding," she said, walking over to Ben and handing him a card.

All traces of her boisterous, fun-loving personality were gone, replaced by a rather fearsome professionalism. "Send me a copy of the contract, and I'll check it out for my client. If everything looks fair and in good order, I'll release it to her to sign." She gave Devin a quick hug. "But this is so exciting! I'm very happy for you and your dad," she said, returning to her normal voice. She shook her finger at Devin. "But you do not sign anything until I've read it over."

Devin nodded, not daring to contradict her. Besides, the arrangement sounded too good to be true. She felt relieved to have someone who would help her make sure it wasn't.

Ben excused himself to chat with Shay for a moment, and Devin hesitated, not ready to let down her guard just yet. She had lived with uncertainty about the shop and her career for so long that she wasn't able to just let go of her worries and celebrate. But the joy she felt was bubbling up inside her and wouldn't be kept down for long.

"Would this be enough to convince you to come to Seattle, Dad? You can give lectures and still help out in the shop when you want to."

"Oh," he said vaguely, rubbing the back of his neck and turning a little red. "I thought about staying close to town. There's a run-down winery in Peshastin that looks worth renovating. I might take a chance on something like that. I could make chocolates for the wine tastings."

Lena made a strangled sort of sound and put her arm around Devin as if bracing her up. "Would this winery happen to be currently owned by a lonely widow or a down-on-their-luck young couple?"

Ron shrugged. "The second one."

Devin looked suspiciously at Lena, and then at her dad. "This sounds like one of Cheryl's projects," she said, not certain that she wanted him to answer. She wasn't sure how much more news she could take today.

"Oh, well, she might have suggested it. And we might be going into this as partners." He flushed again. "Business partners, of course."

Devin rubbed her eyes wearily as Lena and Jacquie burst into laughter. She wasn't sure what to think, except that he had seemed happier lately than he had in years, and that was all that really mattered. They had wanted her to be the one to be able to move forward without carrying guilt and worry about the store, but it seemed that he was going to be the one to do that. And she'd have the shop and her students to worry about. She couldn't have planned it better.

She kissed him on the cheek. "At least promise that you'll come to the school to do some guest lectures," she said. "When you're in between alpaca farms and wineries and restaurants, that is."

Lena grabbed her hand. "I think Devin could use some fresh air after all this. We'll be back in a little while."

She led an unprotesting Devin out of the shop, grabbing their jackets as they went, and onto the sidewalk. Devin sighed, finally able to draw deep breaths again, the cold air chilling her throat. Street vendors were selling roasted chestnuts from brightly colored carts, and a horse and carriage walked down the street past them—signs that the holiday season was truly upon them. This would be a chaotic one, with the shop to run, a move to plan, and classes to anticipate. And Lena. Always Lena.

"This is good, isn't it?" she asked, staying close to Devin's side as they wove through pedestrians. "Amazingly good."

Devin nodded. "I think so. I'm excited," she admitted. "For both of us. Writing a book? Teaching? I never would have thought this would happen."

Lena put her arm over Devin's shoulder and leaned over to kiss her neck, not missing a stride. "A Christmas miracle," she said with a laugh. "What we talked about before…" She hesitated, suddenly serious. "So, it's Seattle in March?" she asked, with hope in her voice.

"Seattle in March," Devin said, with a promise in hers.

CHAPTER TWENTY-TWO

On Christmas Eve, Lena used a pair of tongs to take two slices of schnitzel out of the mesh draining basket, and then she set them on a clean plate. As soon as she had turned away from the counter and back to the fryer, Layla came behind her with a steaming saucepan of gravy and poured some over the meat. She slid the plate in front of Kirby, and he added the sides and used a towel to wipe a few drips of gravy off the plate.

Lena watched them with a smile. One month in, and they were working more smoothly together than she had anticipated. Diners seemed happy, the kitchen was orderly and efficient, and they had even managed to pull off some popular specials, several of which had become fixtures on the main menu.

That wasn't to say there weren't mishaps along the way, and Lena had been gathering plenty of new material for her book. Like the night last weekend when she had put the roasts in the oven but forgot to turn it on. She checked a few hours later to find them raw and room temperature. That meal option had to be scrapped, but luckily Kirby had created a stew with leftover cooked roast, and the hearty dish had been a big hit on the snowy weekend. Some things got burned, some just didn't taste very good, but all in all, they had turned Haus Bavaria into a popular dining option in town.

Cheryl stuck her head in the kitchen door and nodded at Lena. "Hey, Kirby," Lena said. "Do you mind watching the fryer for a few minutes?"

"Sure," he said, coming over to her station. She walked over to the little corner office area and sat down, propping her feet on the desk and taking out a magazine to read. He was watching her with a confused expression and looked about to say something to her, but just then Devin came through the swinging door from the dining room with two people behind her.

"Hey, Lena," Devin said, giving her a casual smile as if they were merely acquaintances who worked in businesses near each other and not so much more. "These are the Comstocks. Brent and Natalie. They were interested in buying our shop, but since we're not selling the brand, they were looking at other businesses in town. I thought an established, thriving restaurant might be a good turnkey option for them, and I know your aunt is planning to sell..."

Lena shook their hands. "Yes, she is, at the end of the season."

"And you're the head chef?" Brent asked, looking a little dubious given that she wasn't doing anything chef-like, while her sous-chefs were scurrying to get the last of the night's orders out.

"I am," Lena said. She waved toward the desk and the fishing magazine on top of it. "Although my role is mainly supervisory. Kirby over there is the one who runs the kitchen."

"Really?" Natalie asked, addressing Kirby. "You look very young to be in charge of such a busy kitchen."

"He's young, but talented. Did you try the stew?" Lena asked, knowing full well that Devin had encouraged them to order it. "It's his creation. Kirby, why don't you show the Comstocks around the kitchen. Oh, and be sure to talk to them about your ideas for serving lunches in the off season and the restaurant's new database."

Kirby was motionless, blushing furiously, but Layla poked him in the back, and he stepped forward. "Oh, okay. Hi," he said, then looked at Lena. She gave him a smile and a wink, and he tentatively grinned back at her before leading them toward the back of the kitchen. She heard him begin to explain his sandwich ideas in a halting voice that slowly grew more confident as he spoke.

Layla smiled at him as he walked away, and then she went over to prep the dessert cart. She had been making the restaurant's desserts in-house for about a month. Her offerings lacked Devin's mastery with flavors and decorations, but no one was complaining about her tarts and cakes. She took the cart into the dining room to serve people, and Kirby was standing by the pantry talking in the animated way he only had when he was talking about a new dish he wanted to make. Lena sat on the edge of the desk and pulled Devin close to her while they had a moment alone.

"That was quite dramatic," Devin said, gesturing at the magazine. "I thought you were just going to let Kirby look like he was doing more work than you were."

"Artistic license," Lena said. "I wanted them to see him in charge."

Devin nodded. "He looks more comfortable now, at least," she said, nodding toward the trio. "I hope this works out for him."

"Me, too. I've been slowly moving more responsibility over to him, hoping he didn't realize it and panic until he was already head chef and couldn't do anything about it. If they want a low-maintenance, already staffed place in Leavenworth, this is a great option. Have you heard from Ben about the plans for the new store?"

She had helped Devin and Ron measure everything portable in their shop, and they had spent hours together designing the new space. Even though the footprint would be smaller than what Devin currently had, Ron had used the same design ability he demonstrated in the shop van's refit to find creative ways to maximize the space.

"He emailed today that he and Marcia love it. The movers the school hired will be here the second of March to dismantle the display cases and help pack everything else. It should only take a day or so, and we'll be on our way to Seattle." She laughed. "It's strange to think of the entire store being transported practically intact to a new city, but I'll be glad to have my familiar tools and everything to help me feel settled there."

"And I'll help in any way I can," Lena said. "You can count on me to be there on March first to eat all the leftover chocolates."

Devin kissed her neck. "Thank you. That was the one piece of this puzzle that I hadn't taken care of yet. What a relief."

Lena laughed, then sobered slightly at the thought of all the good-byes they were facing. She never would have believed it, but she was going to miss her aunt Cheryl, and she knew it would be hard for Devin to leave her dad. They'd be coming to Seattle to visit often, though, and Lena wanted to take Devin to stay in the winery Cheryl and Ron were buying. Of course, a visit to Cheryl's would likely mean they'd be put to work picking grapes or stomping them into wine or something, but at least she was hiring a real professional to manage the vineyards.

Shay and Layla would be following after them and starting school in the summer, and they'd be working in the new store with Devin. Lena was glad that she'd have familiar faces with her, too, and not just the store furnishings.

She reached up and brushed a lock of hair off Devin's temple. "I didn't expect any of this when I came here," she said. "I didn't expect to even like my aunt, let alone come to think of her as a friend. Or to accomplish anything beyond negligent homicide by food poisoning in this kitchen. Or to give a damn about this town or any of the people in it." She sighed and rested her forehead against Devin's. "Most of all, I didn't expect to find you. Or to fall in love."

Devin twined her arms around Lena's neck, pulling her into a slow kiss, full of passion and hope for their future together. "I love you, too, Lena," she said. "And you owe the swear stein another dollar."

Lena sighed. "That thing is not coming to Seattle with us," she said, pushing to a standing position as Layla came back through the door with her now empty dessert cart, Ruben following behind with a tray full of dirty dishes.

Devin just laughed as she went over to help Layla refill her cart with the evening's celebratory staff treats, while Lena and Ruben leaned on the counter and went over the menu. They had only had one public seating tonight, and the rest of the time was left for the staff Christmas party. They were planning a buffet instead of their usual sit-down menu, and Lena was going to try making some puffy potato balls. She hadn't told anyone but Devin that they were meant to be puffy, in case she had trouble with the fryer and they ended up being flat potato pancakes. She'd be happy to pretend that had been her plan all along.

Eventually, once the diners had left, the rest of the waitstaff trickled into the kitchen, followed by Ron and Cheryl. Half of them got to work on the dishes from the service, while the others clustered around the island, lending a hand when needed. The Comstocks politely extricated themselves from the private party, walking out to the front door with Cheryl and leaving an excited and successful Kirby in their wake. At least that was how Lena was interpreting his bright red face and the small smile he gave her before he focused on the roast he was slicing for sliders.

Lena stood at the fryer, splitting her time between watching her potatoes and looking around the room. They were planning a more intimate dinner the next day, with just her, Devin, Cheryl, Ron, Layla, and Jack, but this was the moment that felt truly like Christmas to her. She tried to remember the last time she had felt any magic associated with the season but couldn't come up with a single example. Her mandatory family meals were usually lacking in much sentimentality—and given their jobs, it was common for at least one of them to be called away on any given holiday. This year, though, holiday spirit had been infectious and nearly constant for the past month. She couldn't throw a schnitzel in town without hitting a nutcracker doll, and it would probably be a year before she'd be able to close her eyes and not see the afterimages of twinkly fairy lights. But she had, surprisingly, loved every moment of it. A lot of it had to do with Devin—Leavenworth at Christmas had provided an elaborate and joyful backdrop to their growing romance, and Lena was determined to keep the magic going year-round.

Yes, a lot of her mood had to do with Devin, but it was also Ron and Cheryl and all the rest of this little Haus Bavaria family. She was proud of how far they had all come in just one month, and this get-together was a far cry from the first one they had shared. Ruben was at the grill, turning the bratwursts and chatting with Layla, who was on her usual sauce duty on the range next to him. Ron was helping with the pots and pans, pink-cheeked from the steam of the massive dishwasher, while Devin organized the remaining waitstaff and had them piling plates and flatware on the island. Cheryl quietly came back into the room and gave Lena a wink and a smile before going to help Kirby. The two of them carried on a low, but excited conversation, and Lena felt a sudden wave of unease.

As if sensing her shift in mood, Devin came over to stand by her. "What's wrong?" she asked, following Lena's gaze to Cheryl and Kirby. "Didn't it go well?"

Lena shrugged. "I think it went very well. In fact, I'll probably need to transfer even more responsibility to Kirby, if he's going to be taking over as head chef. Which is just awesome since I didn't want this job in the first place, so what a relief it will be to hand it over to him."

She should mean those words. A month ago, she would have delivered them with confetti and popping champagne corks, but now she felt deflated. She'd actually miss this place, and the realization was uncomfortable.

Devin nudged her with her elbow, not falling for Lena's falsely cheerful words. "Don't give it up just yet," she said. "You have two more months to be the head chef here. You can mentor him and give him more responsibilities, but still keep being the chef until you're ready to let go."

Lena gave her a kiss on the cheek. "Thank you, I will," she said, mumbling under her breath about the *stupid job* and *stupid restaurant* as she turned back to her potatoes. "Oh," she said, pulling the basket full of perfectly golden potato puffs out of the oil. "Look, they actually puffed like they were supposed to."

In her enthusiasm, she said that much louder than she had intended, and everyone in the room laughed along with her, probably all remembering her disastrous first attempts at cooking and describing her food.

"I mean," she added, "naturally they turned out *exactly* as I expected, which I had no doubt they would."

She barely managed to get them on a paper towel covered plate and sprinkled with a little salt before the kitchen piranhas snatched them up. Ruben set a large platter of bratwurst discs and a spicy mustard dipping sauce next to her plate, and those quickly disappeared, too. She and Ruben looked at each other.

"I guess we're eating in the kitchen and not the dining room," she said. "We'd better get back to work."

She turned back to her fryer with a smile, Devin close by her side and loud chatter filling the room around her. She put her free arm around Devin and kissed her cheek. She had come here reluctantly, prepared to hate every moment of her sentence. Who knew that a kitchen full of love had been on the menu for her.

EPILOGUE

Lena sat in her Saab in the cell phone lot at Sea-Tac Airport, waiting for her parents to let her know they were ready for her to pick them up. She tapped nervously on the steering wheel as she waited. Once she had recovered from her surprise that both her mom and dad wanted to come to Seattle for Thanksgiving, she had been a nervous mess. Cheryl and Ron were coming, too, and Lena had desperately tried to get Jacquie to change her plans and come as well, to help act as a buffer between the two couples. Or a defensive wall. Jacquie had promised to call often, but it wouldn't be the same as having her there in person. Devin thought she was being overreactive, especially since Ron would be there to help ease any tension, but she didn't know Lena's family like Lena herself did.

Well, Lena wasn't sure how well that argument stood up anymore. They had been to visit both Portland and Peshastin over the past summer, and Devin and her parents had gotten along surprisingly well. As in, *look, it's our long-lost daughter!* kind of well. Devin had spent hours in their kitchen, teaching her dad the basics of chocolate making, and she and Lena's mom had bonded over her herb-gardening hobby. They had even drawn Lena into their enthusiasm when they insisted that Lena cook some of her restaurant dishes, and all the sibs had come for dinner. It had been a weirdly nice time, possibly helped by the fact that Lena now lived in the next state and not just across town and would be able to leave soon.

Who was she fooling? It was because Devin was there with her.

Even though she was still nervous about the impending visit, she couldn't stop a grin from spreading across her face at the thought of Devin. Lena had fallen in love with her quickly, but she had never had any doubts that her feelings would change once they left fantasyland Leavenworth behind and returned to real life together. What she hadn't expected was the way Devin had flourished since their move. She was still the same person—still kind and thoughtful and wonderful—but when the weight of indecision and sadness had been lifted from her shoulders, she had transformed into a brighter version of herself, like Leavenworth did on the day after Thanksgiving.

She was loving her new teaching job, too, and Lena had the opportunity to work with her at times since the pastry school had been one of the first clients for Lena's new databases. She was creating apps that would help the bakery and Meyer's run smoothly, even with a high turnover of practicum students and constantly shifting inventory. She had unofficially designated herself as taste tester for both shops, and that was fast becoming a fulfilling career move.

Her phone buzzed and she sighed. Yes, everything had been going well. And then The Parents had called. She started her car and drove to the pickup area outside of baggage claim where they were waiting for her.

Luckily, the drive from the airport to the community college was a brief one, and it was easily filled with the typical small talk about their flight—short—and the weather—rainy. She was too stressed to manage a conversation that was much longer. She parked near the food court since the college was letting Devin use the space near her chocolate shop for their dinner. They wouldn't have been able to fit everyone in their small apartment, and Lena thought that having some extra room might allow them all to coexist.

"We're just back here," she explained as they walked through the empty cafeteria. "It's tradition for Ron and Devin to see Thanksgiving as the start of the holiday season, so they've been decorating the...oh, my."

The three of them came to a halt when they came around the corner, and Meyer's Fine Chocolates came into view.

"Subtle," her dad said, after they had been standing there for a minute.

"I know, right?" Lena said. "I'm sure that's what they were going for."

"It's…" Her mother paused, apparently searching for an adjective that would encompass the sight in front of them. Lena had rarely heard her mom at a loss for words, but this would do it.

"It's bright," she eventually finished. "And very beautiful." She raised her voice. "Hello, Devin, dear."

Devin waved at them from her perch on top of a stepladder, where she was adding thick red velvet bunting to the beam across the front of the store, apparently not caring that there was already an evergreen garland in the same space. And a string of dangling icicle lights. Every spare inch of space on the counter was covered with something to do with Christmas or one of the other seasonal holidays that would be celebrated in December. Layla was coming out from behind the counter, forced to contort herself to get past the massive tinsel-covered tree that was partially blocking the way.

Devin climbed off the ladder and came over to greet them and introduce her dad, and Lena stepped to one side, searching for her aunt. She knew her parents would love Ron, but she was worried about what would happen when her mom and Cheryl were face-to-face. There wouldn't be fights or anything unseemly like that, but Lena worried about what the increased tension would do to the party.

Devin left the three parents talking, and she came over to give Lena a kiss. Lena put her arm around Devin and gestured at the beribboned chocolate shop. "You could decorate the entire town of Leavenworth with all that," she said. "I saw your store last Christmas, and I don't remember there being so…much."

Devin laughed. "I was worried Dad might feel sad this year, since we weren't at the old shop, so I might have bought a few dozen extra decorations to cheer him up."

Lena laughed. "And I'm guessing he did the same for you?"

Devin nodded. "After the weekend, maybe we can spread some of it around the rest of the cafeteria. Oh, careful," she said pulling Lena out of the way of Jack, who ran past them in his straddle-legged toddler stride. He had a phone gripped in one of his chubby hands, and Lena heard a disembodied voice coming from it.

"Jack, dear, please hold Aunt Jacquie upright. She's going to be sick."

Lena was about to go rescue her, but Layla beat her to it, scooping up Jack in one arm and the phone in the other. "Hey, Jacquie," she said.

"Oh, Layla, thank goodness. The world was spinning."

Devin laughed as Layla took her two charges back toward the shop, then her laughter faded and she grabbed Lena's hand. "Stay calm," she said. "Everything will be all right."

"It never works to say things like that," Lena said, looking in the same direction, where her aunt was approaching them with a tray of glasses and a wine bottle. Ron hurried over to help her distribute them. It wasn't wine from their new business venture yet, but from another local winery that Cheryl was sampling as inspiration.

Devin tugged on Lena's hand and led her back into the group. The conversation was stilted at first, while everyone was sorted out with wineglasses, and Lena's dad seemed to notice it, too. He was being uncharacteristically loud, as if trying to force them out of their awkward phase. She was about to drag him away from the group when she noticed her mom and Cheryl exchange a glance and an eye roll after he laughed too loudly at one of Ron's stories. Lena's dad caught her eye and gave her a sly wink.

"Oh, smart," Devin said. "Unite them against a common enemy."

The meddler had struck again. As the evening wore on, though, Lena had to admit that she was relieved he had done something. Her mom and Cheryl would never be besties, but they could manage a civil holiday meal together. Jack managed to entertain everyone and fill any gaps in conversation, and Layla even joined in with more confidence than she had shown last year at this time. Lena exhaled deeply in what felt like the first time in days.

She caught up with Devin when she stepped behind the shop's counter to get some more chocolates. "You should leave this tree up year-round," she said, pressing Devin against the wall, using the massive tree as cover. She kissed her, loving the feel of Devin's hands on her waist, encouraging her to move even closer.

"It's handy as a privacy screen," Devin agreed when they broke for air. She looked at Lena with a concerned expression. "Are you more relaxed now? Having fun?"

Lena shrugged. "Yes, despite my best efforts." She grinned. "With you in my life, I'm never going to have a subdued holiday again, am I?"

"Easter was fairly quiet," Devin said. "I'll need to work on that."

Lena laughed and kissed her again, until she heard the sound of Jacquie's voice floating toward them.

"Everyone can still see you, you know," she called.

Lena leaned over to look past the tree, to the table where everyone was sitting, and where Layla was holding her phone toward them. They were all laughing. She looked back at Devin. "I guess the branches aren't as thick as I thought."

Devin gave her one last, lingering kiss. "Next year I'll get an even bigger one."

Lena laughed with her, and took her hand, leading them back to their family.

About the Author

Karis Walsh is a horseback riding instructor who lives in the Pacific Northwest. When she isn't teaching or writing, she enjoys spending time outside with her animals, reading, playing the viola, and riding with friends.

Books Available From Bold Strokes Books

Beautiful Things by Emma L McGeown. A warmhearted romance of missed chances, undeniable chemistry, and a stubborn love that maybe, just maybe, can find its way back. (978-1-63679-934-6)

The Great Popcorn Romance by Georgia Beers. Opposites attract, and Riley Shaw stands no chance of resisting Hannah Kramer's magnetic pull. But opposites know just how to drive each other crazy... (978-1-63679-910-0)

Love Takes a Village by Karis Walsh. As Lena Preiss struggles to manage a busy restaurant in the Bavarian Christmas village of Leavenworth, Washington, chocolatier Devin Meyer brings an unexpected richness into her life, along with her delicious desserts. (978-1-63679-902-5)

Secrets of the Heart by Jenny Frame. When a beautiful stranger starts asking questions about Nikki Sharkey, head of an infamous crime syndicate, Nikki will stop at nothing to protect her daughter Isla. (978-1-63679-653-6)

Talon and the Songbird by Julia Underwood. In a world where survival depends on strategic alliances, Makayla and Talon must navigate not only complex politics but also the dangerous territory of their hearts. (978-1-63679-970-4)

Three Blissful Days by Dena Blake. Kendall Jackson attempts to make her ex regret dumping her by announcing she's dating beautiful park ranger Ivy Patterson. But there's nothing fake about how attracted Ivy is to Kendall. (978-1-63679-707-6)

Chasing Her Scent by MJ Williamz. When Sheridan Rousseau walks into Lisette Mouton's charming little bookstore in Quebec City, she unknowingly holds the key to a mysterious box hidden in a secret room. (978-1-63679-900-1)

Heart's Run by D. Jackson Leigh. Hoping to recover an escaped racing mare, stock transporter Tobie Mason locks horns with local wild horse advocate Maggie Wilkes. (978-1-63679-825-7)

Scandalous by Kris Bryant. When a Hollywood actress trades places with her twin sister, everyone's in an uproar about getting duped, but Lindsay's more concerned about finding out which twin she made out with. (978-1-63679-874-5)

The Art of Love by Ali Vali. When Mimi and Bianca both set their sights on Jolly, sparks fly, loyalties are tested, and hearts collide as they navigate the unpredictable nature of their hearts. (978-1-63679-719-9)

The Secrets of Rhydian Hill by Ronica Black. A doctor in need of a new start. A woman running from a killer. A love story that could end in tragedy. (978-1-63679-880-6)

Feeling Lucky by Krystina Rivers. What happens when, despite suddenly having enough money to buy almost anything, Lucy and Tanner start to discover that maybe all they need is each other? (978-1-63679-876-9)

Iceberg by Gun Brooke. When Lady Arabella hires Zandra, she never expects to find love, especially not as a disaster looms on the horizon. (978-1-63679-908-7)

It Happened One Semester by Aurora Rey. After a Pride night hookup, can eager new Assistant Professor Hudson Greene and Dean of Advising Callie Shaw overcome the odds and ace falling in love? (978-1-63679-814-1)

It's Kind of a Bad Idea by Sarah G. Levine. What happens when an emotionally unavailable serial dater meets the one woman she can't help but fall for—who happens to be the one woman who told her not to? (978-1-63679-920-9)

Thankful for You by Tagan Shepard. Everyone deserves to find their person. Maybe Karen has finally found hers? (978-1-63679-884-4)

What Happens On Location by Nan Campbell. How can Helen produce a successful movie when its director is the woman responsible for the demise of her marriage? (978-1-63679-904-9)

When Love Comes Around by Radclyffe and Ronica Black. Can Maya Sanchez and Nolan Wright trust each other enough to build something real, or will the past tear them apart? (978-1-63679-930-8)

www.ingramcontent.com/pod-product-compliance
Lightning Source LLC
Chambersburg PA
CBHW030513020726
47494CB00004B/1080